In Rembrandt's Shadow

by

Eileen Haavik McIntire

In Rembrandt's Shadow

Published by Amanita Books, Imprint of Summit Crossroads Press, Columbia, Maryland, USA. The publisher may be reached at sumcross@aol.com.

Contact the author at eileenmcintire@aol.com.
Website: www.ehmcintire.com.
Blog: www.eileenmcintire.com

Cover design by Earthly Charms, earthlycharms.com.

ISBN: 978-0-9614519-5-0

LCCN: 2016907999

Acknowledgments

Writing is often considered a lonely profession, but it is not an independent one. I owe a great debt of thanks first to my husband, Roger McIntire, who always provides loving support and guidance.

Laura Cox shared a wealth of fascinating detail on costumes through the ages. The White Oak Writers Group and the Columbia Fiction Critique Group spent hours reading the manuscript, offering criticism and suggestions, and catching those pesky contradictory details. Thanks also to the Baltimore Hebrew Institute and the Joseph Meyerhoff Collection at Towson University and to Rebecca Goldstein, author of *Betraying Spinoza*. I am also grateful for the comments and suggestions of my editors and readers, including Marilyn Magee, Stephen Berberich, Gary Garth McCann, Susan Branting, Dr. Tom Fowler, Peter G. Pollak, and Mark Willin.

This is a work of fiction, but Saul Levi Morteira actually lived in 17th century Amsterdam, and he was one of the rabbis who excommunicated the great philosopher, Baruch Spinoza, for his heretical ideas. My characterization of Morteira and his love for Isa is pure fiction, although he did come from Venice; he did serve as secretary for Elijah Montalto, physician to Marie de Medici, queen of France; and he did accompany Montalto's body to Amsterdam. Morteira's wife's name was Esther, and he had five children.

Writing this book sent me on a fascinating journey through history. Although I tried to be accurate with the historical details, I apologize for any errors that crept in. As always, I appreciate your comments and can be reached at eileenmcintire@aol.com. Please visit my website, ehmcintire.com, and blog, eileenmcintire.com..

- *Eileen Haavik McIntire*

Table of Contents

Preface

This novel continues the adventures of Sara Miller and her new friend Josh Davila that began in *Shadow of the Rock*. Sara's grandmother has left a bequest of $50,000 for Sara to use in searching for her grandmother's brother, Samuel Yulee, lost in the Holocaust.

Sara meets Josh in her search, and he becomes an important link to her lost great-uncle Samuel. They finally discover Samuel living in a pension in Gibraltar.

But both her grandmother and Samuel have unfinished business left from their resistance activities in the Holocaust—a rescued Rembrandt painting buried in a Gibraltar cemetery since 1941. The only clue to the owner of this painting lies in a faded receipt given to Sara as part of her grandmother's bequest.

Finding the rightful owner of this valuable painting and returning it become Sara's challenge for this book, *In Rembrandt's Shadow*.

Chapter 1 – Provenance, 1616

Spanish Netherlands.

Saul peered through the fog at the scattered lantern lights on shore outside Antwerp. No one spoke as the sailors guided the dinghy toward a deserted wharf and then touched the wharf pilings without a telltale bump. They held the boat close to the dock as Saul clambered onto the wooden planks and stood, wrapping his cloak tightly around his body. He doffed his sugarloaf-crowned black hat in false jauntiness to the men who had rowed him ashore.

They pushed off, leaving him stranded. He had never felt so alone and in such peril. He listened as each stroke of the oars thumped against pieces of rotting fruit and vegetables floating in the water. The sounds and noxious smells reminded him of Venice. He felt a twinge of homesickness but that was quickly overshadowed by fear.

The fog grew denser, drifting around him and down the river toward the North Sea. The lights on the ship that waited for him, anchored outside the shipping channel, disappeared. He shivered, although he was not cold, and peered through the darkness at the warehouse. The water slapped against the pilings and a rat scurried away from his footsteps, but no stray sailors or watchmen kept guard on this abandoned quay.

Saul crept down the wharf, thankful that the sea-soaked planks under his boots muted the sounds of his progress. At the wharf's end, he stepped into an alley leading to a road that followed the river toward the sea. He wiped away the moisture that had condensed on his beard and cast a wary eye at his surroundings. Little could be seen through the fog-shrouded darkness. Leaning against the weathered timbers under the eaves of a warehouse, Saul took a tinder box from his pocket, lit a small candle, then pulled out a letter and unfolded it. His hands shook and the ink on the paper had smeared from the damp, so he peered closely to read the instructions once more, repeating them in a low mutter. He must not forget even one detail.

His father had taken the long trek to Paris for the express purpose of asking him to make this journey. He and Montalto had both provided the funds for it. They trusted him to carry out this. . . assignment. Saul didn't know which terrified him the most—that he might fail or that he might be captured.

His father had told him of the horrors his friends had suffered to stay alive through the ravages of the Inquisition in these Low Countries.

"You are used to the ghetto and the restrictions placed on our people in Venice," his father said, "but the government protects us and allows us to practice our religion."

Saul shuddered, remembering his father's next words. "You are going to the Spanish Netherlands. The Spanish everywhere torture and murder non-Christians."

Then his father added, "My friends converted to Catholicism to save their lives and their property, but that was not enough to protect them and ensure their livelihood. They worshipped in secret, cut off from commerce, forced to live on scraps and cast-offs, and always fearful that the next knock on the door would summon them to the Inquisitors."

Saul shook his head. The family no longer had a door upon which to knock. He, Saul Levi Morteira, was to be their rescuer, God save him. He said a silent prayer, touched the letter to the flame, watched it burn and drop to the ground as ash.

Distracted by the task ahead of him, he forgot for a moment

that his man-servant Bernard had stayed on the ship. One person escaped detection better than two. Lacking a servant, Saul used his own boot to scrape mud over the ashes and then stomped on them to make sure no spark was left.

He was to follow the river road until he came to a wayside shrine on the right. He could identify it by the drawing of a bird carved into the back of the shrine near the ground. When he found the bird, he was to whistle three times.

He grimaced as he looked down at his clothes. Rough, simple, and dirty, trousers cinched with hemp string, no stockings. He had left his white cuffs, lace collar, and stockings back on the ship. No studs, no rings. They flashed light like beacons. He suddenly remembered his broad-brimmed hat, the latest fashion in Paris. No farmer would wear such a hat. Saul hid it in the weeds to retrieve on his return.

After a few minutes, the fog lifted, and his eyes grew accustomed to the darkness. Before he left the shadows of the warehouse, he stopped to listen, heard nothing, and silently prayed for guidance and mercy. He brushed off his breeches and set off walking down the road, a simple peasant on his way home.

He made out the shrubs and grasses alongside the road and behind them a few stunted trees. Then he heard a horse and the rattling wheels of a cart. Looking back, he saw the cart fast approaching. He had no time to throw himself into the brush to hide. He stepped aside to let the cart pass, but it slowed and stopped.

"Hola!" A young lad called out to him, then said something in the local dialect.

The boy is offering me a ride.

Saul waved him on as he stumbled like a drunk and turned toward the bushes as if to pee.

The lad muttered a curse, flicked the reins, and moved on. Saul waited in the shrubs until the cart disappeared around a curve. He looked like the poorest kind of Spanish Low Country rustic, but if he spoke—and that boy would remark upon it if he did not speak—he would immediately be condemned as a foreigner. *Best to avoid any such meetings. Best I say nothing to anyone.*

As he walked along the lonely road, meeting no one else, Saul found that he could easily see the road by starlight. He grew more confident and thought with pride how well he had conducted this rescue mission so far and he only twenty. He had resented the imposition of such a trip at first. He knew nothing of these people and was beginning to enjoy his position in Paris.

"I am secretary to the great Elijah Montalto, physician to her majesty, Marie de Medici, queen of France." He proudly spoke the words aloud. Once the family was safe, Saul was to rejoin Montalto in Paris.

Saul chastised himself for the sinfulness of feeling prideful. With all his soul, he tried to be righteous, and certainly in this dangerous situation, he felt humble enough. Still, he would succeed only with prayer and God's help.

These thoughts carried him down the road for awhile, but the longer he walked, the more he despaired of ever finding the shrine.

Then he suddenly spied its white stones in the shrubbery ahead of him. His boots sank in the mud as he pushed aside the scrub to look for the bird incised on the back. He found it with his fingers, feeling the grooves of the design.

This must be the place.

He peered down the road in both directions. Seeing no one, he whistled three times as he had been bid. He waited. Something rustled in the bushes. He listened, wiping the sweat off his forehead. No one appeared. It must have been a small animal. He whistled again as he pushed his way through the scrub to return to the road.

He paced back and forth, losing faith in the mission as time passed. What if the family had been arrested? Weeks had passed since the letter was written.

At last, the brush crackled and rustled as someone moved down the hill toward him. His heart thumped. Was that an enemy, a robber, or a Spanish guard? He breathed a silent prayer. He had never felt so alone. There was no one to help. His fingers touched the knife he carried on his side, and he gulped. He was a scholar, not some ruffian who brawled in the streets. He didn't know how he would use such a weapon.

The stranger pushed through the roadside brambles and reeds, slipped in the mud, and skidded into a fall, landing at Saul's feet. Saul leaped back and fumbled with his knife. "Who are you?" he whispered.

"My clothes, señor," said a low feminine voice. "They caught on the thorns."

A woman? He looked closer as she picked herself up and shook out the faded and torn velvet dress she wore. He noticed where pieces of fabric had been sewn in to enlarge the dress to fit her as she grew. With a pang of sympathy, he realized that it might be the only dress she owned.

Despite the darkness, Saul saw that her face and arms were scratched and bleeding. Her hair straggled in black curls down to her waist and long lashes accented her dark eyes. She was just a young girl, perhaps sixteen or seventeen years old. Not an enemy. His legs wobbled from relief. Saul cleared his throat. "Are you. . . ?"

"You are Señor Saul Levi Morteira, are you not?" The girl curtsied, and he saw her furtive glance down the road.

"Si, I am Saul Morteira of Venice." With an effort, he made himself speak. "You are with the ben Youlis?"

"I am. My name is Isa ben Youli, only now called Isabella Lopez Martinez, you understand?"

His eyes took in the slightness of her body trembling underneath the rags she wore. "Yes, I understand. But where is your family?"

"We have lost everything and hide in the woods near here. We are most grateful that you have come. You can help us flee this place?"

Her desperation touched his heart, and he reached toward her, wanting only to offer what protection he could. With difficulty, he drew back and roused himself to the task.

"I have a ship anchored near here. They wait for you now. The owners are Jewish merchants from Amsterdam. The ship can take you there where you will be safe." As safe as any Jew could be, he amended to himself. "My father has arranged everything."

She searched his face as if to reassure herself that he was a

friend, not an enemy. Finally, she said, "Follow me. I will take you
to my family." She turned to slosh back through the reeds the way
she had come.

Saul followed, admiring her agility as he stumbled along behind.
They waded through the mud and water, which soon gave way to
drier land, and the reeds and marsh grasses became shrubs and
stunted oaks. She led them to an area of dense shrubbery that
seemed impenetrable, but the girl weaved her way through the
bushes, turning back frequently to free Saul from the branches that
scratched him and pulled at his clothes. He glanced down at his torn
breeches. They would never be fit to wear again—even by a stable
boy. He had done well to leave his fine clothes on the ship. Isa
stopped and turned to him, her fingers to her lips.

"Wait here," she whispered and disappeared through the brush.

He waited, surveying the dark shrubbery around him as the tension grew. He knew nothing of these people and had heard only
vague rumors about the horrors they suffered in this country.
Perhaps Isa, lovely as she was, was a temptress in disguise, come to
seduce him. The misgivings, once gaining ground, grew within him.
He felt the urge to turn and flee but was not sure he could find the
road. He had been so bewitched by the vision in front of him that
he had not noticed the path she took.

As he turned his eyes to the heavens to pray for guidance, he
heard soft voices in the brush, then Isa appeared, followed by a
man, a woman, and a small boy, much younger than Isa. Saul saw at
once that their clothes were also faded and worn and without collars
and cuffs. The man and the woman stumbled along, hampered by
the battered trunk they carried between them. They all looked as
thin as the reeds he had pushed aside to get to this forsaken place.

"My parents," Isa said. The boy had stepped behind the parents,
but Isa took his hand and pulled him forward. "And my brother,
Elias." Like the rest of the family, his hair was dark and his skin
deeply tanned. The boy hitched up his short pants, hung his head,
and stared at the ground.

Saul hid his shock at the naked desperation in front of him as he
held his hand out to the older man. "I am Saul Morteira," he said.

"You must be Señor Eliahu ben Youli. My father has told me of the great debt he owes you."

The man grasped Saul's hand in both of his. "Sending his son to our rescue repays whatever debt he owes many times over. We could not survive much longer here. We have escaped the authorities, and the weather has been kind, but fall and winter will come too soon."

His wife broke into tears. "Forgive me," she said. "The fear and lack of food have weakened me. We are thankful for your help."

"You answer our prayers," said Eliahu.

"Our families are old friends," Saul replied. "Of course we must help." He looked at each of them. "I was told there would be seven."

Eliahu did not look at him as he mumbled. "There were seven."

His wife's face again crumpled into tears. She twisted the scarf she wore tightly around her body as she stared down at the ground.

"The curfew for Jews, you see," said Eliahu. "My father had gone to the bakery to buy a few crumbs of old bread, and he was caught. Then they came to our house and took my brother and his wife. The rest of us hid under the floor. When they left, we gathered what we could and fled for the country."

"The Spanish guards did that?" said Saul.

"That is what it is like for Jews in this country." Eliahu spat on the ground.

"Then it is good I have a ship waiting for us," said Saul. "We must return to the river before daybreak."

"Of course, of course." Eliahu took the lead in walking through the marsh on some indiscernible trail, returning them to the road.

Saul's feet felt wet and wrinkled inside his squishing boots. A blister rubbed his heel, making him grit his teeth at every step.

They reached the road but retreated into the brush as a donkey hauling a covered cart approached. A young man plodded beside the donkey and the cart's wheels creaked and groaned in time with his steps.

Saul bit his lip, silently urging the donkey and cart to move past.

They must not wait here long; they must reach the ship before dawn. Delay could bring tragedy to all of them.

When he agreed to rescue this family, he laid aside his resentment and decided to think of it as a challenge and, to be truthful, a bit of a lark. He hadn't fully understood the danger...until now.

Chapter 2 - Gibraltar, 1999

Sara watched the old man as he pursed his lips and shuffled the yellow fragments of paper piled on the table. Beside them rested a long package shaped like a loaf of bread or, possibly, a rolled-up painting.

"The Rembrandt is safe?" the old man asked. A light blue suit hung on his thin body, and he had hooked his cane on the back of his chair.

"It's in a safe deposit box, Uncle Samuel," she said, holding up a key. "At the bank down the street."

Josh sat up and pulled another key out of his back pocket. "We each have one. The painting's safe." He gestured to the package in front of Samuel. "You don't have another painting, do you?"

Samuel placed a protective hand on the package. "I'll tell you about this later."

Sara swept back her short brown hair and no longer felt like smiling. Outside, the bright sunlight had filled her with optimism. Her spirits sang with the knowledge that she was actually in Gibraltar and had surveyed the Mediterranean and the distant mountains from the top of the famous Rock. She had also met for the first time her grandmother's brother, Samuel, the man who sat across the table. He was so serious, Sara's optimism waned. She eyed the package with misgiving.

Uncle Samuel was full of surprises. *Like my grandmother.* Sara remembered how much she had undervalued the passive, secretive woman she had known; how easy it was to stereotype her grandmother as a typical West Virginia housewife—and how wrong that was.

Sara threw a quick peek at the young man sitting beside her. Josh. Dark-haired, tanned, and lanky, Josh looked like a deckhand in those faded, paint-splattered jeans and baggy gray sweatshirt. Probably most people guessed they were college students on tour, but at least her jeans and jacket were neat and clean. He was a grad school dropout, and she had been working in the stifling administrative job she'd found after college. Her grandmother's bequest changed that.

"I'm not sure we can do what you're asking," Sara said.

"It's going to be really tough," added Josh, "since it's been such a long time. . . ."

Samuel sighed. "Yes, it will be difficult. I don't know if you can do it or if anyone can, but we must try. It is right that we try."

Sara scanned the enclosed, glass-covered Moorish courtyard that served as a breakfast room for the old man's pension. Except for her, Josh, and Samuel, the place was deserted and all the tables had been cleared. A pot of coffee and one of hot water bubbled on a hotplate. With the aroma of coffee, the place still smelled like breakfast.

Sara got up, made herself a cup of tea, and returned to sit facing the reception area where the pension's concierge, a tall British woman in an ankle-length black dress, held sway. She had given Sara and Josh a long, strange look when they'd arrived, and then she'd made a phone call as she watched them head for the breakfast room. She'd made Sara feel uncomfortable. Sara sensed the concierge's eyes following them all the way. Why was she so interested? She knew nothing about them or the Rembrandt.

Sara contemplated the old man, a relative she had not known existed until a few months ago. Her grandmother had asked Sara to find him, if he still lived, and left Sara $50,000 in her will to finance the search.

Sara felt proud of her success, but she had not anticipated that it would only lead to a new problem. The Rembrandt. Unsuccessful himself at the task, Samuel had handed to Sara—and to Josh, of course—the mission of finding the rightful owner of a painting that Sara's grandmother had buried for safekeeping in 1941. Sara felt overwhelmed at this impossible task.

How much help would Josh be in this? She was grateful for his aid in finding Samuel, but she didn't know him that well. Would he be up for this job?

He had become a friend and an ally, but nothing more. Now they were partners in the search for the Rembrandt's rightful owner. A frisson of doubt shivered through her. Ever since Samuel had thrust the Rembrandt at them, Josh had become more and more melancholy. Was he having second thoughts about her? Their. . . friendship, if that's what it was? Or was he worried about something else?

Samuel cleared his throat. "So you begin your search. You took pictures of the painting? Made notes?"

"Yes," Sara said. "We documented as much information as we could get from the canvas."

"No one followed you?" Samuel sat back and frowned at each of them in turn.

Sara shook her head. "We were watching for anyone who might seem interested in us."

"We acted like ordinary tourists," Josh added, stretching his long legs under the table, "taking pictures of the mountain and the town." He stared down at his cup.

Sara shrugged at the memory. Like ordinary tourists carrying a million-dollar painting, but to look at them, no one would suspect they possessed anything more valuable than a pocket comb.

She heard the swishing of a skirt, then a shrill voice broke into their conversation. "Excuse me." The concierge. Behind her, a swarthy young man in a dark-green uniform walked in, filled a cup with coffee, and sat at a nearby table.

Hovering by their table like a large buzzard in her black dress, the concierge managed an ingratiating smile. "May I get you something?" she asked. "Pastry, perhaps?" Her eyes swept across the table. "I see you found the coffee," she added, nodding at the cup in front of Samuel.

Samuel turned around to look up at her. "We're fine, thank you," he said with a dismissive wave.

The buzzard withdrew, her skirt swishing as she walked.

Samuel muttered, "Busybody."

Sara frowned. "I don't think we said anything important or useful around her. Anyway, the Rem. . .uh, package is safe."

Samuel looked at them and laughed. "You think so? I don't like it that that woman. . . ," he nodded toward the foyer, "snuck up on us." He leaned forward. "From now on, you must take precautions. Check for signs that your rooms have been searched. Protect those keys." He sat back. "I would tell you to put the keys in a safe deposit box, but. . . ." He winked at Sara.

Sara rolled her eyes. "That would be overkill."

Josh sipped his coffee. "So what are these papers, Samuel?"

Sara watched Samuel and Josh. Behind Samuel, she saw the man at the other table, staring ahead, sipping his coffee, seemingly unconcerned. But was he? She glanced at Josh, caught his eye, and inclined her head toward the other table.

Josh frowned and lowered his voice. He placed a hand on Samuel's arm. "Watch what you say," he said.

Samuel turned around. "Excuse me," he called across to the young man. "We're having a private conversation here. Would you mind moving somewhere else?"

Without looking at Samuel or replying, the man picked up his coffee and walked toward the lobby.

Samuel watched him leave, then turned back to Josh. "Concierge's son. Works here. Now let me show you. . ." Samuel picked up the fragile, yellowed bundle of clippings and papers. "You must go through these papers carefully and look for clues. Some are receipts for paintings that we rescued; some are articles about their owners."

He lay the papers aside and reached across to lay his hand on Sara's. "And you, Sara, have your grandmother's receipt for the. . ." he winked at Sara again, "package. We always gave receipts for the about how to proceed.

Samuel watched her. She smiled at him to hide her doubts. He held his gaze on her for a long moment. "You look so much like my sister Ruth, your grandmother." He turned his head away, but not before Sara saw the tears in his eyes. She placed a hand over one of his. "I miss her too," she said softly.

A moment passed. Josh stared down at his cup. No one spoke.

Then Samuel wiped his eyes with a napkin. He looked from Sara to Josh. "You must understand, both of you, that this endeavor may be dangerous. Much, much money is involved. If word gets out, a lot of people will want to acquire that item, and some of them may be dangerous."

He sat back and picked up his coffee cup. "Your grandmother and I, we suspected that someone in our group was a traitor. Our enemies knew our moves, and then the Nazis trapped us and killed four of us outright and threw the rest of us into the camps. Your grandmother and I were separated. Until you showed up at my door, I thought she had not survived the camp." He paused and then added softly, "But I always hoped."

Josh laid a hand on the case. "Don't worry. We'll be careful."

"You must." Samuel took a deep breath and stared down at the table. "No one, not your parents, Josh, nor yours, Sara, will thank me for giving you this assignment. I am afraid for you, yet. . . ." He shook his head, "it must be done, and I cannot do it."

Sara laid a hand on his arm. "It's no longer your decision to make or your responsibility," she said, speaking more certainly than she felt. "I have to finish the job my grandmother began. She trusted me to do that."

As she picked up her teacup, Sara realized the truth of her statement. She could not retreat. Her job was only half done. A tremor of fear raced down her back. She looked up to find Josh, arms folded, chair tipped, frowning at her.

"We're in this together, you know," he said. "Both our families are involved. It might have been your Great-Uncle Samuel and your grandmother who rescued the paintings, but my family were part of the pipeline to protect those paintings."

Samuel's eyes flicked from Sara to Josh and back again. Samuel cleared his throat. "There is one other thing. . ."

Sara couldn't believe her eyes. Samuel was blushing.

"I made a mistake here." His eyes toured the ceiling before turning down to his hands, folded on the table.

Sara held her breath.

"I did not expect the painting ever to be retrieved or the owner found," Samuel said. "And one night, after too many glasses of wine, I spoke of it to some people here. The concierge was listening along with the others who may have passed the story on. I don't think any of them paid much attention to this old man, but I mean what I say when I ask you to take care."

Sara sat stunned into silence.

"How long ago was this?" Josh asked.

"A couple of months ago," Samuel said. "They're still around, including the concierge and her son."

"I'm glad you told us. We'll keep an eye out." Sara studied the concierge, seemingly busy with a ledger on top of the reception desk. "Probably no one has connected your story to our arrival."

"Sure," said Josh, but Sara heard her own doubts in his voice.

Samuel picked up the loaf-like package. "This will help. It is," he winked at Sara, "a decoy."

Josh shook his head. "No, you don't, Samuel. You're not going to lure people away with that and get yourself killed."

Sara pushed the package aside. "Put that away. You don't need to worry about us," she said. "There are two of us. We haven't seen anyone interested in us."

"Not yet," said Samuel. "But you can't see everywhere. No, I make amends with this. It will buy you time, if nothing else."

Sara glanced at Josh, not sure what to say.

Josh pursed his lips, stared at the ceiling, and finally looked at Samuel. "All right. But be careful and watch out. Lock your door, don't go out alone, keep your eyes open."

"Such advice you say to me, I say back to you." Samuel pushed away his coffee cup and stood. "We all must take care. I'm glad we have that settled, and now I think we go out to lunch."

They ambled down the street to a nearby cafe. On one side, the great Rock of Gibraltar loomed behind the streets along the coast, and cable cars overhead made their way up to the top of the Rock and back again. On the other side of the street, the Mediterranean spread out across the straits to the Atlas Mountains of Morocco. Sara walked between Samuel and Josh, her gaze traveling from the mountain slope to the sea. She felt the history around her and caught now and then the scent of oranges from the roadside trees.

After lunch, they returned with Samuel to the pension, greeting the concierge at the entrance but ignoring her inquisitive stare.

Samuel leaned on his cane in the doorway as Josh hailed a cab, but as the cab pulled away from the curb, Sara looked back to wave at Samuel and saw another car pull out behind them. She watched it in the rearview mirror, hoping to see it turn off. It did not. It followed them to their hotel, then passed by and sped on its way.

"A fire?" asked Isa. "Here on the road?"

Saul gazed at the soggy marshland around them, then at the road. "We need to signal the ship."

The family dispersed to find dry twigs that might burn, and Saul gathered them into a small pile and lit it with his tinder box, adding more bits of dry driftwood and dead grasses as they were found and brought to the fire.

"This will do well for our purpose," said Saul. "Isa, you walk down the road one way and Elias the other. Keep watch. If anyone comes, run back here and tell me. Whisper." He turned to Eliahu with a grim smile. "We should hope they have nothing to do."

Eliahu nodded as if he had no strength to speak. His wife looked on, her hands clasped, eyes closed, lips silently moving.

As Isa and Elias ran off, Saul stepped back and forth in front of the fire, alternately shielding and exposing it to the ship.

"They see us," said Eliahu, pointing out at the ship. "They are waving a lantern."

"Good." Saul left them to walk around a bend in the road to find Isa. "No one comes?" he whispered.

Isa came toward him, gesturing at the road behind her. "No one."

Saul felt his legs weaken at the sight of her. Even the darkness did not hide her beauty. He longed to stroke her dark tresses, run his hand down the smooth, soft texture of her face, gaze forever in her huge, dark eyes. . . . With an effort, he broke off his thoughts, snuck another peek at her as he joined her in walking back to the fire. Their lives were in danger here. He must protect Isa, but any moment could spell disaster. They still had too many minutes before the dinghy got to them, and then as many minutes back to the ship. At any time someone could spot them, raise an alarm, and send the guard galloping down the coast to imprison them.

But even as he scolded himself and argued against such folly, he found himself watching Isa's graceful movements, as she was, dressed in rags, unadorned by fashion or jewelry. He had heard it said that beauty was only skin deep, but Isa had shown how competent she was, too. He longed to touch her. Again he scolded himself.

This would not do.

To distract himself, he moved next to Eliahu, staring out at the ship. "Looks like we're safe for the moment," Saul said as if that were the only thing on his mind.

"Someone from the ship is rowing this way," replied Eliahu, peering through the darkness.

"Good." Saul would be glad to get out of this godforsaken country. He had known discrimination and the hatred of others toward people of his faith, but not such rampant ostracism, robbery, and murder as these people had suffered. He pulled out his watch and once more held it close to read the time. Almost five o'clock. They would be out of here and into the North Sea by the time anyone was about. They should reach Amsterdam in a day, perhaps, if the weather held. Isa would be safe in Amsterdam.

Such a contrast between the two countries. Holland in the north was in full flower. Wealthy, busy, vigorous, liberal and, compared with other countries on the continent, fairly tolerant of all religious beliefs. It stood as a model for how a country should be run.

Not like this obese and constipated hag of a country, old in its thinking, grasping and selfish in its governing aristocrats. The Spanish Netherlands. What an abomination!

He heard loud voices and boots stomping down the road toward them and then saw Elias running to the fire, his face frightened, one hand pointing back down the road. "Someone comes!"

Saul put his fingers to his lips. "Get your sister," he whispered and listened. Farmers? Soldiers? Coastal guard? They were coming this way, but so far they were beyond the curve of the road.

Saul quickly stomped on the fire to put it out with his boots and then scattered the ashes. He squinted at the river to locate the dinghy on the dark water and found it only about halfway to shore and barely visible. He heard the rhythmic dipping of the oars. Seeing no fire, would they take the cue and hold off? Hopefully, being offshore they would see those men and stay away. He said a silent prayer and ran into the shrubs to hide with Eliahu and his family. Thorns tugged at his clothes and pollen from the tiny blossoms made his nose itch.

Isa gripped his arm as they watched a band of five men approach, staggering as if they had drunk too many pints at a tavern in Antwerp. They wore ragged army uniforms, and a sword hung at each man's side. The men halted at the remains of the fire Saul had lit. One probed the ashes with his foot. Another walked into the bushes, coming so close that Saul smelled the beer and sweat. Isa pulled her dark curls across her face to hide its whiteness, and they all held their breath. The man stared out at the marsh as he relieved himself. Then Elias sneezed.

"What?" the man shouted, parting the shrubs.

Saul pushed back, but the thicket behind him was too dense. None of them could retreat into the shadows. They were all exposed. Trapped.

The soldier grabbed Elias and yelled to his companions.

Elias bit the man's hand and tore himself free. Saul punched the man in the jaw and tripped him. Elias gaped at the soldier sprawled on the ground, but Saul grabbed the boy's arm.

"Swim to the boat!" Saul whispered.

Taken by surprise in their muddle-headed state, the four other soldiers gawked, then galvanized into action. One grabbed Isa as she ran past and clamped his arms around her as she struggled to break free.

Saul and Eliahu, pushing Elias and Isa's mother toward the river, glanced back at Isa's cries.

The four other soldiers drew their swords and waved them menacingly as they lurched toward Saul and Eliahu.

"Go!" yelled Saul as he dodged the stumbling soldiers to reach the man who held Isa.

Elias grabbed a handful of sand and ran after Saul. Then Isa threw her head back into the ruffian's nose, leaving him howling as the blood spurted. Saul wrenched Isa free with one hand, slid a foot behind the other man's ankle and pushed him backward. As he fell, Elias threw sand into the man's face. Then Elias ran past the other soldiers throwing handfuls of sand into their eyes.

Saul and Isa ran toward the river, pushing Isa's mother who hesitated at the water's edge, looking back at the trunk they had abandoned. "Our things," she moaned. "All our precious things."

The soldiers were left crawling to the water to wash their eyes or cursing as they sat on the road. None of them carried firearms, and their swords and knives were useless as the distance widened between them and Saul and the ben Youlis.

The sailors in the dinghy strained at the oars against the tide toward the ben Youlis who flailed their arms and tugged on collars and sleeves as they helped each other slog through the cold, shallow water in their sodden clothes. When they reached the boat, they hung onto the sides waiting their turn to be hauled onboard by the rowers.

No one spoke on the ride to the ship. Saul sat in the dinghy, cold and uncomfortable in his sopping boots and britches. He thought of his good hat, still back in the bushes, then permitted himself a brief look at Isa. Her ragged dress clung to her thin body as she shivered between her mother and Saul on a bench behind the rowers. Saul silently praised God for Isa's rags. Layered petticoats would have drowned her. Isa's mother kept one arm around Isa and the other around Elias. They clung together for warmth in the chilly night air. Eliahu sat behind them, hunched over, hugging himself. Saul heard him repeating a litany of prayers and said another silent prayer of gratitude that Isa was safe.

The breeze had freshened, kicking up the waves as the rowers crossed the channel back to the ship. More than once, Saul was thrown against Isa or she against him in the pitching of the dinghy. He would have paid for rougher seas.

He pulled his cloak around him and gazed at Isa obliquely. After all, what was the cost of a pair of boots, breeches, and even a good hat when the reward was such a vision?

They approached the ship, and Saul looked up at the men hanging over the gunwales, staring down at them. The captain puffed his pipe and stood on the bridge, arms folded. Saul saluted him. They would soon be away from this oppressive country and into the freer air of Holland.

Once they reached Amsterdam, he would find a coach to

Whatever it was, Sara was not giving up. She would go it alone if she had to. Josh could certainly choose to go back to St. Thomas. She walked to the window and surveyed the street in front of the hotel. A car was parked across the street, and two men stood on the sidewalk, smoking cigarettes and staring at the hotel entrance. A chill raced down Sara's back. Were she and Josh under surveillance? She stepped back from the window. She'd never seen those men before. Probably they were waiting for someone who would soon appear, and they'd drive off. But what if Samuel was right about dangerous people wanting the painting? She peered down at the two men, then picked up a pen and wrote a brief description of each, hoping she was being overly cautious. She'd recognize them if she saw them again. She hoped.

She pulled the table away from the wall so she and Josh could conveniently sit on each side and spread out the papers Samuel had given them. The ragged cluster of yellowed notes were receipts like the one Sara's grandmother had left her. The faded, hastily written names, addresses and items on each of the six receipts were as illegible as on her grandmother's receipt. It was just a carbon copy, of course, and a poor one at that. Could anything be done to make it more legible? Sara didn't think so.

She laid the receipts aside and turned to the stack of faded and torn articles about Jews who had recovered their stolen artwork. None of the articles mentioned any Rembrandts.

Sara picked up the list Samuel had prepared of organizations involved in finding stolen and lost art. She was surprised it was so long. The first thing on the agenda was to contact these groups. That was a job for the Internet, since the list was just that, with no addresses or phone numbers supplied.

She heard Josh's knock and opened the door. "No messages for me," he said.

His eyes used to light up when he saw her, but now his expression remained bleak and his eyes looked everywhere but at her. Sara's spirits plummeted. Was he planning to drop out of this project? Could she handle it alone?

She looked down at the papers. "None for me either." She

hadn't expected any. She snuck a look at Josh. "Is anything wrong?" she asked.

He shrugged. "Not at all," he said but his frown and listless gaze out the window spoke otherwise. Sara kept her eyes on the papers as she debated how to find out what was wrong. Something was.

He finally pulled a chair over to the table and picked up the last list, the one with the members of the resistance group to which Samuel and her grandmother had belonged.

"Those people stayed in places all over Europe," Sara said, depressed at the immensity of the task and the thought that if Josh's attitude didn't improve, she might be pursuing it alone. "Small hotels, pensions, boarding houses, apartments."

Josh rocked the chair back and waved the list. "But didn't Samuel say they were all originally from St. Thomas, friends who grew up together?"

"He did." Sara sat across the table, pondering the papers spread out before her. "They might have focused on Denmark since St. Thomas had been a Danish colony years before. When did the Nazis invade Denmark?"

His interest sparked like a struck match. He sat upright and snapped his fingers. "I think it was 1940. Took over Norway that year too."

Sara glanced at him, glad to see a bit of enthusiasm. "How do you know that? "

"I told you. History major." Josh shrugged. "And World War II movies." He drummed his fingers as he stared off into space. "So yeah, if Samuel's little group from St. Thomas was trying to save anybody's stuff, they might focus on the Danes."

He picked up the list again. "Although," he tapped his chin, "we did find the painting in Gibraltar."

He leafed through the papers. "Samuel added a note here that says by 1942, all the group members, including himself and your grandmother, had been captured or killed."

Sara reached for the list. "Let me see it."

Sara felt tears come to her eyes as she read her grandmother's name. Ruth Yulee. A name Sara had never heard spoken. Until her grandmother's death last year, Sara had not known her grandmother had once lived by that name. For a moment, Sara felt a deep sense of awe and sadness as she read this proof of the adventurous and courageous woman her grandmother had been before the Nazis and the camps had broken her spirit. How odd, cruel, and unpredictable life was. She regretted every moment of impatience she had ever felt at the woman she had thought was another boring West Virginia apron-wearing housewife.

Sara frowned. "Do you suppose anyone else survived?" she asked.

"I doubt it, but we can search for them." Josh was perusing another list. "It would be a big break if one of them did and remembered more than Samuel does."

"Or had been one of those who actually handled the art and gave out the receipts." That could have been her grandmother. The thought gave Sara goose bumps.

"We can try to decipher those later." Josh sat up and stretched, yawning. "I thought we would see Samuel and try to convince him to return to his family in St. Thomas. We'd be gone a couple of days. Instead. . . . "

He thought they'd only be gone a couple of days. That might be what's wrong. A twinge of jealousy unsettled her. Was he missing a girlfriend? He'd never mentioned one, and no one she met in her brief visit to St. Thomas had mentioned any women in his life.

He picked up a handful of papers and stood. "There's an Internet Cafe down the street. Let's begin looking up the names and organizations on the Internet first. If we get phone numbers, we can call them."

"Fresh air, that's what we need." Sara grabbed a notepad and the clipped receipts and slid them back into Samuel's notebook. "We'd better keep all Samuel's papers with us."

She stepped to the window and looked out. The car was still parked across the street, but now the men sat inside. She motioned Josh over and pointed to the car. "Been there since we got back."

"Don't like it," he said. "We'll have to find a back way out."

"Yes, let's," said Sara. When she reached the door she stopped.

"Just a minute." She pulled a hair out of her head and placed it on top of the clothes inside her suitcase.

Josh nodded. "Good idea."

Sara shrugged. "A bit hackneyed. An experienced spy would watch out for this, but I don't think our guys are experienced or very smart." She surveyed the room. "Do you suppose Samuel's right? That we are in danger?"

Josh shrugged. "He's an old man, living in the past, but I'm worried about the people at the pension who heard his stories." He waved at the window. "And I don't like the looks of that car."

"I'm hoping Samuel doesn't get hurt because of the decoy."

Josh laughed. "What a crazy idea. A decoy, of all things."

"He's seen too many movies," Sara said, closing the door behind them. On their way out, they headed toward the back of the hotel and left by a delivery door leading to the alley running alongside the hotel to the street.

The Internet Cafe was a hole-in-the-wall shop selling souvenirs and postcards at the entrance and time at the computers on a table in back. Sara and Josh each took a computer and began searching the names on Samuel's lists. Since the lists originated from Samuel's memory and were sketchy to begin with, the task was as difficult as Sara anticipated.

She chose to research the names of the resistance group members. Of the twelve names on the list, two were accounted for— Samuel and Sara's grandmother. Somene else might still be alive, and they might know something about where the painting came from. She went to AskJeeves.com first with little expectation of success. Names could have changed or they might be living in nursing homes or with relatives and so unreachable.

Giving up on AskJeeves.com, she logged onto a genealogy site to track down some of the names and their descendants, but with only names, common ones at that, and no birth or death dates, this resource was useless. She visited sites listing Nazi concentration camp victims, but the numbers were immense. She tried a new search engine, Google, to look for the names, but it brought up pages of similar names of people, none of them likely, almost all of them probably dead. She glanced at Josh. "I'm not having much luck, are you?"

He shook his head. "Let's go back to the hotel and call the numbers we have. We might find a relative if nothing else."

They returned to the hotel through the back alley. Sara immediately checked the hair on her suitcase. Still in place. Josh had entered behind her and noticed the blinking red light on the phone.

"You've got a message."

"Who would be calling me here?" She picked up the phone and listened to the messages, nodding with pursed lips.

A minute later, she put down the receiver and looked over at Josh.

"Well?" he said, leaning against the wall with folded arms. His face had returned to its bleak look.

She brushed the hair out of her eyes. "Mom wants a call. . .and so does your mother," she began. "And Samuel has left town."

"What?" Josh stared at Sara in disbelief.

"Actually, he's at the airport right now waiting for a flight out of the country." She handed him the receiver. "You listen to the messages. Tell me what you think."

He listened, then slowly hung up the receiver. "He sounds scared."

Sara nodded. "I thought so, too. He thinks someone is onto him."

"No one knows we found the Rembrandt."

"That concierge is sharp and nosy. She might have figured out what we're up to."

"The manager at the bank where we left the painting?" Josh thought a moment. "No. He might think we had something valuable but wouldn't know what it was. Anyway, he deals with such stuff every day." He paused, then added, "I've only talked to my mom briefly since we arrived and didn't mention the painting. What about yours?"

Sara groaned. "Of course, I called my mother yesterday and told her what's going on here. My mom worries. She doesn't have many friends or socialize easily, but my brother Dave. . . ." Sara bit her lip. She should not have mentioned anything about the Rembrandt to her mother. Of course, she'd tell Dave and knowing him, he might already be lining up buyers for it. Sara would have to avoid talking to him for awhile.

Josh pulled at his ear. "Samuel might have spoken to my parents. After all, he grew up with my grandparents. My mother always called him Uncle Samuel, even though they weren't related. I don't think they would say anything to anyone," Josh said, but he looked worried. "It's those people he talked to at the pension. I'll bet he's waving that decoy like a flag, trying to lure potential thieves to him and not us." He laughed as he shook his head. "Be just like him."

"I'm sure Samuel is off to be with his family in St. Thomas," Sara said. "He'll be okay. He belongs there anyway." She walked to the window and stared out at the street. "If the people in his resistance group were from St. Thomas, he should know their relatives. He could ask them if they know anything about this."

"He lived there for many years, you know." Josh paced the room. "He must have explored that angle. We can call my folks tomorrow. Maybe he'll be there."

"I'll call Mom." Sara looked at her watch. "Six hours time difference. Almost midnight there, but she's a night owl."

"Meanwhile, I can go through the other papers in the bundle Samuel gave us. The receipts, especially, and think about what else we might do here in Gibraltar."

"I plan to get phone numbers for all the organizations that deal with paintings lost in the Holocaust and talk to them. We need to brainstorm and put together a plan." She picked up the phone but set it down again as she saw the worry on Josh's face. He had gone to the window and leaned on it, staring down at the car still parked out front. This time it was empty.

"What's wrong?" Sara asked.

"I-I'm not sure I want to go through with this." Josh ran his hands through his shaggy, dark, wavy hair. "I've been thinking about it," he added. "There may be repercussions that. . . ." He paused. "The truth is. . . I'm afraid."

Sara froze. Was Josh backing out? She didn't want to take on this job by herself. "So am I," she said. "Even though the Rembrandt is safe and Samuel's on the way home with a decoy. My brother Dave might want to interfere, but he's back in West Virginia. Even if Dave told all his buddies back in West Virginia, what could they do about it?"

"Maybe you should call him," said Josh. "Warn him not to say anything to anyone."

She shook her head. "He might get too interested. No one here could actually know we have the painting. Samuel is the one they'd go after although I hope that's not so. Are we being followed? Those two men parked in front of the hotel concern me." She did feel uneasy and glanced at Josh, staring out the window.

"They aren't there now," said Josh. That sad and worried look seemed welded to his face..

"So what are you afraid of?" She asked again.

Josh sighed and turned away from the window. He frowned, stared down at his feet, and shook his head. "We might find out more than we want to know."

Chapter 5 – Provenance, 1616

Amsterdam.

The merchant ship with its passengers plunged through the rough waters of the North Sea toward Amsterdam. Despite the ship's rolling, Saul refused to keep to his bunk, preferring the bracing winds and salt spray of the deck. Isa left her family, all fighting seasickness below, to join Saul on his walks.

"The seas are rough. My parents are thinking that death at the hands of the Spaniards would not be as bad as the sickness they suffer here," she told him.

Saul could not help his heart turning over as he greeted her, glad of her company and pleased that she seemed to enjoy his. The valiant effort she had crafted to make such repairs as she could to her dress, using a shawl to cover the stains and tears, filled him with pity.

He looked down at her. "Perhaps so, but this sickness is only temporary."

"We are all grateful to you," she said seriously. "We had no more resources and were starving. It would not have been long before we were found and arrested. . .or killed."

"I was glad I could help." He wished to take her hand. "It was but a small service to ensure your safety and well-being." He could not be more explicit and thought back with irony to all his protests and anger at being sent on such a mission. He remembered telling his papa that it would likely prove a waste of time and money. Money. These people would need clothes and housing and work. How this would be accomplished nagged at him. He could not afford to help out of his own pockets.

Saul pushed this thought aside to enjoy the pleasure of walking along with Isa against the wind in a companionable silence. The coveted position of secretary to Monsieur Montalto in the court of the queen of France no longer seemed so important. Certainly not as important as a smile on Isa's face. He turned away so she would not see the adoration in his eyes.

"Will there be any trouble when we leave the ship in Amsterdam?" Isa asked. "We have nothing but the clothes we wear. We were forced to leave our trunk and everything it contained on shore with the soldiers."

Saul looked down at her ragged dress, the torn shawl that she hugged around herself. Her shoes, too, were battered. In fact, her entire family could pass as the worst kind of beggars. All his misgivings surfaced. This would not do, and it meant that his mission was not yet over. What would he find when they arrived in Amsterdam? Had his father made the necessary arrangements? Where would his father have found the money to pay the tradesmen, order the furniture, and purchase a home for this family? Had he found sponsors for them among the wealthier members of the synagogue?

What was the tie that bound his father to this desperate family? He was from an Ashkenazi family, originally from Austria. The ben Youli family came from Spain and then the Spanish Netherlands and so were Sephardic. Yet whatever the debt his father owed this family, he had refused to speak of it. Saul was to obey. Perhaps one day, he would pursue the matter with Eliahu, as his father-in-law, as family. Then he might learn the truth.

He looked out at the sea, listened to the creaks and groans of the ship, and smelled the fresh salt air. He said a silent prayer of gratitude, before glancing down at Isa. The family must be properly clothed and housed, and work must be found for Eliahu.

As the ship approached the spires and crowded buildings of Amsterdam, the seas calmed, and the family stepped out on deck to watch the ship drop anchor. Small boats filled with produce and crates barely made way for it. While the family watched the bustling activity of the men taking down the sails, Eliahu drew Saul aside.

"Words can not express how grateful we are to you." Eliahu spoke softly so none of the others would hear. "But we have nothing, and now I fear we must ask for more help."

"I understand." Saul stared down at his feet, thinking how hard this supplication must be for a proud man. "No need to speak further." He looked down at his own clothes, well-made and fashionable. White stockings, lace collar, and cuffs with studs, all tailored to mark him as a gentleman of some standing. All kept in excellent condition by his man-servant Bernard. After witnessing the privation of the ben Youlis, Saul glanced in appreciation at Bernard, leaning on the gunwale and staring out at the town.

"Whatever you can do, it must be considered a loan," said Eliahu. "It will be repaid."

"You are not to worry. I am sure my father has made arrangements for you." Saul stopped walking and looked at Eliahu. "My servant and I will take the first boat to the docks, and visit my father's representative there. We will return as soon as possible with the necessaries." Saul hoped that would be true.

Tears sprang into Eliahu's eyes. He looked away. "Pardon me, my friend." He dashed at his eyes. "I have spent many days with not enough food or rest and too many worries."

"I know." Saul resumed walking along with Eliahu. "I hope those days are past. Please don't trouble yourself about debt. My father assures me he is pleased to help an old friend." *If he has not provided for them, I will apply to the synagogue.*

Eliahu grasped Saul's hands and shook them. "May God bless you and your father."

Saul paid the sailors to row him and Bernard ashore where he passed through the customs house without trouble and entered the city. He felt grateful that here in the United Provinces, barriers to Jews practicing their religion were removed in 1614.

He walked proudly without harassment to the Beth Jacob Synagogue, wearing his white cuffs and closed lace-trimmed collar. He

He stood awkwardly, watching her, wanting to say what was in his heart, but he could not.

Finally, Isa looked up at him. "We are all so grateful to you. We wish you a pleasant journey and hope you will be well."

Saul cleared his throat. "And I, you," he said. "I hope you will be happy here."

"You rescued us from hell. We now live in paradise and our dearest wish would be that you could stay with us." The last words were said so softly that Saul barely heard them. Isa turned back to her embroidery.

He watched her a moment, then fearful that he might betray himself, he turned and walked out to the carriage. "Go. Now," he said and stepped up into the coach to take his seat. Bernard followed.

The coachman flicked the reins. The carriage rolled forward on the stones, but all Saul's thoughts centered on that beautiful face bent over a square of cloth fortunate enough to be in her hands.

Chapter 6 - Gibraltar, 1999

"Is anything bothering you?" Sara asked Josh again that evening.

"No, of course not," he said. But something obviously was.

By the next day, he was even more uncommunicative and morose, frowning at the floor, pursing his lips, and pacing.

Scared and worried, Sara attempted to break through the barrier with a cheerful face and comments. His responses were monosyllabic, even at breakfast in the hotel dining room. Sara carried back an offering of pastries from the buffet table, but they produced only a fleeting smile.

He waved aside Sara's efforts to develop a plan, so she ate the rest of her breakfast in silence and tried to dream up one on her own. She felt abandoned and found Josh's attitude difficult to accept, but she'd only known him a few weeks. Was this the way he really was? Faced with obstacles he gave up? Was that why he gave up graduate school?

As she sipped her tea and mulled over what to do about Josh, two men approached their table and hovered. She looked up at them. "Yes?" They looked like the men in the car outside the hotel. The description she'd written down fit. She'd been too upset about Josh to check for the car this morning.

"You are Ms. Miller?" asked the thinner man in what could possibly be a German accent. He was bald with sandy eyebrows and thin lips curved into an ingratiating smile. The other man was stouter and shorter. Both wore business suits, no hats.

"Who are you and what do you want?" asked Josh, standing.

"Please, may we join you?" The thin man didn't wait for an answer but slid onto a chair. He looked at Sara and then at Josh. "I am Mr. Blank."

The other man took the opposite chair. "And I am Mr. Smythe." He studied his fingernails.

"Yeah. Right," said Josh, frowning as he sat back down.

Blank? Smythe? Fake names, Sara thought, studying them. What did they want?

"We're tourists," Josh said, "and we're not buying anything from you."

Mr. Blank chuckled. "You must listen to our proposition. You will find it most interesting."

Sara sat back, stared at Josh, and did not respond.

"You have a. . . ," Blank hesitated, "a package of interest to us. This package is only a problem for you. For us, it is a family matter."

Smythe narrowed his eyes. "A family matter indeed."

Blank frowned at him and continued. "We can handle its. . .uh. . .delivery appropriately and pay you handsomely for it."

Josh leaned his chair back. "We have nothing of interest to you."

"And why would you think we do?" Sara asked.

Blank smiled. "Samuel Yulee is my good friend. He told me about it and suggested that I contact you. He thought you would prefer that I take care of it."

Sara glared at him. Whoever these men were, they did not know Samuel well, and they had certainly misjudged her. And Josh. They were fishing. Were they friends of the concierge or had they heard the story from someone else? Were they at the party where Samuel talked about it? If so, how many others were going to come sniffing around?

"As I told you," Josh said, "we have nothing of interest to you."

Blank turned his cold eyes to Josh. "That painting belongs to my family," he said with narrowed eyes and stabbing fingers. "You are stealing it."

"Tell us about your family," said Sara, to defuse the situation and get a clue from whatever story they told.

"Our family owned the painting and lost it to the Nazis in. . ." Smythe hesitated, his eyes looked up and down at her. "In 1940. We are merely claiming what was stolen from us."

"We need documentation from you about that." Sara now stood. She was through with these bullies. "If you cannot furnish documentation, give us your name and address and the reason why you think we have your painting. Otherwise, we cannot do business with you."

Smythe rose with flushed face and glared at Sara. Sara glared back. He looked as if he were ready to hit her. She refused to flinch.

"We want that painting," he said through gritted teeth, "and we will get it. You will spare yourselves much trouble by letting us buy it from you." He stared at Sara and added with slow calculation, "You would not like to get hurt."

"Are you threatening me?" Sara's voice rose. Josh reached over and laid a hand on her arm.

"I think this interview is over," he said.

Blank spoke. "You misunderstood Mr. Smythe. Of course we are not threatening you. The painting is an heirloom handed down in our family and stolen by the Nazis. We would simply like to get it back."

"And as I told your friend, Mr. Smythe," Sara said between clenched teeth, "we need complete documentation or corroboration to that effect. You may leave your contact information with us."

"All our papers were lost many years ago." Smythe shook his head. "I cannot supply the documentation. That is why I offer you a reward you will find most sufficient for its return."

Sara looked at Josh before replying. His face was expressionless. He was waiting for her. "I'm afraid not," she said. "We cannot relinquish the painting on that basis."

Smythe sat back, frowned at her, and twiddled his glass. He glanced at Blank. After a moment, Smythe stood. "Very well."

Blank's snake-like eyes slid from Josh to Sara as he, too, stood. "Good day," he said and followed Smythe out of the dining room.

Sara watched the two men leave and then looked at Josh. "One of the people who heard Samuel?" she asked.

"Could be. Or a friend of the concierge." Josh drummed his fingers on the table. "Boobs. Both of them."

"We haven't seen the last of them either." Sara pushed away her breakfast plate. She was no longer hungry. She sat back and studied Josh. He was as adamant as she was in refusing Blank and Smythe's offer. If he had lost interest in the project, he could have urged her to hand the painting over to them. What was wrong with him?

Perhaps she needed to reassess him and his role in this adventure. If he continued to be so unpleasant, she could proceed without him. Perhaps she really didn't like him much after all.

Maybe he needed a break. The last few days had been intense.

Then she surprised herself by saying, "Let's go out for a walk along the Mediterranean. I'm still so thrilled to be here." Had she actually suggested going for a walk along the sea? The idea, much less the walk, would have brought on an intense panic attack two months ago. The strange panic attacks she used to suffer at the sight of any body of water had disappeared as mysteriously as they had arrived. She felt liberated and, for once, in control.

"A walk sounds good," said Josh, but he cast her a searching look. "You're sure?"

"Of course," Sara said. Had Josh seen her fear? She thought she had covered those attacks well. Was he that perceptive? She snuck a glance at him, but he was staring glumly down at the carpeted floor.

Josh led her out of the dining room.

They crossed the street to the sidewalk alongside the sea. Sara scanned the street for the mysterious car but it was no longer in front of the hotel. "I don't see Blank or Smythe or their car around," she said.

"They're probably lurking, though." Josh scanned their surroundings. "They aren't going to give up that easily."

A frisson of fear traveled down Sara's back. What would Blank and Smythe try next? Josh took her hand as they strolled down the sidewalk, but the his face was grim. Sara attempted to start a conversation, but it died stillborn as Josh, lost in his own thoughts, didn't respond.

After awhile, they stopped to watch the fishing boats in the distance, then sat side by side on a low concrete wall. They dug their shoes into the sand and stared out at the sunshine sparkling like diamonds on the water. Behind them, cars rolled by on the street that followed the coastline. On the other side of the street, two- and three-story pensions and shops stood, the green slopes of the Rock of Gibraltar behind them.

"What's wrong, Josh?" Sara asked. "I know something is bothering you. Is it me?"

Josh roused himself enough to look at her and shake his head. "You? Of course not." He picked up a pebble and skipped it out on the water. He didn't say anything for a few minutes. Sara waited. Finally, he turned to her.

"I'm sorry. I haven't been much company lately. I'm so worried."

Sara studied his unhappy face. "Worried? Why?"

"You see what this means, don't you?" asked Josh, casting his eyes down at the sand, his slumped body matching the hopelessness on his face.

"Another adventure, I think," said Sara, hoping her enthusiasm would snap Josh out of his funk.

He stared out at the water. "Is that how you see it?"

She turned to him. "What are you worried about? Please tell me. I'm eager to get started, but if you have reservations, I should know. We have a lot of work to do."

Josh shook his head, the picture of melancholy, picked up another pebble, and threw it out on the water.

"What is it, Josh?" asked Sara, now alarmed. She waited.

Finally he said in a low voice, "I love my family, Sara."

Sara had not expected this. Had she said anything against them? Of course not. Why would she? They had been most gracious to her. Perhaps he was homesick. "They're nice people. I love them too, and I'm glad I found them." Where was he going with this?

She took his hand and squeezed it, then she let it go. "And I'm glad I met you."

Josh brushed his hand across his eyes. "Would you still feel that way if you found. . .that is, you learned that they had done something wrong? Very wrong?"

Sara paused in her natural rush to reassure him. Would she? "I don't know, Josh. They weren't Nazi sympathizers, were they? I can't think of anything worse than that." She looked at his downcast face. "What did they do?"

He sighed. "I'm afraid of what we'll find."

"Afraid?" She saw the slump of his shoulders, the uncertainty in his eyes. The excitement of their discovery still thrilled her but had vaporized for Josh. He now seemed crushed by the weight of it. "What do you mean?" she asked.

He didn't reply for a few moments, then shrugged. "Think about it, Sara. I can't get the questions out of my mind. How did my family get its money? It takes a lot of money to open an art gallery in downtown Charlotte Amalie."

"But your family has been there a long, long time. Plenty of time to build up a business."

"One would think." He kicked at the sand with his foot.

"What are you afraid we'll find?"

"Sara, we've learned that your grandmother and Samuel were involved in smuggling art belonging to Jewish families out of Europe during the Holocaust. My grandparents must have been part of the chain. What happened to all that art? Was it eventually returned as promised? We know one painting wasn't. That Rembrandt. Did other art get waylaid? Didn't you wonder about Abe Carilla—the man we met in Florida? How come Carilla's family never received the painting they had entrusted to Samuel's group?" He threw another pebble into the sea.

"And how did my parents get so wealthy?" he added bitterly.

Sara stared down at the sand. "Oh. I see." No wonder he had been so distracted and depressed. Not a girlfriend, not a problem with her, not a lack of interest or enthusiasm. He was grappling with concerns much bigger than anything she had considered.

"Yes." Josh stabbed the sand with his foot.

Josh's father and mother. Not them. Their parents. Josh's grandparents. Sara had never met them, but his parents had such a high standing in their community. She liked them. She couldn't believe they were dishonest. "Why don't we ask them?"

Josh snorted. "Oh, sure. Ask them."

She looked at him. "Why not?"

Josh shook his head. His shoulders sagged as if they couldn't carry the weight of his thoughts. "Because…because they could tell me the truth and show me how they built the business bit by bit and honestly, but maybe that's not how it was. Maybe they stole that art, sold it, and kept the money for their business." He looked at her. "In which case, they would lie. How would I know?"

"I see," Sara said again, as they both stared down at the sand.

"Yes," Josh repeated, frowning as he picked up another pebble and threw it out on the water.

Sara looked at the fishing boats motoring in the distance. "So we have to trace not only the painting we found but also check on what happened to all the others as well."

"Oh sure, that'll be easy." Josh folded his arms and kicked at the sand.

Sara glanced at him. "I didn't say it would be easy, but Uncle Samuel is depending on us. And your family's reputation is at stake. We need to develop a plan and start working it."

"What if I don't like what we find out?" He gazed across the water, his eyes blinking in the bright sunlight. "Do you think I want you to know I'm descended from thieves?"

"That doesn't mean you're a thief." Sara took his hand and squeezed it. "I don't think you or your family are thieves, but we do need to learn the truth."

Josh shook his head. "So how do you propose we do that?"

"We talk to your family. Get their records—they must have kept them. They probably returned the paintings to the rightful owners, but maybe they didn't know how to return some of them. Maybe they couldn't read the receipts either. First, we'll have to find out what did happen, then we do whatever needs to be done—if anything." Sara looked at Josh. "If they sold any of those paintings, and they probably did not, it was because they couldn't locate the owners. In that case, if we do find the owners because we have some of the receipts, your parents might make amends or pay back what the paintings were worth."

Josh dug his shoe into the sand and frowned.

Sara grabbed his arm and forced him to look at her. "Right now, you don't know anything, you only have suspicions. I say we look for the truth and deal with it, or you'll live with those suspicions forever."

"Look for the truth. . ." Josh repeated.

"Samuel is leaving this job to us. He would have known if your family or my grandmother had benefited from stolen art. He would never have given us this. . .this mission if he suspected your family of such dealings."

"Maybe. . ." Josh shook his head. He pushed himself off the concrete wall. Sara also stood and took his hand.

"Of course." She began walking back to their hotel. "Samuel would have known. Let's get back to work. We can ask him to send us an accounting of what paintings were returned and what happened to those that couldn't be returned. It's an obvious question and no one should have any problems with it."

"Unless something else happened to those paintings. . . unless someone doesn't want us looking into this question." Josh paused, then added, "Like my parents."

Chapter 7 - Provenance, 1616

Tours, France.

The carriage rolled on across the meadows of the Low Countries and then to France taking Saul back to Paris and his duties as secretary to Monsieur Montalto. Saul felt unsettled, restless, and impatient. He jumped out of the coach whenever it stopped, whether they needed to change horses, rest, or buy meals at taverns along the route. The journey seemed endless.

He thought back to the year before. His feelings had been quite different on that journey from his home in the Venice ghetto, stifled by tight quarters and narrow canals, to the post with Montalto in exciting and cosmopolitan Paris. The thrill of traveling through towns and countries he had only read about kept him at the coach window, where he soaked in every sight.

The taverns and inns brought other experiences. He had enjoyed the boisterous camaraderie and drinking every evening, but he had taken one look at the louts snoring in the sleeping rooms allocated to men and decided to pay extra to sit in the parlor at night instead. His man-servant slept with the other servants as usual. For most people, traveling was to be endured as necessary, in carriages that rattled every bone, dirt that snuck into every crevice and fold, and manure-laden mud that stuck to even the finest shoe.

He laughed grimly. On this trip from Amsterdam, he barely tolerated the boredom, and the tavern camaraderie now seemed menacing, veering toward boisterous bullying and challenge that frightened him. The sight of new places on the road no longer thrilled him. Through the interminable hours, his thoughts did not stray far from Isa's large brown eyes and full bosom. He knew years would pass before he achieved the stature worthy of claiming that delightful girl as his own.

On the fifteenth day, he arrived in Paris at his employer's splendid mansion, built to befit the physician to the queen and reflect the owner's prestige. Saul had seen grandeur in Venice, but in Paris he lived with it. He would have liked to scoff at such ostentatious wealth, but he loved climbing the marble steps leading from the road up to the mahogany door. What would Isa think of such splendor? Would she be as impressed as he was by the spacious foyer so well lit by a magnificent crystal chandelier overhead? Would she marvel that the slender golden chains from which it hung could suspend such weight, even when filled with enough candles to light an entire city? He imagined leading her into each of the well-furnished parlors on each side of the foyer, and both of them mounting the central massive staircase of polished oak ascending to the floor above. He would like to share with Isa the honor of living in such a palace. She would see how he enjoyed the deference of the well-trained servants.

He woke from his daydreams, exhausted by his restless thoughts and the travail of his journey. He wished for a respite of a week at least, but as he entered the mansion, the head steward immediately gave him a letter from Montalto. He read it with dread, feeling a profound weariness. Montalto was requesting Saul to travel on to Tours. Saul groaned. Tours. Another seven days' journey at least, and he was expected to leave early the next morning. He had no doubts that Montalto would then barrage him with the work accumulated during his absence. Perhaps, if he were kept busy, he would not think so incessantly of Isa.

His position as secretary, which he had felt honored to achieve, now rankled in its absolute necessity to live in France rather than Amsterdam. He chafed at the limitations that had charmed him three weeks before. Then he had hidden his irritation at being ordered to the Spanish Netherlands. He ran a hand across his eyes. Was this to be his life from now on? Ordered hither and yon by his employer and his father with no regard to his own health and happiness?

Nevertheless, early the next morning, he trudged out to the carriage with Bernard and climbed into the coach for the tedious trip to Tours.

As the sun set on the seventh day, they arrived at the town house where Montalto was staying. Even though it was not yet dark, the house shone as if every candle had been lit. Montalto's valet, wringing his hands and shaking his head, met Saul, tired, dusty, and irritable, at the door. The valet barely remembered to take Saul's hat and cloak. A feeling of dread hung in the air like funeral drapes, halting the reprimand that sprang to Saul's lips. The other servants paid little attention to him as they whispered together in small groups at the foot of the stairs.

"He is dead, monsieur," the valet said without preamble. "He is dead. What are we to do?" He gripped Saul's hat and cloak in trembling hands.

Saul did not comprehend at first and responded in a cold voice meant for servants. "Dead? Pray tell me, who is dead?"

"The master, sir. The master. Monsieur Montalto." The valet looked at Saul with frightened eyes. "He is dead. What are we to do?"

Elijah Montalto, physician to Marie de Medici, queen of France and second wife of King Henry IV, was dead? Impossible. "But I left him three weeks ago. Surely he cannot be dead. Are you sure?" Saul looked up the stairs where two maids hovered in front of a closed door. He turned to the valet. "Is that his room?"

The valet stared up at it. "Oui, monsieur."

The door opened, the maids stepped aside, and two men walked out. The first one saw Saul, gazing up the stairs at them. "Monsieur Morteira?"

"Oui," said Saul. *Who were these men?*

"You have heard. . .?" asked the other one.

Saul felt the floor heave under his feet. He reached for the banister. "So it is true then?" he asked, recognizing the man behind as Montalto's solicitor, Monsieur Bloch. His square, white, lace-edged collar framed a narrow head with a mustache and pointed beard. The doublet embroidered with rosettes and the white shoes painted in similar rosettes showed him to be a man of elegance and fashion.

Both men nodded. "A sad affair," said Monsieur Bloch.

Saul stared up at the men from the foot of the stairs. "How did this happen?" And, he wondered, what would now be required of him?

"I was called to the bedside by his coachman. He had been taken violently ill. I could not save him." The man in front walked down the stairs. He also wore the large square collar over doublet with breeches, white stockings and shoes, but his outfit was as austere and somber as the expression on his face. "I am a physician and colleague of Monsieur Montalto's. Eduardo Leger."

Saul stepped aside to let the men pass as he bowed in acknowledgement. "What should be done?" he asked.

Monsieur Bloch gazed at the assemblage around Saul. "I suggest that we meet in the parlor." He pointed to a room at the right of the stairs and addressed one of the maids. "We require brandy and a cold supper."

The maid curtseyed. "Oui, Monsieur." She disappeared into the back rooms, followed by the other servants.

"Over here, gentlemen." Monsieur Bloch led them into the parlor. "We have much to discuss."

Saul followed in a dazed state. What would he do now? *I am no longer employed. Should I even return to Paris?* Montalto's valet brought in glasses and brandy, poured for them all, and left.

"When did he die?" asked Saul. "Had he been ill? He was in good health when I last saw him."

"Monsieur Montalto died almost an hour ago after a short illness," said Monsieur Bloch, the solicitor. "We do not know the exact cause." He turned to Saul. "As you know, he was of our faith and must be buried as soon as possible."

"Of course." Saul drummed his fingers on the table, thinking of

Montalto and the plans, the dreams, he had left undone. *And now I am to bury my employer. All the power he had over me, over the queen, over France, has dissolved like salt into the sea.*

"He is to be taken to the Jewish cemetery," Bloch referred to the papers in his hand, "in Amsterdam at Ouderkerk aan de Amstel." He looked at Saul with cocked eyebrow. "You must make the arrangements. His funeral service will be at the Beth Haim Synagogue there."

Amsterdam! Despite the shock of such news, Saul's heart leaped. Someone would have to accompany the body. He was the logical choice. "I have come from Amsterdam. I am familiar with that city."

He struggled to keep a solemn demeanor in the face of such news. The cold supper arrived, creating a diversion.

After they had eaten, Bloch again picked up the papers and peered at Saul over them. "Unfortunately, Monsieur Montalto had no family here and as secretary you will be the logical person to take charge of his affairs. Under my supervision, of course. You are familiar with his correspondence and business?"

"Of course," Saul said.

"Good." Leger nodded. "So you will do what you can to conclude any pressing matters. We have many arrangements to make, but you must leave by tomorrow."

"I will prepare the estate and legal necessities for the family," said Bloch.

"And I can leave tomorrow," said Saul. He no longer felt weary. He could take a thousand trips such as this one if they took him to Amsterdam.

He escorted Bloch and Leger to the door and then asked the valet to show him to his room. The next day he arranged for transporting the body to Amsterdam without delay and for shipping his own meager possessions to Amsterdam. This time, Saul made no plans to return to France.

What a strange coincidence. What did it mean? There was something mystical about it, as if God in his infinite wisdom had set in motion this strange sequence of events. That I should be the one who rescued the beautiful Isa and her family; that I should be the one to take them to Amsterdam and to settle them in the city; that my employer, who would have retained me in France, was now to be buried in Amsterdam, and that I, Saul Levi Morteira, should be the one to accompany Montalto on his last journey; all of this must be part of a great plan. Could it be part of God's plan for me? What else could it mean?

He said a silent prayer and asked for God's blessings on Montalto's soul.

Saul determined to make Amsterdam his home. With the death of his employer, he would appeal to his family in Venice for help. The thought suddenly occurred to him: he and his family were Ashkenazi Jews from Germany; most of the Jews in Amsterdam were Sephardic from Spain and Portugal. Isa's family was Sephardic, too. Would that be a problem? Worrying about this occupied him for two hours of the journey before he decided that since he was fluent in both Spanish and Portuguese, he should be able to fit in well with the Amsterdam Jews.

He sat back in the coach to count his assets once again. He was well-educated and profoundly immersed in the laws and rituals of his Jewish faith. He was well-suited to the academic life. All this lent weight and substance to his bearing. He could acquire the stature of a rabbi, a teacher, and because he had strong views on how schools should teach the Torah, perhaps he could found an academy. He saw the road ahead clearly.

All this will make me a worthy contender for the hand of the beautiful Isa. His heart gladdened at the thought and he determined to speak to the rabbis at the synagogue of Beth Haim immediately upon the discharge of his duties for Monsieur Montalto.

Chapter 8 - Gibraltar, 1999

"We're not going to get anywhere trying to hunt down survivors of the original resistance group," Sara said, waiting for Josh's reaction. Had she convinced him that the truth was better than suspicion? Was he now committed to this project?

Josh sat at the table in Sara's hotel room, shuffling the papers. He looked up. "We've got one in the bag. Samuel. We should have pumped him more."

Josh was ready to press on. Sara felt giddy with relief. "We need to make sure he got home okay," she said. "Now that we've had that threatening visit from Blank and Smythe, I'm worried about him and his decoy." She checked her watch. "Do you have a number for him in St. Thomas?"

Josh looked through his wallet and retrieved a small slip of paper. "Got it . I'll call him." He walked to the phone, dialed numbers, and waited. He looked over at Sara. "No answer."

"I don't like that." Sara thought of the car that might have followed them from Samuel's pension and of his sudden departure. Could Blank and Smythe have been in the car or somebody else? Had Samuel truly gone away on his own or was he forced away by someone or something? Was he okay?

"I'll call my mom. Maybe she's heard from him." Josh dialed again and waited, smiling at Sara. "He doesn't have a mobile phone and his home phone's been turned off."

"Ask her if she or your dad knows anything about the Rembrandt." Sara winced at the look Josh threw her.

"We should cover all bases," she added defensively.

She turned back to read through the papers, not wanting to cramp his conversation, but her ears perked up when he asked his mother about Samuel.

"You've heard nothing?" Josh asked. He raised an eyebrow at Sara. "Do you have any idea where he might be?" Sara saw a frown appear as Josh listened. "We need to talk with him as soon as possible. Let me know when he shows up. I'll keep you posted on where we are."

He listened another moment and Sara saw him swallow as he glanced at her. Then he said, "By the way, Mom, do you know anything about a Rembrandt painting of a rabbi as a Moor? It was one of the paintings lost in the Holocaust."

Sara waited, hands clenched, as Josh listened. His hands twisted the phone wire and he stared down at the floor.

"Okay. Thanks," he said. "Love you, too, Mom." Josh put down the phone and shook his head.

"No sign of Samuel?" Sara asked.

"Nope." Josh sat back and put his hands behind his head. "Samuel always played things his way. He may be trailing that decoy all over Europe. I'm not too worried. . .yet."

He reached for a pen. "My mother said she'd dig out the old records on the rescued paintings and get back to me. You're right, Sara. We need to find the truth about the Rembrandt and all those other paintings."

Sara turned away from Josh to hide her relief. Josh was onboard now. She hoped Samuel was all right and simply off on some jaunt.

"Speaking of Samuel, I'm sure Blank and Smythe aren't through with us," Sara said. "They give me the creeps. What do you think they'll do next?"

Josh paused, pen in hand. "Might depend on how they found out about us. Through Samuel at the party where he had too much wine? The concierge? Some other means?"

"Unless they've spent almost sixty years hunting for the painting, which I doubt, it has to be someone at Samuel's pension." She was beginning to feel that at the pension, Samuel may have been like a leaky bucket, always spilling something.

"But they don't know where that painting is." Josh stretched his arms out. "We made a big mistake, Sara, when we talked to those two obvious crooks."

She stared at him. "What?" They'd revealed nothing to Blank and Smythe. "What mistake?"

He sat up and rapped on the table. "We knew what they were talking about."

"You're right." Sara put her head in her hands and groaned. "We should have pretended ignorance. They got us."

"So they know we have it, but they don't know where." Josh cast his eyes around the room.

"And they were so busy watching us that they missed seeing Samuel leave with the decoy. It was their red car in front of the hotel."

Josh nodded. "If they'd seen him, they'd be after him instead of us." He looked over at Sara. "I'm glad they missed him." Josh shook his head and sighed. "He's too fragile—his bones would break easily."

Sara stared at him as his meaning became clear. "You think they'd beat him? That's horrible." She shivered. "That means they'd beat us, too, torture us if they caught us in a vulnerable place." She picked up the lamp on the table. "What are we going to do?"

She examined the lamp and dropped her voice. "I don't see any bugs. That is, if I'd recognize one when I saw it. I suppose they might try to plant one on us or in our rooms."

Josh laughed. "If they had smarts, but I don't see any signs of a break-in, do you? Or a search?" He pointed to the lamp and whispered. "The painting is large enough that it would be easy to see if we had it. If they did break in, that is, and if they wanted to plant some bugs." He looked under the table then he walked over to the television set and turned it on loud. "If they did, that should confuse them," he said, lowering his voice. "They don't seem the type to know anything about sophisticated listening devices."

"They wouldn't find the painting, so then what?" Sara whispered, tapping a finger on the table. "They'd spend a few days listening for clues on the bugs."

"Yeah." Josh said. "Buys us a couple of days. We need to change hotels."

"Or rooms," said Sara. "We should stay here in case Samuel calls. I'll go down and talk to the desk clerk."

Half an hour later, they had moved their belongings to other rooms across the hall, which Sara thought would serve their purpose, and were back on task.

Josh picked up the papers from Samuel's notebook and leafed through them. "Samuel's resistance group had to be organized in some way or have important connections. People wouldn't hand their valuables to somebody on the street. The owners of the property were given receipts and expected to reclaim their belongings at a future date."

"True." Sara said. "Samuel said most paintings and other property were shipped to your family's art gallery." Sara saw Josh's body tense. "I've seen your Dad's office. He has records on everything else, and I don't believe your family is anything but scrupulously honest. You're right. Your grandparents would certainly have kept records of what they received and how they disbursed it. Surely they would. . . ."

He stared out the window to the blank wall of the other building. "But it's been sixty years. Would my parents have kept them ?"

Sara walked to the window and turned around to look at Josh. "I don't know, but we need that list and a full report. If Samuel gets back there, he could ask your parents for us—tactfully, of course—and then fax the records to us. We could match them to these receipts." In deference to Josh's feelings, Sara hid her excitement. Maybe they were grasping at straws, but she felt they had taken a tiny step forward.

She leaned over Josh's shoulder, saw him hesitate and felt his pain as he wrote down the questions to ask Samuel. She ached to ease the pain but wasn't sure how. Finally, she said, "Your family would have done a great service, Josh."

"It's a place to start," he said. Sara knew what he was thinking. These records, if his family still had them, could establish a path from the original owner to Josh's family and then back to the original owner or his heirs. The result? Case closed. Josh's family found innocent of any wrong-doing.

Or not.

Neither of them spoke. Josh stared at the wall, his mouth set in a grim line.

"Let's move on," Sara said, rushing to alleviate the awkward silence between them.

"Yeah. Here's another question. What happened to the paintings that couldn't be returned?" He narrowed his eyes at Sara. "For my family's sake."

Sara stared absently out the window. "Of course. I have a bunch more. How did they get hold of the art in the first place? How was it shipped to them? This was wartime."

"How did they recruit members to the group?"

Josh rapped the table. "And why did he think there was a traitor in the group?"

"That's right." Sara stepped back and folded her arms. "Another question."

Sara walked back to her side of the table and sat down. "Did he keep in touch with any of the other resistance members after the war?"

Josh leaned back in his chair and stretched. "He more or less answered that. He didn't or he would have a more current name and address on one of those lists."

"And he would have known his sister, my grandmother, was alive," added Sara.

"I don't see the point of pursuing any traitor in the resistance group." Josh shrugged. "He or she would probably be long dead by now."

"Could have descendants." Sara said. "That may be why Samuel made the decoy. I have another idea," she said, tapping her pen.

Josh threw her a lopsided grin. "Yes, you are full of them."

Sara ignored the comment. "We only need to locate the rightful owner of the Rembrandt. That's what we should keep in our heads. That's our top priority. Too easy to be distracted by a lot of other issues."

Josh folded his arms. "So...?"

"So we talk to experts on Rembrandt paintings. Maybe we can establish a provenance that way. Find out who the most recent owner was."

"If it is a genuine Rembrandt."

Sara brushed this aside impatiently. "Yes, if it is a genuine Rembrandt or in the Rembrandt school. Or even if it's a well-known copy." She looked at him. "It is an old painting."

Josh nodded. "And it was painted by a skilled artist."

"Right." Sara agreed and then wrote a note to herself. "We need to go back to the Internet Cafe to look up Rembrandt experts. "Does it matter if it's a genuine Rembrandt? What if it's a copy or done by a student in Rembrandt's studio?"

Josh sat back, rubbing his chin with his hand. "I don't know. As you said, we only have to return the painting we have to its rightful owner. Whether it's genuine or a copy or whatever doesn't matter."

"We are on a bit of a hot seat here, you know," said Sara, fanning herself with the sheaf of papers.

"How so?" asked Josh. He tipped his chair back and folded his arms.

"The owners could say their painting was an original, but we gave them a fake." Sara frowned.

Josh brought his chair back to an upright position. He shook his head. "I don't think so. For one thing, if it's an original, there's got to be a provenance showing a chain of ownership. He'd have to be able to prove he owned an original in the first place."

"Of course the painting has been out of circulation for half a century," Sara said. "They would only have our word for how we found it. Would that void its provenance if we had one?" Sara studied Josh. He knew more about paintings than she did, surely. He must have learned something at his parents' art gallery. She knew nothing. She couldn't even say what might be a good painting or a bad one. She picked up the pen and tapped it in staccato rhythm on the desk. "Right now we don't have anything that might serve as a provenance. Doesn't it usually stay with the painting? How will that affect the painting's value?"

"I don't know." Josh propped his chin on his hand. "And whoever the owner is could conceivably have had an authentic and a fake or a copy from an apprentice. They could claim the painting we found, which was the genuine Rembrandt, was actually the apprentice's copy that they also owned, that we'd stolen the original and given them the copy. Then they'd want compensation...from us."

"The possibilities are downright scary, when you put it like that." Sara shivered.

"Yeah. But I say we plow ahead anyway." Josh pulled a Coke out of the small refrigerator in the room. He raised an eyebrow at her.

"No thanks." She stared down at her hands, thinking of her grandmother's bequest. Her grandmother had expected her to finish the job. "I agree. We have to go ahead. It's the only way we'll find out your family didn't get rich on the misfortunes of others." She looked up at Josh. "Which I don't believe for a moment," she added and then said, "I hope your mother is going through those records."

"I hope." Josh walked to the window and stared out at the street below, sipping his Coke. "I want the complete story from both of them."

Sara picked up a pad of paper and her purse. "I'm going back down to the cafe and start getting phone numbers for the organizations on the list Samuel gave us. I'll also look up Rembrandt experts. An expert might know who was the last owner of our. . ." she glanced at the door, "our package."

"I'll go with you." Josh followed her out the door. "Blank and company have us under surveillance. Maybe someone else, too. Like Samuel said, we should stick together and watch our backs."

Chapter 9 - Provenance, 1623

Amsterdam.

Saul walked down the marble steps of his house on Sint-Anthonishuis. His thoughts lingered on Isa and her family, a few blocks away. Seven years had passed since that night on the coast of the Spanish Netherlands. Seven years. They had all done well in the tolerant environment and prosperous economy of Amsterdam and the United Provinces.

He had as well. His academy was flourishing, and he was becoming well-known and respected as a rabbi.

He stopped for a moment to feel the balmy breezes and sniff the scent of flowers. Spring. For this special night, he had shed his rabbinical garb and dressed carefully in the latest fashion, lace-trimmed, wide white collar, full sleeves with vertical panels in black and white, and full black breeches and stockings. Even his black, heeled shoes were new from the cobbler. He hoped to impress them all.

The time was right to approach Isa and her father on the subject of marriage. Isa. An excellent wife for a rabbi. Beautiful and accomplished, although at twenty-three, she was well beyond first blush. She had had other suitors, of course. He had seen them and discreetly inquired about them, but Isa had shown no preference, and none were of any concern. Certainly none approached his own learning and status in life. Attaining that status had kept him from being the most attentive suitor he might have been, but no man could be more worthy of Isa's hand.

He thought that both Eliahu and Isa's mother, even her brother Elias, favored his suit. Isa, beautiful Isa, she of the dark-brown eyes, full lips, and shining black hair he longed to caress, Isa would soon be his wife. No one could have any objections. His heart was full, and he greeted everyone he met as he walked down the street.

As smitten as he was, he could not help the unbidden thought that crept across his mind—and not for the first time. Isa was intelligent, perhaps too intelligent for a woman, and tended to be headstrong. He would have to teach Isa her place. She must not question his authority as she sometimes did now. But that was only girlish flirting. Of course, she would soon learn proper deference when she became his wife.

He was so engrossed in his thoughts that he almost passed the steps of the ben Youli house. He turned back, climbed the steps, and rapped on the door with his walking stick. A young maid answered and curtseyed.

"Welcome, mijnheer," she said. "May I take your hat?"

He handed it to her and she regarded it with awe. It was the latest in fashion with a lower crown and wider brim than before. He had turned up the brim on the right to give it a jaunty cock but dispensed with the plume. He had bought it on impulse, unusual for him, but Isa had teased him about being too stodgy the week before.

He followed the maid into the front parlor where the family was gathered. Eliahu, stout and rosy-cheeked, looked like the wealthy merchant he now was. He came forward to greet Saul, shook his hand, patted him on the back, and drew him closer to the family. Isa smiled at him from her chair. The young Elias stood in back and bowed slightly to him in greeting.

"Welcome, my dear friend Saul," said Eliahu. "We are pleased you can join us tonight." He grinned at his family. "We have a celebration!"

"A celebration?" Saul asked, looking down at Isa. She blushed and stared at her hands. She wore a broad, white, cartwheel ruff around her neck, setting off her lovely face, and a dark gray dress with the front tucked up as was the fashion to reveal a fetching pink petticoat beneath. In Saul's eyes, she looked more beautiful than any woman he had ever met.

Eliahu's wife, no longer bone-thin and haggard, entered the room. "Welcome, Saul. We have good news tonight!" She beamed and laid a hand on Isa's shoulder. She also wore the large white cartwheel ruff around her neck, but her full-skirted dress was beige showing no petticoat.

"You have been so busy of late," Eliahu said, "that we have not enjoyed the pleasure of your company. We must catch up on the news. But first, you must meet my assistant, Joseph Laredo." Eliahu brought forward a sturdy young man of cheerful demeanor, who seemed about thirty. He had been standing in back with Elias next to the fireplace. He wore a dark-green doublet and matching breeches. He grinned at Saul and reached out a hand. Saul shook it. He remembered meeting Laredo on the street, walking with Isa on some errand or other but had considered him of no consequence. A low clerk, employed by her father.

Eliahu turned to the maid standing in the doorway. "We will have the bottle of wine now with bread and cheese." He rubbed his hands. "So, my friend, how is everything?"

Saul forced himself to smile at them all as a gracious guest should, but a grim foreboding clutched his soul. "I am wondering what we are celebrating," he said. *What could it be?* Did Eliahu complete a lucrative business arrangement? Was he promoting his assistant? Perhaps they were rejoicing in some great accomplishment by Elias.

The wine and glasses arrived. Eliahu poured and passed around the glasses. When everyone had a glass, he lifted his. "A toast," he said, smiling at Isa, "A toast to my daughter Isa and her betrothed, Joseph Laredo. L'Chaim!" They lifted their glasses in a salute and drank them down.

Saul kept his face blank, but his ears buzzed. He could not breathe. He forced himself to lift his glass with the rest, and he drank it in a daze. His mind refused to accept what he'd heard. It was incomprehensible. Was this a joke, perhaps? One cautious look at the others, seeing them as if through the bottom of the glass, told him the unbelievable truth. They were celebrating Isa's coming marriage to. . . . He had to struggle to remember the name. Joseph Laredo. Saul glanced at him. Laredo was slight and dark, probably another Sephardic Jew, as the ben Youlis were. *Could I have misunderstood? Surely God would not be so unkind.*

Feeling as though he were mired in thick gravy, Saul sat through the dinner and the after-dinner conversation, acting as if he, too, were happy at the upcoming nuptials, his face frozen in congeniality. He left at the earliest possible moment and walked through the night fog for hours before finding his way home. He sat up, trying to read but could not concentrate and when he finally went to bed, he could not sleep. *Had Isa not seen that all I had worked for here in Amsterdam was for her and her alone? How could she not understand how much I adored her?*

And her family. Did they not know the cruel joke they had played on me? Was this what they called gratitude?

The next morning, he walked back to the ben Youli house, rapped on the door and, rolling his hat in his hands, told the maid that he wished to see Isa out on the steps. He barely kept his tone civil and ignored the odd look from the maid. When Isa appeared, he asked her to walk with him. She hesitated. With any other woman, Saul might have assumed she worried about the propriety of such a request, but not Isa and not the casual, egalitarian Dutch.

"I wish to congratulate you on your coming marriage," he began, but the words were tinged with the cold bitterness he found hard to conceal.

"Thank you," she replied, gazing down at the sidewalk.

"I did not know that you were considering such a. . . ." He found the sentence hard to complete. ". . .a man. To marry, I mean. I had never met him."

How had she met him? Had Eliahu, that treacherous fool, thrown them together? Joseph Laredo. A mere shopkeeper. An assistant to a merchant. Then the self-acrimonious thoughts began. *I should not have waited so long. I should have courted her more. Been more ardent. Could she not see how much I loved her? How can I endure life without her presence?*

They walked in silence.

"We would not have done," she said at last. "You and I, I mean."

Saul stopped and looked at her in surprise. "Why do you say that? I should have said we were perfectly suited."

"You are disappointed now," Isa said, "and I did not mean to hurt you, but I would not want a husband who would not listen to me. My ideas and opinions meant nothing to you except as material for correction. You saw only an image of your own making. You will realize in time that I could not be the wife you desire." She stepped forward to continue their walk.

He followed her, dumbfounded. "You are sadly mistaken. I have always found you a captivating companion. I had waited before declaring myself until I had the financial resources for marriage. Perhaps you feared that I had bestowed my affection elsewhere?" He watched her face. *Did she know how difficult it is for me to say these things?*

Isa shook her head with a sad smile. "I have always known you cared for me, and I will always care for you and be most overwhelmingly grateful to you."

"But then, why?" He stopped walking to look directly at her. "Why?"

She matched his gaze. "Because you are a rabbi, a man of faith with strong beliefs, and I cannot help but question our beliefs and our faith. I have seen the hatred and the persecution that stains the very core of every religious belief, beliefs that we can never be sure are absolute truths and so must be subject to question, doubt, and humility. Instead, religious beliefs of every stripe and color tear Europe and even our own country apart."

"You must know God's plan is an enduring commitment to our people," said Saul, shocked to his soul. "We cannot question God's will. His laws are as revealed to us through the Torah. You must not question that." The look she gave him enraged him. "You are but an ignorant woman. You cannot argue religion or philosophy or politics with a learned man." He paused and then added, "such as myself."

"Dutch women are different," Isa said. "Some of us do argue and question."

"The Torah is our law. It is not to be questioned." Saul repeated firmly, appalled at himself for stooping to discuss such important matters with a woman.

"But we are surrounded by Catholics, Calvinists, Lutherans, and so many more who have scriptures that differ from ours, and they, too, believe them fervently. Most barely know of the Torah." Isa spoke softly. "How can you find the truth with blind faith and no discussion of all these ideas?"

"I can not argue with such as you," Saul replied. "You speak blasphemous lies, but you are only a woman and can be ignored. You would do well to keep your thoughts to yourself. Our religion is not the result of chance or the product of power politics."

They returned to the ben Youli house in silence. Isa stopped on the steps and looked at Saul. "I had hoped we could be friends."

Friends! Saul forced himself to smile at her and replied coldly, "Good day. I wish you success in your marriage."

As Saul walked back to his own residence, he gritted his teeth in anger and frustration. He had spent years pining for a woman who refused to accept his authority as a man of learning and a rabbi of stature. *She would never have made a good wife for me. Never. In that, she was perfectly correct. She had the instincts of Eve. She had eaten of the fruit, and she was lost.*

He desired marriage and children. His thoughts turned to another young woman of his acquaintance. Esther. Quiet and acquiescent. She knew her proper place and kept it. He set his lips in a tight, straight line, climbed the steps to his house, and savagely flung open the door. Esther would make a fine wife. He slammed the door shut behind him.

Chapter 10 - Gibraltar, 1999

As Sara exited the elevator ahead of Josh, she saw Blank reflected in the large mirror behind the front desk. Josh bumped into her as she drew back.

"What. . .?" Josh began as Sara turned to him with her fingers on her lips and pointed to the mirror. His mouth made an "O."

Sara walked silently towards the back of the small hotel and found the door leading into the alley alongside. She and Josh hurried down the alley onto the main street.

"They mean to watch us," Sara said as they walked toward the Internet Cafe.

"We're going to have to change hotels," added Josh, "as soon as possible."

"Later," said Sara. "Right now we have work to do."

They spent an hour at the Internet Cafe, hunting down experts on Rembrandts, the names of Rembrandt paintings and subjects, and biographical information on the artist. They printed out much of the information and returned in hopeful spirits through the alley to their hotel.

The concierge called to them as they passed. "Mr. Davila, I have a telephone message for you." As she handed Josh the message, she looked at Sara. "Ms. Miller, yes? Someone has been here asking for you." She rummaged through a sheaf of pink message slips. "Here. She asked that you call her." She handed Sara the message.

Before Sara could ponder who would ask for her in Gibraltar

where she knew no one, the concierge added, "Also, that young man over there." She waved toward a man wearing a business suit and sturdy brown boots. He was engrossed in a magazine. Next to him sat Blank, imperturbable and watching.

Blank's presence was disturbing enough, but when Sara recognized the other man, her mouth dropped open. She stepped back and closed her eyes, hoping she was mistaken. She opened them again and saw that he was not an apparition, but a reality.

"Oh no," she whispered. "Dave."

Her brother. Direct from West Virginia. Here to take control.

Sara managed to keep the anger out of her face as Dave looked up and noticed her. She ignored Blank.

"Hi, Sara." Dave clumped toward her in his heavy boots, a huge grin on his face.

"What brings you here?" she asked, submitting to his hug. Surely he didn't think there would be money in this for him. She stepped back.

"Whoa. That's not much of a welcome, Sara." Dave straightened his shoulders and jacket.

"I'm surprised to see you." Sara noticed his suitcase. A large one. How long did he plan to stay?

"Took off work. Thought I'd better make sure you don't get into trouble over here," Dave said. "I know something about investments and insurance and with this big find of yours. . ."

Josh walked over and introduced himself.

"I'm Sara's brother. Came over to help," Dave produced an uneasy grin with his hand shake. "Glad to meet you."

Josh put his hands on his hips. "Big find?" he asked with arched eyebrow, looking from Dave to Sara, a question in his eyes.

Sara saw the question. Surely Josh didn't think she was conspiring with Dave to steal the painting. She studied Dave. "It's not ours," she said. "We're searching for the owner."

"Oh come on, after all these years?" Dave took Sara by the elbow and steered her to the elevator. Josh followed.

"We don't want to talk down here," Dave said. "I got a room down the hall from yours."

Sara shook off his hand. "I'm afraid there is nothing in this for you or for us. We need to find the owner, return the painting, and then we'll be done. I'll be back home searching for a job"—she felt a shiver of dismay—"and you will be, too, if you don't get back to work."

She turned away from him as the elevator began its ascent.

"See? That's why I'm here." Dave spoke to Josh, man to man as if Sara weren't there. "My sister doesn't have any practical business sense, none at all. Not like us. I'm sure you'll see it my way."

Josh folded his arms and looked at him. "Really?" he said. "She's done pretty well so far."

Sara waited for him to tell Dave the fact: there would be no money in this for any of them. To her chagrin, he said nothing more. Dave flashed her a smug look. That he was so confident he would prevail made her so angry she couldn't speak. She stared down at her shoes. Dave always had been a bit of a bully. Now it looked as if the fight would be all hers. She couldn't count on Josh's support. He was so irritating, but then he was worried that this search might have serious consequences for him and his family..

She did not feel the same qualms. Josh's family was an honorable one. They would not be involved in profiteering on stolen art. His mother, his father—they were nice people. She remembered their kindness and how pleased they were to meet her. She thought of their gallery—light and airy. Judging from the size of their home, it must be profitable. They did not need to steal paintings--not if the robbery was all in the past, done by Josh's grandparents. Money was not the only issue in this search.

Seeing Dave reminded Sara of his desperation to escape his humdrum existence as an insurance salesman in Martinsburg, West Virginia. She had also felt that desperation to escape her own job, a stifling but safe administrative position. Her grandmother's bequest had given her a respite, although Dave had tried to claim half of it, but still what was she to do with her life after this adventure? *I need to find a meaningful career, and I have no ideas, so far. She lifted her chin. But I have moved on, and I know I cannot go back.*

She shook her head. So then what?

They walked into Sara's room. Dave took the upholstered easy chair, pushed it over to the table and shuffled through the papers with a raised eyebrow. "What's all this?" he asked, looking at Sara.

"Nothing of interest to you." Sara took the papers away from him and sorted them into a neat pile. "We're working on them," she said. "Don't mess them up."

"Well, excuse me." He sat back. "Hey, is there any Dr. Pepper in that refrigerator?"

Sara checked. "No Dr. Pepper. A Coke?" She handed it to him.

Dave opened it, swallowed a large gulp, and tipped his chair back. "So where is this painting now?"

"It's safe," said Sara. "Stored away where no one can get to it." As she said this, she scanned the room. If someone was listening in, that was a good message to send. She sat in the desk chair and pulled it up to the table. Josh leaned against the wall, arms folded.

"You sure? It's got to be worth a lot of money." Dave's eyes darted around the room as if he might spy the painting on the table or under a shelf.

"Might be a fake," said Sara.

Dave shook his head. "Not if it's been hidden away for umpteen years. Don't think so."

Sara glanced at Josh, who was watching them both, a slight smile on his face. She took a deep breath. "Dave," she said, "Josh and I are going to find the owner of the painting and return it. That's all there is to it. There's no money in it, probably no reward, although that would be nice. I'm using the rest of Grandma's bequest to finish what she wanted me to do. You might as well go home now." How many times did she have to repeat this to him before he got the message?

Dave swigged his Coke, rocked his chair, and studied her. Then he cast an inquiring look at Josh.

What was Dave thinking? How he could spin out his involvement? Sara knew he wasn't going to go home, and she knew she wasn't going to win this argument. The question would precipitate into minimizing Dave's interference while she and Josh worked on the problem. And that would be irritating and difficult.

She peeked at her watch, folded her arms, and frowned at Dave. "I need a rest and shower before dinner. You guys scoot, and I'll meet you in the lobby at seven. We can go to that Italian place down the street."

"All right." Dave shoved his chair back and stood. "Where are you staying, Josh?" He snuck an amused glance at Sara.

He thinks we're staying together. She pushed Dave's suitcase toward the door.

"Next room," said Josh, waiting for Dave to leave, but Dave waved his hand and maneuvered Josh into leaving first.

Sara knew what was going on. Dave didn't want them making plans without him. Sara stood in the doorway, watching Dave enter his room, then she closed and locked her door, walked to the phone, and called Josh.

"Glad to meet your brother, Sara," he said when he answered the phone. "Seems like a nice guy. Concerned about you."

Sara sat on the bed. Josh was being tactful, a new side to the man, and she appreciated the kindness. "Thank you," she said, "he is okay most of the time, and I owe him. I had a bad time growing up with neighborhood bullies. He was always there, but I'm afraid we have a problem."

"I'm afraid we do," Josh said. "How about meeting me down-stairs. . . ." He paused. "That is, in the alley for a minute to discuss Dave."

"You want to meet outside?" Sara asked. "Why would we do that?" Then she understood. Their phones might be bugged. In which case, the eavesdroppers just heard this conversation, but Dave would be of no interest to them. She could visualize Dave eavesdropping outside her door, though. "Okay. I'm leaving now."

"Be quiet so you don't tip Dave off."

"Right." Sara looked out her door and saw Josh waiting. They walked quietly to the stairs, then down and out to the alley.

Josh leaned against the side of the hotel. "You know your brother. What is he likely to do?"

Sara shrugged and stared down the alley at the pedestrians on the street. Yes, she knew Dave. Interfere, that's what he'd do. He wanted the money and didn't have the same scruples she had on how he got it. She sighed. "I think we'll have to be careful what we say around him. He'll want us to sell the painting and give him part of the money. He'll pester us and ridicule our plans." She hated to say such things about her own brother—he had his good side, but she couldn't let him manipulate Josh.

"I understand," Josh said.

Sara shook her head. She hoped he did.

"However, there is one other little thing," Josh said.

Sara sighed. "What other little thing?"

"Samuel called."

"Samuel called? He did?" Sara felt a huge sense of relief. Samuel was all right. "Where is he?" She walked down the alley to sit on a bench in front of the hotel, gesturing for Josh to join her. No one else was around except a few passersby and no one showed interest in them.

He sat down next to her and stretched out his legs. "Got a message. I'll call him right now." He pulled a cell phone out of his pocket. Seeing Sara's expression, he added, "Picked this up earlier today. What about that message you got?"

Sara still held it in her hand. She scanned it. "It's from someone named Mrs. Pickford. Do you know her?" She noticed the area code. Gibraltar. Local.

"Never heard of her. How about calling her out here after I call Samuel? They didn't bug this phone."

"Good idea. I'm worried."

"Me too." Josh said as he punched in the numbers. Sara waited as she tried to make sense of one side of their conversation. Josh finally ended the call and turned to Sara.

"Okay. That was Samuel," he said. "He's quite the cloak-and-dagger man."

Sara sat on the edge of the bench. "What do you mean?"

"He's back in St. Thomas, said he'd ask for whatever records my parents have." Josh paused. "Hard to get a word in edgewise, you know?"

Sara smiled. "I'm glad he's okay."

"I hope so," Josh said. Sara heard the concern in his voice. "Samuel said he was followed into the Gibraltar Airport. As he was checking his bags, he set the decoy down, and someone swiped it. He didn't see who. He says someone is onto us, and by now they must have discovered the package only had a rolled newspaper in it, so they'll be looking for us."

"Oh no," said Sara. "What's he going to do?"

"He's leaving St. Thomas tomorrow, didn't unpack his bags, and he's going to leave a false trail. Hopes he can still get whoever it is off our backs and onto his."

Sara's stomach flip-flopped. "I'm glad he didn't get hurt this time, but I'm worried about him. They must know he doesn't have it, and I'm glad that points to us rather than him, but we're in a dangerous situation. And whoever they are, they're in Gibraltar. How desperate are they?"

"And who are they?" added Josh. "Blank and Smythe, if that's their real names, are watching us. Did they swipe the decoy? Who else knows of our connection to Samuel?"

"Your family and mine, and the people at Samuel's pension."

"Especially the concierge and her son and whoever else she talked to."

"Your turn to call Mrs. Pickford." Josh handed the phone to Sara.

She read the message again before tapping in the number. For people who flew into Gibraltar a couple of days ago, she and Josh were suddenly too popular.

A British voice answered. "'Allo?"

Didn't sound familiar. "You wanted to speak to me? I'm Sara Miller."

"Yes, Miss Miller. I'm the concierge at Samuel Yulee's pension. He left us suddenly, but his things are still in his room. Will he be returning?"

It's the buzzard. What should I say? Sara felt suspicious of such unwarranted attention. How did the buzzard know where they were staying? Why would she ask for her? Why not Josh? What did she really want? Sara stared at the phone, trying to decide what to say.

"Miss Miller?"

Drat. The buzzard was pushing for an answer. "I don't know, Mrs. Pickford. Let me get back to you." Sara ended the call.

The more she thought about the message, the odder it seemed. The buzzard must have heard Samuel's stories. She might even have put Blank and Smythe on their trail. Although. . . . Sara remembered the dark young man who'd followed them into the breakfast room. The buzzard's son. Was he after the painting too? None of them had succeeded, at least so far, so the buzzard was trying a different route. Sara mulled over the possibilities as she handed the phone back to Josh.

"So who was she?" Josh asked.

She looked at him. "The concierge," Sara said, "Mrs. Pickford. The buzzard."

"What did she want?"

Sara described the conversation. "I don't know what Samuel plans to do with his room and stuff at the pension—if he left anything behind, which I doubt, but she wasn't interested in that. She really wants to know where Samuel is and hopes to weasel information out of us."

Sara crossed her arms and stared at the cars parked on the street. She didn't recognize any of them, but she knew Blank or Smythe was sitting in the hotel lobby right now.

"What did you tell her?"

"That I'd get back to her."

"Good." He paused. "Seem to be a growing number of people on our trail."

"Makes me nervous," said Sara. "How far are they willing to go to get that painting?"

"It's worth a lot of money."

"We've got Blank, Smythe, and the buzzard watching us." Sara began walking back down the alley toward the hotel's back door.

Josh followed her. "They haven't tried any rough stuff yet, but what will happen when they get tired of waiting?"

"I don't want to think about that," Sara said. "So who else is interested in the painting?"

Josh looked at her. "Your brother. Dave."

Sara nodded. "And whoever he talked to."

There was a long pause.

"We've got to get out of this hotel and out of Gibraltar," said Josh finally.

Chapter 11 - Provenance, 1636

Amsterdam.

Lying in bed, hair covered by a nightcap and covers piled over her even though a warm breeze wafted through the window, Saskia van Rijn listened to her dear husband Rembrandt downstairs talking to the widow who rented these rooms to them. Saskia supposed the widow's two daughters were somewhere about the place.

She heard male voices too. Remmy's students must have dropped by.

She had no desire to leave the bed, nor did she want the tea and bread left by the maid. A tear drifted down her cheek. Rumbartus would be nine months old now. Their first child. He should be almost walking and starting to talk. Instead, he lay in the cemetery, dead at two months. How had she borne the pain?

The pain had made Remmy's heart heavier too, but he had buried himself in his work. She had no interest in the tasks she used to enjoy. What did they matter? Their two rooms hardly required housekeeping, and the widow ran the house quite well without her help.

Saskia heard his steps coming up the stairs. Another attempt to cheer her up. She combed her hair with her fingers, brushed the tears aside, and sat up, forcing a smile on her face.

Rembrandt tiptoed into the room, then seeing she was awake, burst forward in a show of good cheer. "My dear, you mustn't stay in bed so late. The summer lingers, and the day is warm."

He walked to the window and took a deep breath. "Ah, the scent of dew-soaked grass. We can walk to the market." He picked up the cup on the nightstand. "But your tea is cold." He turned to the door and called, "Freja!"

The maid appeared in the doorway. Rembrandt handed her the cup. "Bring us a pot of hot tea, please."

"Of course. Perhaps madam would like a boiled egg? A slice of ham?" Freja straightened the blankets around Saskia.

"Just tea," Saskia said, smiling at her husband with sad eyes. "I'll be down soon for breakfast." She threw aside the covers and put her feet on the floor. "You needn't worry about me, Remmy. See? I'm up now. Go back to your students."

The maid departed with the cup. Rembrandt kissed his wife on the cheek and squeezed her hand. "That's better. Have your breakfast and then join me in the parlor. I expect a new client to visit. It was more convenient for him to stop by here than to come to my studio. Of course I agreed. You can talk with me while I wait."

Saskia smiled slightly. He was trying to be kind, but he felt the sadness, too. He used to joke and laugh. A year ago they had moved to this large house in the fashionable Nieuwe Doelenstraat neighborhood of Amsterdam. They had been so merry together. She must rouse herself—she could not weigh him down. He had too much to give. His paintings were the marvel of Amsterdam—and not only Amsterdam but all of Holland. He was so. . .so busy. He didn't have the time to think about their little boy. But she, she had too much time. . . .

The maid appeared and Saskia made a show of drinking it. They all worried about her.

She dressed and dragged herself downstairs. The cook dropped a spoon in surprise when she saw Saskia enter the kitchen.

"I will take breakfast now," Saskia said and walked into the dining room.

She opened the dining room windows to let air and light in. Perhaps a bit of late summer would counter her depressed spirits. She sat at the massive table, forcing down a boiled egg with a slice of bread spread with butter and cheese, and listened to the hum of conversation in the parlor across the hall. Remmy must be talking to his students. Perhaps she should become more involved in his business. She could do sums. She heard a loud rap on the front door. One of the students answered it.

"Mijnheer van Rijn?" The visitor asked, his voice deep and heavy with a Spanish accent.

"Ja." That was the student. "This way."

She heard Remmy stand and greet the visitor. Probably shaking hands now. She walked over to hover in the doorway. She recognized the visitor, although she couldn't recall his name. One of the Jewish merchants. A Sephardic immigrant. He was quite elderly, stout with a heavy white beard, but his cloak, gloves, and shoes were all fashionable and well-made. The buttons adorning his doublet and breeches also spoke of wealth as did the patterned lining of his cloak and the pointed lace trim on his collar. Perhaps he sought a portrait for his family.

"My name is Eliahu ben Youli." The man held his wide-brimmed but featherless hat in his hand and bowed. "You are Rembrandt van Rijn?" The student came forward and took the man's hat and cloak.

Remmy answered the bow. "I am. Will you sit? My servant will bring you tea." He saw Saskia standing in the doorway and nodded to her. She caught the message. She could play the part. It was important for Remmy to look prosperous and well-established. No one need know they only rented rooms here. She curtseyed. "Ja, mijnheer," she said and left to summon the maid. Saskia returned quickly to her post in the doorway as if she were an attendant waiting for further orders.

"What may I do for you?" Rembrandt asked the visitor.

Ben Youli sat in one of the upholstered chairs in the well-furnished parlor. Rembrandt occasionally borrowed the chair for his subjects. Ben Youli accepted the cup of tea from the maid with a nod before turning to Rembrandt. "I have a commission for you."

Rembrandt sat in the tall wooden chair he used when sketching. He held a pen and sketchbook in his hands even now, but his attention was on this potential new client. "And what might that be?" he asked.

"My family wishes to repay Rabbi Saul Levi Morteira a debt of gratitude. He has become a man of consequence in our community." The visitor sipped his tea.

"Yes, I have heard of him," said Rembrandt, nodding his head.

Saskia searched her memory. Had she ever met this Rabbi Morteira? She had few acquaintances among the Jews of Amsterdam although Remmy enjoyed their company and occasionally included them in his Biblical paintings.

Ben Youli settled into his seat. "My family and I wish to commission a portrait of him as a gift for his home. Your reputation as a painter and a painter of Jews is well-known to us, and most fortunately, the rabbi lives nearby."

Rembrandt scratched his chin and squinted at ben Youli. Saskia recognized this delaying tactic. Remmy was trying to size up this client. "Have you spoken of this to him? He would have to sit for me in my studio."

"I have," said ben Youli, "and he is agreeable, although he stipulates that the painting be instructional—perhaps you can paint him as a Biblical figure. Also," ben Youli cleared his throat, "I understand that you can make sketches of him quickly and paint the portrait from those. He is a busy man with many demands on his time."

Saskia leaned against the doorway. She had seen Rabbi Morteira as she went about her business at the market and passed by him once in the street with a group of students. She had thought him rather pompous and full of himself and heard others call him "a fanatic" and a "ruthless inquisitor." Yet he had earned the gratitude of Mijnheer ben Youli. How would Remmy paint such a man as this rabbi?

Rembrandt folded his arms. "As it happens, I, too, am a busy man, but I will make time for Rabbi Morteira." He winked at Saskia, watching from the doorway.

Saskia smiled. Of course he would make time for any commission that promised a large sum in guilders.

"And the price for such a painting?" asked ben Youli.

"Two thousand guilders."

Saskia gasped. That was a monstrous sum. It would drive away this commission.

Ben Youli frowned. "I will pay fifteen hundred guilders."

Saskia watched Rembrandt pretend to consider, then he shrugged slightly as he turned to ben Youli. "For you, I will say sixteen hundred guilders."

"Very well," ben Youli said. "It will be framed too, then, and ready for mounting on the wall?"

"Of course." Rembrandt fidgeted on the seat. He shouldn't act so restless, Saskia thought. He will offend the patrons.

Ben Youli sat back and sipped his tea. Saskia recognized the signs of a man comfortable with the terms and satisfied with the result. Only a few details now needed to be concluded.

"When may he call on you for sitting?" ben Youli asked.

"I am finishing up several commissions, but I can put those aside to sketch him." Rembrandt rose. "He may come when he will." Saskia saw that Rembrandt yearned to return to his studio.

Ben Youli took the hint, set aside the tea cup, and rose also. The maid brought him his hat and cloak, he bowed to Rembrandt and was shown to the door.

After he left, Saskia entered the room. Rembrandt turned to her. "So, we receive another commission. What did you think, my pretty little bird?"

"I think," she said and smiled at him, "I will buy a new hat."

"Splendid." He took her arm. "Are you ready for a walk on this beautiful day?"

Chapter 12 - Gibraltar, 1999

Sara walked between Josh and Dave to a popular Italian restaurant featuring red-checked tablecloths decorated with candles on top of chianti wine bottles.

"We have restaurants like this back in West Virginia," Dave scoffed as his eyes darted across the room.

Sara ignored him and greeted the hostess who led them to a table, but supper began as a grim event with Josh and Sara hostages to Dave's good humor.

Sara could tell he was pleased with himself. He probably thought the painting was as good as his right now. He had assessed the situation and, swayed by his redneck buddies, figured that Josh, being male, should be in charge, even though she still had money left from Grandma's bequest and was paying their expenses. He had tried to wheedle the money out of her back in West Virginia and failed. She imagined the chart he'd mapped out in his brain: Impress Josh with his businessman's logical experience. Use Josh to influence Sara. Get painting. Sell it. Get money. Go home.

He really should know better, but Sara could tell he was desperate. She wondered what Josh was thinking. He had concentrated on the meal and avoided raising his eyes to look at Dave or her. She surveyed the restaurant. Most of the patrons wore casual slacks and shirts or blouses. Her little group stood out with Josh in his paint-splattered torn jeans, ragged T-shirt, and sweatshirt, she in clean jeans, pink blouse, and sweater, and Dave wearing a gray zippered jacket over a flannel shirt, jeans, and leather boots. She could feel the stares and then the easy dismissal of them as Americans. She didn't see anyone she recognized, but she didn't think any of the people who contacted them had given up.

Now to play the knight's move. Dave was not a good chess player, but she was and her favorite move was the knight's non-linear leap to surprise her opponent. The knight's movements made her think of a bird flying away in a three-dimensional world to foil a cat stalking it in a two-dimensional one.

She laid aside her napkin and cleared her throat. "You know, Dave," she began, "we're not staying here in Gibraltar."

"What? You're not?" Dave sputtered. His eyes flicked to his wallet, lying on the table next to his plate.

Josh looked up at her with a raised eyebrow. He glanced at Dave's wallet, then winked at Sara. Perhaps they could make the trip too expensive for Dave.

"We've got reservations on the first flight to Paris tomorrow." Sara willed Josh to stay silent. They would make the reservations as soon as they got back to their rooms. Maybe they'd get the last two seats available, leaving Dave out, which would be a lucky break.

"But. . ." Dave's eyes turned to slits. "When did that happen?"

"Yesterday," said Josh to Sara's relief. He had understood at once.

"But why?" Dave looked from one to the other. "That's going to be expensive, traipsing all over Europe. Anyway, what will you do about the painting?"

Sara rested her chin on her hand. She was enjoying this. "We need to get out of Gibraltar, and we're likely to find an expert on Rembrandt in Paris," she said. "Someone connected to the Louvre."

Dave sat back. "So you're going to take the painting to him?" His eyes gleamed, and he leaned forward. "That means you'll have to take it out of its hiding place." He cast a winning smile at Sara. "I'd sure like to see it."

"Sorry. It stays here," said Josh, "in storage. We have the subject, notes, dimensions, and photos of it. Enough that its provenance could be traced, if that's at all possible. We're not asking if it's a true Rembrandt, where they would need to see the actual painting."

"Seems like an awful lot of trouble," Dave swiped his mouth with the napkin, "for a painting that's been lost for sixty years. Its owner has got to be long dead. Might as well be yours. Maybe the owner stole it in the first place. You don't know."

Sara stared off into space. "I think I'll have gelato for dessert."

"Me too," added Josh, motioning to the server.

Dave looked from one to the other. "All right. What time's that flight?"

"Morning," said Sara. Surely there was a morning flight to Paris.

Dave threw down his napkin. "I'll make reservations soon as I get back to the room. Where are you staying in Paris?"

Sara glanced at Josh. He shrugged. Dave meant to hang onto them. She resigned herself. She couldn't tell her own brother to go away as much as she'd like to. This wasn't kid stuff. "We don't know yet," she said. "We'll decide when we get there."

Josh roused himself to say, "That way we'll throw off anyone who's following us."

The night was balmy for October, so after dinner they walked along the Mediterranean before returning to the hotel. Sara headed for the alley.

"We're going in the back way?" asked Dave.

"Better this way," said Josh.

But the alley was now dark and halfway to the hotel door, they stumbled over a pile of clothes. Sara pulled out the tiny flashlight attached to her key ring and shined it on the pile. She drew in her breath as she realized that it was not a pile of clothes. She peered both ways down the alley. No one else there. Her hands started trembling so much she could barely hold the flashlight. Its light bounced on the pile.

"It's Smythe," she said. She knelt to feel for the pulse in the carotid artery. Nothing. Her hand touched something wet and sticky. She shined the light on it. "Blood," she said, waving away its metallic smell. She pulled a tissue from her pocket and absently wiped her hand. Her teeth started chattering. Memories overwhelmed her. She had stabbed a man once to escape a vicious assault, and the fear that she'd murdered him haunted her for months. She had not, but later she learned someone else had dealt him a crippling blow. That was before she'd met Josh, but the anxiety and dread still lurked deep in Sara's psyche. She forced herself to stand and leaned against the wall. She had nothing to do with this, she told herself.

Josh knelt next to the body and felt the man's wrist.

"Blood?" Dave backed away from them.

Josh stood. Sara felt his concern as he looked at her face, heard her chattering teeth. He put his arm around her, and she leaned against him and stared down at the body. "He's been shot," she said.

"I'm getting out of here," Dave turned to run.

"We can't get involved in this," Sara said. "He's dead. There's nothing we can do for him."

Josh squeezed her hand. "Do you think Blank did this?"

Sara shrugged, took one more look at the body, shuddered, and held Josh's hand as they followed Dave in heading for the hotel entrance.

"We should call the police," she said.

Josh glanced at her.

"Anonymously," she added.

"Not yet. Let's check our rooms first."

"But we can't leave him there."

"There's a pay phone at the Internet Cafe," Josh said, his face grim. "I'll make the call after we check our rooms."

Blank. What if he were still in the lobby? Did he know what had happened? Had he killed Smythe?

"I really don't like thinking we might be next." Sara folded her arms and rubbed them as if she were cold.

"Killing us won't get them the painting," said Josh.

Sara cleared her throat and added, "But torture would."

She saw Dave waiting for them at the entrance. "Go to your room," she said to him. "We'll see you in the morning."

"Fine," Dave said, "And what are you going to do?"

Sara shook her head but didn't reply. They walked across the lobby to the elevator. Blank was indeed sitting there, reading a magazine and munching on a candy bar. He looked up and winked as they passed.

Sara ignored the wink. Surely he wouldn't sit there placidly reading a magazine if he'd killed his partner. But if not him, then who? The stakes in this game had gone up.

She tried to act casual and unconcerned and saw that Josh was doing the same. Dave looked upset and worried—and guilty. Fortunately, Blank was the only witness. They took the elevator up and left Dave fumbling with the key to his room as they walked down to Josh's.

"Wait here," Josh said as he unlocked the door, but as he opened it, someone behind the door pulled it all the way open with one hand and grabbed Josh's arm with the other, flinging him across the room onto the floor.

The man stepped out from behind the door and motioned to Sara with a gun. "Get in," he said.

Sara stood frozen, gaping at him, then staring at Josh, sitting on the floor, rubbing his arm and groaning. She couldn't make her mind work. Did that man really have a gun? Was that Josh on the floor?

"Get in," the man repeated, reaching for her arm. Sara stepped back. The man raised the gun as if to shoot.

That galvanized her. She was not going to die here if she could help it. A graphic vision of the blood-soaked dead Smythe crossed her mind.

"Don't shoot!" she cried as she scooted in past the gunman. Her eyes darted around the room, looking for anyone else and saw that Josh's suitcase had been dumped on the bed and the clothes scattered. The gunman seemed to be alone. He was young and swarthy. Sara recognized him as Mrs. Pickford's son. The buzzard must have passed on to him what Samuel had said at the pension cocktail hour, and he'd listened to them in the pension's breakfast room. He wasn't wearing a mask. That had ominous significance.

She knelt down beside Josh. "Are you hurt?"

He shook his head. "Thought my arm was broken for a minute."

Relieved that Josh was probably not hurt, Sara stood and looked at the gunman. "What do you want?"

"Sit down," he said, using the gun to motion to the floor.

Sara stalled as she contemplated the floor. If she sat there, she would be at a severe disadvantage. Hard to attack from that angle and she meant to attack. She took a deep breath to summon the courage to sit in a chair instead of the floor, all the while expecting a bullet for her defiance. "I can't sit on the floor," she said as if she were disabled. "Who are you?"

"Never mind. I've come for the painting." He now sat on the edge of the writing desk, one leg swinging back and forth, the gun held loosely in his right hand.

"What painting?" asked Sara, gripping the chair arms.

"Don't bother lying. I know you've got a Rembrandt, and I mean to have it."

"Did you kill that man in the alley?" Sara watched for any sign of guilt—she couldn't imagine two killers at the same hotel. He must have done it. He was a killer. A shiver of fear churned her stomach.

The gunman grinned at her question but didn't reply. Instead, he asked her again, "Where is the painting?"

She casually looked around for anything she could use as a weapon. She felt Josh press lightly on her foot with his shoe. She pressed back, meaning she understood. He was okay and ready to fight. And so was she. But how? Right now the gunman had a definite advantage.

He slid off the desk and stood menacingly tall, pointing the gun directly at Sara. "I don't want to get rough, but I will," he said. "Where is the painting?"

"It is secured," she said. "There's no way you can get it."

She saw the gunman's eyes narrow. "Where?"

She felt Josh moving but dared not look at him. She had to create a distraction, but what? She swept a hand across her hair and unbuttoned the top button of her blouse. Anything to keep the gunman's attention on her and off Josh. His gun wavered.

"Very nice," he said with a grin, then he pointed the gun at her again. "Where is it?"

She needed to keep talking. "It's in a bank vault," she said. "Absolutely safe. Requires four of us, all named, photographed, and fingerprinted for secure identification, to remove it from the vault." *What a whopper.* She was taking a chance that this man had never had a safe deposit box. Probably never even had a checking account.

"You've got to be kidding," he said. "There are only two of you. Three counting the old man."

In the distance, Sara heard the distinctive sirens of police cars. Had anyone discovered the body and reported it? The sirens came closer, then very close, then stopped. The blue lights of the police cars flashed on the walls in the room.

"I'd get out of here if I were you," said Sara.

"Don't try anything." The gunman maneuvered past them to raise the unscreened window and poke his head out. Momentarily distracted, he didn't see Josh slip off his shoe and hurl it at the man's head, which startled him into cracking his head on the bottom of the window. Rubbing his head, he stepped back into the room as Sara lifted the heavy bed lamp, swung it into the man's groin and then used it to smash his gun hand. He dropped the gun as he fell to the floor.

Sara ripped a tissue out of her pocket, covered her hand, picked up the gun and threw it out the window into the darkness.

The man now moaned in a fetal position on the floor clutching his stomach. Josh pulled the sash out of his robe and quickly tied the man's legs together at the ankles. The man lifted his head and retched.

"I'll get my stuff and meet you downstairs," Sara whispered. "You get Dave. We're out of here as of right now."

Sara ran to her room, gathered all her possessions, threw them into her suitcase, picked up the notebook with Samuel's papers, and met Josh knocking on Dave's door. "Everything okay?" she asked.

"I rolled him into a sheet, too," Josh said. "Take him awhile to get out of all that." He banged again on Dave's door.

Dave opened it, half undressed, and stared at Sara and Josh. "What's up?:

"We're leaving here immediately," Sara said. "I'll explain later. Get your stuff and go downstairs. Now. Meet you in the lobby."

She started down the stairs. "To the airport?"

"To the airport."

"We'll have to avoid the police, if we can," Josh said. "We can't afford to get detained while the police sort out the murder."

A few minutes later, Dave emerged from the elevator, red-faced and breathless. "This better be good," he muttered.

"I'll rouse the manager and check out," said Sara. "I'll say my brother insists we join our family in Spain."

Josh looked at his watch. "It's late, but they'll just think we're crazy American tourists. Maybe we can get away with that."

Blank must have gone home or was hiding from the police. They turned away from the police cars and walked to the next street to find a cab. "The airport," said Josh.

The cab driver, a young man in sweater and cap, turned around to look at them. "The airport, she not open at night," he said in a heavy Spanish accent.

They looked at each other. Finally, Sara said, "Take us to the Airport Hilton, then, if there is one."

"Si, señora." He sped off down the street. Sara saw the Hilton sign only a couple of blocks away, then turned to look back. She couldn't see anyone following them. A few minutes later, they were hauling their baggage into the hotel.

Sara turned to the other two. "I'll get rooms here for the night, then I'll use their business center to check on flights out of here. You two can share a room, can't you?"

"Sure," said Dave, looking at her purse. "That's Grandma's money you're using." He frowned at her. "You said you already made plane reservations."

She waved him away. "A mistake."

She booked the rooms. "We need to get out of here as early as possible. I'll see you at breakfast tomorrow morning at seven."

She and Josh left Dave at the elevator and wheeled their suitcases to the business center.

"While you're making the reservations, I'll look for more experts on Dutch and Renaissance art," said Josh.

The business center was brightly lit, open, and empty, so all the computers were available. They each took one.

Josh's search was quickly successful, and he soon printed out a list. To Sara's dismay, she found that only flights to London, Birmingham and Manchester left from Gibraltar. Nothing to Paris. No trains or buses either. For those, you had to walk across the border into Spain. They couldn't afford to be so vulnerable. She finally rented a car to be picked up early the next morning. They'd figure out what to do from there, but right now, they had to get out of Gibraltar before the gunman, the buzzard, or Blank found them.

After breakfast, they picked up the rental car for the seven-hour trip to Madrid. Sara watched for anyone who seemed interested in them and their movements, but no one followed and their pursuers would not know for hours that they had left Gibraltar. In Madrid, they booked a flight to Paris.

No gunman. No Blank. No police. She wondered if the alley they had thought to be a safe escape from the hotel was actually known to be a haven for thieves and Smythe's murder the result of a robbery. She couldn't wrap her mind around the idea that a man was murdered for the Rembrandt.

They arrived in Paris in the early evening. For her own peace of mind, Sara halted in the lounge at the gate to watch people disembark. Who else was on that plane?

"What are you waiting for?" asked Dave.

She knew she was being silly, but that gunman had terrified her. He could so easily have killed them. He lived in Gibraltar. He knew what the transportation scene was like. He knew they couldn't leave Gibraltar by plane until the next day. They could have been discovered at the Hilton. They could have been followed. Even to Paris. He and Blank, alone or in cahoots, meant to get the Rembrandt, and they might already have murdered Smythe for it.

So she was being extra sure, but as she watched, the faces hurried by, often looking down or away from her or rummaging in purses and pockets for keys, perhaps, or baggage receipts. As the disembarking passengers dwindled, Sara turned to join Josh and Dave to go through immigration and pick up their baggage.

Paris prices were expensive. Even so, Sara deliberately booked herself and Josh into a small luxury hotel in the third arrondissement, near the Musée des Arts. No one would be watching them here. Dave complained about the cost, implying that Sara should pay for his expenses too, but she held firm and he grudgingly paid for a room there as well. Sara watched him irritably. Her strategy to drive Dave to return home was not working. He meant to cling to them.

The next morning, they all clambered into Sara's room while Josh phoned the Renaissance and Dutch art experts in Paris he'd found online, hoping one of them would give them a quick appointment. The result was discouraging. He finally found one on a list of secondary experts who was willing to give them an appointment for three that afternoon.

They ate a late lunch and then returned to their rooms, but Dave weaseled his way into Sara's while Josh went to his own.

"Gotta tell you about Mom," Dave said.

"I spoke to her yesterday. She's fine." Sara leaned against the wall, arms folded.

"She always says she's fine." Dave sat on the couch, lounging there as if he meant to stay. He looked at Sara. "But she isn't getting any younger, you know. I'd like to give her a nicer life, wouldn't you? Security. Maybe even travel."

"Of course."

"You could give her some security and so much more. Come on home now, Sara, even without the Rembrandt. You can use whatever you haven't wasted of Grandma's money to help us all out."

Sara sighed. "Dave, I know it irks you that Grandma gave the money to me and not you, but she gave it to me for a purpose. She trusted me, and I've worked hard to honor that trust. But I'm not finished yet, and, as I keep telling you, the painting does not belong to me. There is nothing I can do about that."

"Of course it belongs to you. You found it." Dave paced back and forth. "Law of salvage or something like that."

"If you think you can persuade me to sell it and keep the money, even if it's for Mom, you are absolutely wrong. Anyway, I am not the only person concerned in this. Josh and his family are involved too." She opened the door and gestured to the hall. "Please go home. You can't do anything here."

He threw her an injured dog look as he left, adding as he walked down the hall, "go do what you want, but let me know when you're ready to go meet that so-called expert. I'd still like to tag along."

Sara closed her door, locked it, and called Josh.

"So how'd it go?" he asked.

"He's trying every manipulating trick he can." Sara felt disloyal speaking against her own brother. She would prefer to help him out and to support her mother. Of course she would—after she'd finished the job she had to do. She didn't like the manipulation, and she especially didn't like confrontations. Dave knew that, and he was used to bending her to his will.

What he didn't understand was that she bent when the stakes were low, and she wasn't too interested in the outcome. Now the stakes were high, and he was going to find his tricks didn't work. She hoped.

"We have to guard against him." She swallowed and added, "I will need your support in this."

"Good. Thanks for saying that." He paused. "Didn't know how to play it. He is your brother, after all."

Sara smiled. Sometimes Josh was so perceptive and maybe that's what counted. "Thanks for backing me up last night."

"Going to Paris? In my mind anyway. Especially after we found Smythe. Gibraltar is a dead end. Sorry. No pun intended."

"I'm so glad you understood." She sat down at the table and took a deep breath, trying to relax. "You anticipated the need to go to Paris too?"

"Sure. No argument there."

"There's one other thing." Sara swallowed and gripped the phone. "Did you notice anyone familiar on the plane? Someone you've noticed before? Someone who might be following us?"

She waited through a long silence. When Josh didn't respond, she added, "I think we outwitted them, but . . ."

"Me too," Josh said at last. "Can't be sure. . ."

"Me neither, but I hope we left that crowd in Gibraltar. See you later." Sara hung up the phone and walked to the window to stare down at the passersby. Sometimes she liked Josh a lot, but neither of them had a clear idea of how to proceed. They'd have to make it up one step at a time, watching out for the predators and handling what happened next.

Chapter 13 - Provenance, 1655

Amsterdam.

Rabbi Saul Levi Morteira returned to his home on Sint-Anthonishuis after a wearying day at the academy. The man-servant took his cloak and left to fetch the brandy. Feeling his weight and his years, Morteira walked into the study and sank into the large comfortable chair near the fireplace. His wife Esther had the chair built especially for him. It was constructed of heavy wood to accommodate his bulk and thickly upholstered in dark blue wool. He removed the plain collar and the cuffs, laid them on the small table next to the chair, and stretched his hands out toward the fireplace to warm them.

He looked up at the Rembrandt hanging to the right of the fireplace. As a gift from the ben Youli family, the painting brought back such a mixture of memories it was at once a pleasure and a rebuke. What a callow youth he had been to be so swayed by a lovely face. He had long since ceased to feel pain and longing when he saw Isa in the streets. She was as cordial to him as he was to her. Ah well, God works in mysterious ways.

He sat back and stroked his beard, now streaked with gray, rousing himself to take the glass of brandy from his man-servant. The comfort of the chair, the heat of the fire, the warmth of the brandy, all lulled him into a relaxed state of reminiscence as he looked up at the painting.

How devastated he had been when Isa rejected him to choose a man who was simply a merchant, beneath her in every respect.

He, Saul Levi Morteira, had waited until he could offer her all a woman should want—status, security, a fine home, a handsome income, his own companionship for eternity. Yet she refused him. More, she refused him on intellectual grounds, as if they were equals. That a woman, a mere woman, rejected him for such a reason still staggered him, after all these years, shaking to the core all that he had understood about women.

The folly of her choice still rankled, for his beliefs, correctly formulated as they were on a strict interpretation of the Torah, were not subject to change. She would not accept, had never accepted with true womanly modesty, the fruit of his profound study and thought. The years had not taught Isa her place.

Last week—he shook his head as he thought of her insolence—she had trekked through the wind and sleet to plead with him to reconsider his condemnation of Spinoza. And on what grounds! That Spinoza should be allowed to write and talk about his blasphemous philosophies as free speech? No! To air such ideas was to give them credibility. A devil's playground for fools. It must not be permitted, and he, Saul Levi Morteira, had done what he could to throttle that licentious so-called philosopher. He was proud to support the vote of excommunication for this Baruch Spinoza.

How insupportable to remember that he, Saul Levi Morteira, a rabbi, had once considered that heretic a fitting husband for his own cherished daughter. He laughed. That idea was thankfully abandoned as Spinoza's true colors showed themselves.

Saul sipped his brandy and considered that the severe excommunication forced upon Spinoza was fitting punishment for the kind of secular beliefs that he espoused. Worse, he wrote and spoke of them to others as if they were worthy of discussion. He promulgated dissension and disbelief among the faithful, and that must not be permitted.

Saul stared into the fire. A fleeting memory crossed his mind of the disappointment, the flash of. . .anger on Isa's face when he rebuffed her. He supposed such rebellious ideas had always been in her lovely head behind those beautiful eyes.

No matter now. That was all behind him. He had led a blameless life of selfless devotion to his religion and his people. Esther had proven to be a good wife. She had borne him five children, all grown now. Spinoza was of no consequence. He had moved to a village where he worked as a lens grinder. Saul chuckled. A much more fitting occupation than philosopher for such a heretic.

His eyes again looked up at the Rembrandt, its colors glowing in the firelight. Himself as a Moor. A Moor! He remembered the grim humor with which he had insisted on that subject, harking back as it did to Spain and the Inquisition that had brought him and ben Youli's family together. Rembrandt had acquiesced, of course. He liked such costuming. His studio was full of odd fabrics and objects.

Saul frowned at the painting. Even now, despite the years that had passed, it unsettled him, causing uncomfortable thoughts, painful thoughts, thoughts that pierced the comfort of his happier memories. It was the sackcloth he wore for his bitter mistake.

His man-servant poured Saul another glass of brandy. With a grim chuckle, Saul considered leaving the painting to the academy. It could hang alongside the one in which he was painted as Abraham, a more proper rendition he had commissioned, wishing to see himself as a religious subject. That painting was at least educational and, properly, should belong to the academy and hang in the assembly hall.

He lifted a glass to the painting on the wall. If it had not been a gift from Isa's family, he would not have consented to it or kept it. Hung on a wall in his own house, the painting seemed immodest. He knew rabbinical scholars who objected to any "graven images," although with such a master as Rembrandt living in the neighborhood, that objection hardly applied.

The painting did not belong here. He was an old and sick man, no longer needing the lessons this painting had taught him over the years. He did not want this painting to be counted among his possessions, but who should receive it? His children did not want such a dreary painting, even if it was of their father. The painting would become a burden to keep out of respect for him. They would not think they could sell it. It would only gather dust in the back of their attic until finally handed on to some other family member unfortunate enough to have space for it.

The problem remained. Who would be the most fitting and proper person to receive such an unloved yet valuable object of art?

Chapter 14 - Paris, 1999

Since they were new to Paris and its subway system, the Mètro, Sara herded Josh and Dave, who insisted on joining them, out of the hotel shortly after lunch for their three o'clock appointment. She had studied the Paris Mètro map and led them through the underground maze to the correct train and then out through another maze at their destination to exit onto a wide promenade lined with aging plane trees and small shops.

"How did you do that?" asked Dave. "You've never been in a subway before and neither have I. Miracle we got here." He looked at the street signs. "You sure this is right?"

Sara didn't correct him. She had traveled more than he and the Washington, D.C., subway system was familiar to her and similar to the Paris Mètro.

She watched the slow trickle of other passengers who exited the Mètro at this station, nodding to Josh with raised eyebrow at the people around them. He shrugged but shook his head. She didn't recognize anyone either.

She checked the address number of the shop in front of her. It was No. 359. "The address we want want is 375. This way," she said and took off down the street, leaving Josh and Dave behind to catch up.

The street was not crowded, which made it easier to scan the faces around them, but she stopped at several stores to window shop, using the store windows as mirrors to look for any interest in their activities. Everyone seemed to be going about their regular business, so Sara felt safe leading Josh and Dave down the street to No. 375.

She paused at a shabby storefront two blocks from the Mètro station and again checked the number above the door. No. 375.

"Can this be right?" she said. It seemed an unlikely place for a Rembrandt consultant, even a secondary one. She appraised the musty display of artifacts in the window, frowned, and glanced at Josh.

Josh looked from the number painted on the door to his notes. "Yep, this is the right address," he said, squinting through the window.

Dave snickered. "This is the office of your Rembrandt consultant?" He laughed. "Not promising. Don't see much money here. He can't be a dealer in expensive paintings, much less a Rembrandt." Dave turned away. "Let's get out of here."

"Maybe he's a professor," Josh said, "and scholar. And only a part-time consultant on Rembrandt. There's probably not much call for his expertise." He peered into the shop. "I suppose there aren't that many Rembrandts to discuss."

"Yeah," Dave stood back, hands in his pockets, and sneered. "Rembrandt's been dead a long time."

Sara ignored him, but she felt disappointed, too. An expert on fine art should have an impressive office, maybe one connected to a museum. He wouldn't rent space from a. . .a junk shop. Even if he owned this shop, wouldn't he want it to be more imposing to impress his wealthy clients?

Josh whistled and stepped forward to open the door, but it didn't budge. "Locked?" he said in surprise. He checked his watch. "We're a few minutes early, but it's the middle of the day. Wouldn't a shop be open?"

Sara rang the doorbell. They waited. She rang it again. She heard rustling inside and then watched a middle-aged woman in a simple black dress emerge from the dusky interior and peer at them. The black dress reminded Sara of the buzzard, but this woman looked wispy and benign. "Un moment, s'il vous plaît." She rattled the chain as she withdrew it, then Sara heard the rasp of a key turning, and the door opened. "Bonjour." She looked Sara up and down. "Americaine, oui?"

"Oui," said Sara. "Bonjour." Everyone here seemed to know at a glance that they were Americans. "We don't speak French. Parlez-vous. . .uh. . .anglais?"

"Mais oui." She opened the door wider. "You would like to see our collection, n'est-ce pas? Bon." She stepped aside to let them enter.

Sara scanned the dusty array of curios and old furniture. The place smelled as if mice called it home. She walked forward to peer at the dark display of paintings on the wall. She didn't know much about fine art, but surely none of these paintings qualified as the work of a master.

"Are you looking for anything in particular?" the woman asked. "If we don't have it here, we have many, uh, connections and, I'm sure, can find exactly what you want."

Josh stepped forward. "We are here to see Monsieur Ardon." He spoke slowly and carefully. "We have an appointment, and this is the address he gave us."

The woman frowned. "Mais oui. But of course. This is his shop and his office is up the stairs." She shooed them toward the back of the shop and pointed to a dark and worn wooden staircase painted a grimy brown. "Up there." She turned her back on them.

Sara watched her relock the front door. Were they now trapped in this dirty, mouse-ridden hovel? What would they find at the top of the stairs?

She was the last to climb up to a hallway lit by a dim bare bulb. "Twenty watt. Maybe fifteen." Dave grumbled. "I'm not impressed."

"Shhh," Sara said. She also felt let down by the dreariness of the place, but she walked to the door at the end of the hall, trying the doorknobs on the other two doors as they passed along the way. Both were locked and no light showed under either door.

At the last door, light glowed through the old-fashioned window of frosted glass on the upper half. "Dr. Jean-Louis Ardon" was stenciled on the glass.

Josh took her hand, squeezed it, and then knocked. She heard a chair scrape against the floor, then a moment later, the door opened.

The light from the room behind him made the man a silhouette. Sara blinked.

"Bonjour. You are my three o'clock appointment? Come in, come in."

He turned and shuffled back to his chair as they followed him into a large room lined with walnut bookcases. They overflowed with papers, pamphlets, and books. Framed paintings rested on the floor, leaning against walls and bookcases. Only a few faced outward, all portraits of subjects wearing clothes of another century. A conference table took up the middle of the room. Ardon had placed his computer at one end and stacked papers on each side.

He gestured to the table as he rolled his chair over to it. He set aside a stack of what appeared to Sara's eyes to be engravings. She tore her eyes away from the engravings to study the man they'd come to see. The Rembrandt expert was a portly, bald man with white eyebrows, and he wore faded blue jeans and a pilled gray sweater over a white undershirt. She had expected someone younger, more professional-looking. Maybe he was eccentric or a puttering retiree. Whatever he was, he was a disappointment to Sara who'd looked forward to meeting someone erudite, cultured, and learned. Yet he was listed as an adjunct art consultant specializing in Dutch and Renaissance art, including Rembrandts, on the websites of several reputable European museums.

She glanced at Josh, and he returned the look with a slight shrug. So he too had reservations. Dave dropped into a chair at the table, drummed his fingers on the chair arm, and frowned as he surveyed the room.

Ardon leaned back in his chair and beamed at them, quite comfortable in his domain and amused at their expressions. He gestured toward the two other chairs, both covered with dust. Sara swept the dust aside with her hand as she sat. Josh didn't bother. She smiled to herself. Why would he in the clothes he wore?

She observed with distaste the dirt and disarray and tried not to smell the odor of dead rodents. She felt depressed. This man would be useless.

"How may I help you, my children?" Ardon asked, his voice oily and smooth. He sat back, his fingers laced together over his ample stomach.

As Sara tried to overcome her dislike, Josh began. "Dr. Ardon, we found your name on the Internet and need your help. You are an expert on Rembrandt, are you not? You're a consultant with the Louvre?"

He sat back and shrugged. "Some say so. Do you own a Rembrandt?"

Sara heard the sneer in his voice and ignored it while hiding her surprise at his accent. It was as American as theirs although it had a New England sound to it.

She stepped in. "We have a Rembrandt painting that was buried for sixty years to protect it from the Nazis during World War II. We would like to know its provenance in order to return it to its true owner."

She did not mean to sound irritable and condescending, but this man looked more like a used car salesman than an art expert. What was he thinking about them? What would he do with what they told him? Would he be a friend or an enemy? They were entering territory that felt more dangerous every minute. She couldn't bear to find another dead body. Smythe must have been killed in a random robbery. She hoped they'd left the Pickfords, Blank, and everyone else who was after their Rembrandt back in Gibraltar.

Now they were telling this stranger that they possibly had a genuine Rembrandt. Even if he were the expert they expected, this place did not inspire confidence. A Rembrandt painting would be quite a temptation to anyone. She studied the sad, cluttered room. He needed the money.

Ardon scratched his chin. "I see." He leaned toward Josh. "Well, son, do you have this Rembrandt with you?"

"It's in safekeeping," said Sara. *And it's going to stay there.*

"If it is as you say, and I must say I find your story hard to believe, you must take great care with such a fragile treasure." Ardon
leaned back and twiddled his thumbs. "So how am I supposed to
tell you about this Rembrandt if I cannot see it. It should be in the
hands of a conservator, in a climate-controlled vault. Where do you
have it? In a grocery bag?" The skepticism on his face matched the
sarcasm. "And I will insist on seeing its provenance."

Sara ignored the insult as she drew several papers out of her
purse. "Here's the information we have on it, and several photos,
taken of the painting on the front and the drawing on the back. We
measured it too. We're hoping you might recognize it from the
subject matter or the photos."

"I see." Ardon perused the photos. He picked up a half-chewed
cigar, looked up and grimaced at Sara's appalled expression.

"I don't smoke anymore." He stuck the unlit cigar in his mouth
and continued to read through the papers, stopping once to exam-
ine the photo. He peered at Sara over the top of his glasses. "You
say here that it seems to be a study of Rabbi Saul Levi Morteira
dressed as a Moor."

"That's right. And on the back . ."

"Is a pencil drawing of Morteira dressed like Abraham. I see, I
see." Ardon leaned back in his chair and stared out the far window.
"Morteira dressed as Abraham is quite a famous painting." He
rubbed his hand on his chin. "If what you have was an early study
while on the front is a finished and authenticated painting. . ." He
whistled.

"It's signed by Rembrandt in the corner. . .at the bottom," Sara
said.

Ardon smiled at her. "Of course, my child, but who signed it?
Someone trying to pass off a copy as the real thing? Maybe. . ." He
studied his fingertips, but his sudden look at Sara chilled her.
"Maybe. . .you?" He turned the same cold, penetrating look at Josh.
"Or you?"

Sara reared back, shocked. "Us? Why would we do such a
thing?"

Too late she realized what he was saying. *Money. Lots of money.*

As she stuttered to refute this charge, Josh spoke. "You're right. Someone could be tempted to do that, but not us."

"Of course not," Dave added. "We wouldn't even consider it. Why, that would be fraud."

Sara watched Dave turn the idea over in his mind.

Ardon waved the cigar. "I'm not accusing you. The signature could have been added by an apprentice, perhaps, in 1654 or 1730 or 1850, any time after it was painted to support the claim. Someone could have added it to a genuine Rembrandt if the great man himself had neglected to do so." He stopped to chew on the cigar. "And you do not have its provenance which makes it of dubious value."

"Look," Sara said, "we don't want to sell it or display it, we simply want to locate the rightful owner and return it. It had been hidden for safekeeping and rediscovered a few days ago. We thought you might know the painting and its provenance—since you are an expert on that art period."

"Whether it's genuine or fake, it needs to be returned," Josh added.

"Sure," said Dave, leaning back in the chair and acting the role of impartial observer.

Ardon licked his lips. "Still, I should see the painting. Where did you say it was?"

Sara shook her head. "You must have listings of all Rembrandt's paintings here, surely." She looked at Ardon. "As an expert on Rembrandt, I mean. Find the paintings that resemble ours, give us a list along with the owners and their addresses. I'm willing to pay whatever you charge."

Dave sat up. "Sara!" he sputtered.

"But where is it?" Ardon asked, turning to Sara. "You can tell me that. And where did you find it?"

Sara shrugged. "I guess there's no harm in telling you that we found the painting in Gibraltar. It was hidden there around 1941, and it's now locked away in a safe place." She resisted the idea of taking out the safe deposit key hanging on a chain around her neck and waving it at him.

Ardon now paid full attention to her instead of Josh, studying her with those greedy eyes as if she were a pigeon in a pot. Sara shivered. He would throttle her for the key if he got the chance.

She lifted her chin. "The key is in safekeeping also." Let them think that. If anyone had any ideas about kidnapping them and forcing them to give up the Rembrandt, it added another layer of difficulty. The thought seemed melodramatic as she looked at the pathetic little man in this rat's nest of an office. But then more and more people seemed to be interested in them and the painting and someone stole the decoy from Samuel. And murdered Smythe.

Sara noticed Dave clenching his fists and heard him mutter, "Safe deposit box. It's in a bank." His look at Sara was calculating.

Ardon drummed the fingers on one hand. The other still held the repulsive cigar. "Of course." He pushed his lips in and out.

"If you did see the painting itself," asked Sara, "could you tell then if it was a genuine Rembrandt?"

He chewed on his cigar, staring at the three of them before shaking his head. "Perhaps. Certainly, I could be more helpful if I had the painting rather than a few photos." He picked up the photos and tossed them aside. "Unfortunately, frauds can be quite well done." He shook his head. "The only way we can be most sure whether it is genuine is to have a complete provenance of its ownership from the time it left Rembrandt's studio until the present. Certain tests can be performed on the painting that may also be conclusive." He chuckled. "But I would need the painting, you see."

His eyes slid from Sara to Josh. "You know, my friends, un-scrupulous persons. . . not you, I'm sure, are turning up regularly with frauds they claim to be art stolen by the Nazis."

With a sigh, he swiveled his chair around to the computer, turn-ing the monitor so they couldn't see it. For a few minutes, he tapped keys and scrolled with the mouse as he studied the monitor. Sara moved over to view the monitor, but Ardon waved her away. She watched him irritably and knew Josh was just as annoyed.

Finally, Ardon stopped scrolling and looked up at Sara. "I can't find any citation for your painting, which is Saul Morteira as a

Moor, but I've found a website entry with a picture of Rembrandt's completed painting of Morteira as Abraham that is in a private collection. I'll print out the online photo of the painting, so we can compare it with Rembrandt's rough sketch of Morteira as Abraham from the back of the painting you have." He frowned reproachfully at Sara. "Of course, you've only shown me photos, not the actual work." He picked up the photo Sara had brought as if it were a bag of dog poop, then he turned back to the computer and clicked "Print."

He laid the printout next to the photo. As he studied them, he frowned and muttered to himself. Sara held her breath. Finally, he looked up at them. "The drawing shows his sure strokes. . .could be genuine. . .the artist changed the pose a bit, but on the whole, the drawing on the back resembles the final painting and reflects his style, dexterity and strokes. I can't believe a fraud would have such a thing." He shook his head. "I need to see your original drawing to be sure, of course." He glared at Sara.

Sara leaned forward to study the printout. "Can you give us the name of the owner of this painting?"

He laughed. "Would that I could but I cannot give out the names of my clients. I will contact the owner, ask if he knows anything about your painting, and let you know." He sat back and again laced his fingers over his stomach. "Best I can do right now. . . given the circumstances."

Sara leaned back and folded her arms, disgusted. Ardon was playing games. The painting was probably owned by a museum and that information could easily be obtained by a computer search. She'd do that herself later. Ardon was not into sharing information, just getting it.

She watched Ardon's expression as Josh, who had not recognized the game, continued to ask questions. "You're sure you can find nothing about a painting of Morteira as a Moor? The owner of that one is the person we want."

Ardon shook his head. "I don't know what to think. We have records of all his paintings and their provenances. . . we thought." He sat back and opened his hands. "I have nothing on the subject of your painting." He picked up his dead cigar and waved it at them. "And that leads me to believe that your painting is a fraud, my children." He peered at them through narrowed eyes and chuckled.

"Can't be," said Dave. "You're lying so you can get your hands on it."

"Hold on, Dave," said Sara. She turned to Ardon. "We are considering that possibility," Sara said, "although it looks genuine and seems very old and with that drawing on the back. . ."

"Whether it is a fraud or not," added Josh, "we still want to return it to its owner. That's why we're here."

"Most admirable." Ardon sat back and stared at his cigar. "I will contact my sources for you and discuss this with my colleagues. Where are you staying?"

Josh gave him the name of their hotel before Sara thought of an alternative. Did they want this man to know where they stayed? Her stomach felt queasy as the gunman in Gibraltar flicked across her memory.

Ardon scribbled the name on a scrap of paper. "How long will you be there?"

Josh glanced at Sara. "A week, perhaps."

"A week!" Dave shrieked. "I can't stay there a whole week."

"Sorry, Dave." Sara winked at Josh. "But, yes, probably a week. We have a lot of work to do since we've come up with nothing so far."

Ardon stood. "We'll see, then. I'll contact you if I learn anything. Now my fee. . ."

Sara pushed back her chair as she also stood. "Send us your bill along with any new information you learn. I don't have any money with me."

A frown crossed his face. He sighed. "Very well. Good day to you." He stuck the cigar in his mouth, waved them toward the stairs, and pulled his keyboard forward, turning his back to them.

Chapter 15 - Provenance, 1660

Amsterdam.

Isa sat, stiff from the aches and pains of age, in a padded upright chair, reading in the parlor when her maid entered the room and curtseyed. "There is a man at the door who wishes to speak with you."

"What is his name, Greta?" Isa laid her book on the table, straightened her broad white collar and arranged the folds of her full-skirted black widow's dress. Her hair, white now, hung in long ringlets on each side of her face.

"Rabbi Saul Morteira, madam," she said in an awed voice. "He says you know him, that you will see him."

Saul! He had barely said two words to her since that walk so many years ago. When she saw him in the street, he ignored her or tried to. An uncomfortable memory of her plea for Spinoza surfaced. It was a pity they could not have remained friends, but she didn't blame him. She had not meant to hurt him, but the situation was impossible. She had tried to hint to him that her interests were elsewhere, but he had never learned to listen. They were both so old now. None of that past history mattered anymore. What had driven him to this visit?

Isa looked at the maid. "I do know him, and I will see him. Show him in, Greta."

Greta curtseyed again and left.

Isa surveyed the room and was pleased. Despite Saul's dire predictions, Joseph had been good to her, and he had done well, leaving her a wealthy widow. Their home reflected their prosperity. She imagined it through Saul's eyes. He would be waiting in the foyer with its checkerboard of black and white marble tiles covering the floor. Then Greta would lead him into this room with its expensive Persian carpets. A fire lent warmth and cheer, and heavy brocaded draperies kept the chill out. Isa reached up to straighten the three paintings of merchant ships at sea that added interest to the walls. Those ships had belonged to her late husband. A pleasant room. Saul would like it. She stood to receive him, standing straight despite her arthritic back and painful hips.

A moment later, Saul hobbled into the room, wheezing with the effort and leaning on a cane. His face brightened when he saw her. "Hello, Isa."

For a few seconds, Isa couldn't speak as she studied this very old, stout man, his face obscured by a bush of gray beard. He looked much older than he did a month ago, when she'd seen him in the street, and he seemed ill. She hoped her face did not reveal her shock. She stepped forward to welcome him. "Good evening, Saul."

He bowed slightly as he assessed his surroundings. "May I sit down?"

She waved at the large, upholstered chair by the fire. "Please. Greta will bring us tea and pastries." She gestured to Greta, who again curtseyed and backed out of the room. Then Isa moved to the chair on the other side of the fireplace. "How are you?" she asked.

He grimaced. "As well as can be expected for my age and condition. And how are you, my dear?"

"I am well, thank you."

"I was sorry to hear about your husband."

"Thank you." She had adjusted to widowhood. Why was Saul here? What could he want? Surely he did not think to pursue her now after all these years. Once he had loved her, and she had rejected him. Cruelly, she realized later, yet she had not intended to be cruel, and her family had never once thought of him as a suitor for her. Their actions were innocent.

She thought of Spinoza. Saul had ruined him and yet for Saul, it was justified on the highest of grounds. He had rebuffed her pleas for clemency on Spinoza's behalf. How fortunate that they had not wed. Married to the rigid bore in front of her would have killed her, maybe not physically, but her mind and spirit would have died. As she contemplated him, she realized he was studying her as well.

"Congratulations on your new book," she said, seeking something to say. "*The Tratado*. I hear much talk of it in the synagogue. You have done well."

"Thank you." Saul inclined his head in acknowledgement. "I call it my magnum opus. It is a treatise on God's providence over Israel and the eternity of the Law of Moses."

"I am impressed," said Isa. "A fitting subject for you." *Scholarly and dull.*

Greta brought in the tea and a plate of pastries. They busied themselves with that for a moment, which gave Isa time to adjust her thoughts.

"How may I help you?" she asked. Surely this was not a simple social call.

He smiled. "Direct as always, I see." He hesitated. "Many years ago, your family commissioned from my illustrious neighbor a painting of me. You gave it to me as a gift, and it has adorned my home for many, many years."

Isa looked down at her hands. "We, my whole family and I, remain grateful to you for rescuing us from certain death in the Spanish Netherlands. We wanted to give you a gift that was irreplaceable."

Saul took a sip of tea. "That you did, my dear. That you did."

"We hope you have enjoyed it," Isa said tentatively. Where was all this leading?

"Rembrandt has fallen on hard times, but his paintings have not. It is a valuable painting. He is a genius. That painting holds many memories for me, both painful and pleasant. I feel it holds the same for you and your family." He paused. "I am in my last days." He held up his hand to stop her protests. "Yes, yes, I fear it is true. I would like to give the painting to you because of its memories for all of us." He looked down at his feet and said softly, "I would not like to be forgotten."

Isa sprang to her feet and knelt by him, taking his hands. "You will always be remembered by me and my family. We may disagree, but we all loved you."

He did not speak for several minutes. Isa watched him struggle with his emotions, unfamiliar emotions in such a reserved man. She looked aside to give him privacy. They had rarely seen each other except in passing on the street for many years, but he had been a part of her life and thoughts since that night on the North Sea.

He picked up his tea cup and cleared his throat. Isa retreated to her chair.

"I brought the painting with me," he said. "It's in the foyer. I would like you to have it." He looked at her again, as he used to so long ago, when they had been friends. For a moment, Isa felt as if all the bad feeling that had passed between them had been washed away, leaving only the good.

A brief smile crossed his face. "I would like you to have it," he repeated and hesitated, "I would like you to remember me."

Isa could not mistake the message. He was speaking to her, and her alone. His words did not include her family. She could not refuse such a heartfelt gift. She answered in kind.

"I will treasure it," she said, reaching over to squeeze his hand.

He raised her hand to his cheek before releasing it.

She blushed in confusion and sat back, flustered, in her own chair. "Greta," she called to ease them over the sudden awkwardness.

Greta appeared in the doorway. "Yes, madam?"

"More pastries, please, and hot tea. This has grown cold." Isa waved her away and then stared down at her hands, seeking something to say. A vision of the life she might have led crossed her mind, but such a life would have been impossible. They were an unsuitable match and their lives would have been a misery. Yet, she realized, she did love him as, she knew, he had always loved her.

Chapter 16: Paris, 1999

Sara and Josh, with Dave straggling behind, left Ardon's office, crestfallen from the seemingly useless visit, and walked down the promenade to a sidewalk cafe.

"Where do we go now?" asked Sara, ordering tea and a croissant sandwich.

"Seems to me," said Dave, kicking a pebble into the gutter, "if you can't find the owner, it's yours." He glared at Sara, a sly smile on his lips. She refused to comment.

They dawdled over their drinks and sandwiches, watching the passersby, and returned to the hotel later that evening.

"We need a good night's rest," said Josh as they entered the hotel. "We'll pick up fresh in the morning."

Sara greeted the concierge as they walked by, but she called out, "Bonjour, Mademoiselle, did you see le monsieur who wished to speak with you?"

Sara stopped and turned to her. "Moi? You mean me? Someone wished to speak to me?"

"Oui, voila." The concierge waved at the door. "He arrived a short while ago. I thought he'd wait," she leaned across her desk to scan the lounge, "but he must have decided to leave." She shrugged at Sara. "Ah well," she sighed, "if it's important, he'll be back."

Sara glanced at Josh, who shook his head. "What did he look like?" she asked the concierge.

The concierge shrugged. "Young. He seemed, " the concierge hesitate, "uncomfortable, pardon me, madame, but he parlez la francaise very well. Perhaps you make friends here, no?"

"Merci," said Sara. *Could it have been the buzzard's son? Could he have followed them here?* She walked to the door and searched the street, but the street was crowded with pedestrians showing no interest in her.

She eyed Josh without expression as she returned to the lobby. "Merci," she said, nodding to the concierge. "I don't see anyone looking for me. Call me if he comes again. S'il vous plaît. If I'm not here, please get his name."

Sara's curiosity was aroused. Who could that young man who spoke French be? Surely no one could have followed her here from Gibraltar. She thought of Abe Carilla, who had followed her from one Florida town to the next as she searched for Samuel. Carilla had been harmless. Why hadn't this mysterious person now looking for her caught up with them and introduced himself? They hadn't walked fast and had kept a wary eye out for anyone showing an undue interest in them. They made no effort to shake off followers and saw none.

"I don't need anything more to eat but I do need down time," said Josh as they went up the elevator. "See you guys tomorrow."

Dave dug his hands into his pockets. "Think I'll go back down and take a walk before I go to bed. Look around."

"All right." Sara hurried to her room and shut the door behind her. A few minutes later, she heard a light knock. As she opened the door, Josh slipped into her room with his finger on his lips.

"What. . .?" Sara stepped back.

"Shhh. Don't want Dave to think we're meeting in case he's still around." Josh stepped over to the window and surveyed the street below. "There he goes." Josh smiled at Sara. "He's okay, Sara, but his agenda is different from ours."

She grimaced. "I know. So what's on your mind?" As she said that, a wayward thought surfaced. What was on his mind about her, about their relationship? Sometimes she felt so close to Josh, but most of the time they acted like pals, buddies. Is that what they would come to in the end? Just pals? With a start, she came back to the present. "What did you say?"

"I want to go back to Ardon's office tonight and break in to check his database for myself."

Sara gaped at him. "Are you crazy? What if we're caught. This is France, for goodness sake." *Josh couldn't be serious.*

"You know, of course," she raised an eyebrow at him, "that would be against the law."

Josh frowned. "Yeah, but Ardon's whole set-up seems weird to me. That curio shop is full of junk."

"Yeah. And he's a fine art consultant. An odd combination."

Josh paced in front of the window, rubbing his chin and staring down at the floor. "Did you notice how he kept the computer screen away from us, so we couldn't see it?"

"Of course I did," Sara said, "but it could have been easier for him to look at it or maybe there was other confidential stuff on the screen. It wasn't necessarily because he was hiding anything."

"I want to see those files." Josh pulled out a chair from the table and straddled it, folding his arms on the back. "He's an expert on Rembrandt. Why wouldn't he have information about our painting in his files?" He waved his hand. "But if he convinced us that the painting was a fraud, he could then offer to 'take it off our hands' at a low price. He's already suggested that he needs to see the painting itself to verify its authenticity. Once out of the safe deposit box, it would be fair game for any thief. I don't trust him."

Sara picked up a paper clip and fiddled with it. "We made a mistake going to Ardon. He's very peculiar, and he felt sleazy to me. Like a con man." She didn't want to think about breaking into Ardon's office. She'd never done anything like that in her life. The idea sent goose bumps up her arms. She wondered what the French police would do if they were caught. What were French jails like? She felt itchy to think of them.

"I had the same feeling about him. We were too fast on the trigger in seeking him out," agreed Josh. "My parents own an art gallery. You'd think I'd be more savvy about things like this." He shrugged. "Never paid any attention. Running an art gallery was never my plan. We probably should go to an expert at the Rijksmuseum in Amsterdam. Home territory for Rembrandt."

"Finding the painting's provenance is one way to track down the owner," said Sara. "Another way is to see if anyone is searching for it." She walked over to the table and picked up one of Samuel's papers. "Uncle Samuel wrote down a number of organizations trying to trace the stolen art. I've been going through that list, but no one seems to have any information relating to a painting like ours."

Josh stroked his chin. "Meanwhile, we're here in Paris."

Sara looked at her watch. "It's late, but we could still go out and reconnoiter tonight to see if any lights are on over the shop. Someone might live there." She felt appalled at herself. She was actually getting used to the idea of breaking and entering.

"Good," Josh said. "If we see any problems, we'll go back to our hotel."

"If we knew exactly what kind of data was stored on Ardon's computer. . ." Sara was thinking out loud.

"We'd be in a better position to negotiate, if that becomes necessary, and thwart whatever strategy Ardon might dream up to get the painting. After all, Smythe might have been murdered because of it."

Sara shook her head. "I hope not."

Josh leaned over to gaze out the window. "Dave's coming back. I don't think we should involve him."

"The less he knows, the better." Sara walked over to stand next to Josh and watched Dave enter the hotel. "We can sneak out of here at midnight and go over to the shop. Do you know how to get in?" Sara thought about lock picks. Where would you get such a thing?

"Oops." His eyes dropped. "That does pose a bit of a problem, but that door and lock looked flimsy to me. I'll bring a screwdriver and force the lock."

Sara shook her head. "I've got a better idea."

"Okay. That part is up to you." Josh walked to the door. "I'll run out and buy a disk for copying his database."

"Too bad you can't access it from the Internet cafe."

He shook his head. "I'm not that kind of computer geek. Midnight tonight. Now I've got to get back to my room before Dave gets here." He slipped out the door, blowing Sara a kiss as he left. She stared at the door. *What did that kiss mean?*

She turned back and walked to the table, thinking about Josh. She did like him. She enjoyed his company, and she understood his concern about his family. He had a personal stake in returning the Rembrandt, as did she. She heard the elevator open in the hall and then Dave's boots tromping to his room.

Poor Dave. Life was such a struggle for him. Her own job had been tedious and boring, but her grandmother had rescued her from that. . .for now. She loved the challenge of the search. The travel. Meeting Josh and working with him.

This is the kind of thing she should be doing. How could she turn this into an occupation? She had to avoid the kind of life Dave was living, even if he did have a new car, nice apartment, and the latest electronics. He was a slave to his possessions.

She checked her watch. In four hours it would be midnight. Her stomach turned over. She wondered how flimsy the lock would actually be.

Chapter 17 – Provenance, 1670

Amsterdam.

Aged and infirm, Isa fussed over the afternoon pastries and cakes set out for her nephew, Elias ben Youli, who was named for her brother, his father, as was the Sephardic custom. He was the last of her family. Her father, her mother, her husband, her brother, and even her own children were dead. She still wore the black dress of mourning for her children and adorned it only with the wide white collar and cuffs. A long widow's veil hung from the back of her head. Her heart felt heavy. She should not have lived so long. Even Saul had been dead ten long years.

Her nephew Elias was a strong young man. He would marry and have children. The family would live on. She shook her head and sighed, straightening the folds of her dress. She would not live to see that day. Now he took his family's fortune to join the Jews in Morocco. Morocco of all places! A barbaric land ruled by despots. She had no desire to visit such a country even if her health would allow it. For a moment, the gnawing hunger and bone-deep fear she had lived with every day in the Spanish Netherlands swept over her, bringing with it the pervasive anxiety that had always been with her and sapped her spirit. Times were so unsettled.

Elias had never known hunger or the terror that came with every knock on the door. He had been nurtured in a benevolent climate of prosperity and tolerance. He must be warned to watch his tongue. The courts of Morocco, the courts everywhere, did not lean toward tolerance and good humor, nor were they friendly towards Jews.

With the waning of Holland's prosperity, she no longer had much to give him, but she did have one heirloom, a painting considered of much value. In these unsettled times, it would not fetch much, but still, a Rembrandt would command interest at least. Elias knew its history and its connection to their family. Surely he would prize it as she did.

Greta entered the room and curtseyed. "Mijnheer ben Youli is here."

Elias burst into the room. "I am. How are you, Tante Isa?" He turned to the maid who had stepped aside in trepidation. "Get us a pot of tea, will you, Greta?" Elias turned her around and gave her a gentle push out the door. She giggled.

Isa took him in her arms and kissed him on both cheeks, buoyed by his energy and enthusiasm. "So good to see you again, my dear." She sank back into her chair and gestured to the other one. "Please sit. I am anxious to hear all about your plans. Amsterdam is not good enough for you?"

"I wish to see more of the world, Tante Isa. I am going to Venice. . ."

Venice! For a moment Isa's thoughts wandered. Saul came from Venice, but he had settled in Amsterdam. She had often wondered why. Looking back now, she supposed it was because of her.

". . .and then to Rome and Egypt and Morocco. I have friends in the Jewish community of Fez. I can find work with the merchants there."

"I see," said Isa, studying him. She wondered what the rest of the story was. Had he met a young woman from one of the Jewish families in Morocco? The country had sheltered so many refugees from the Inquisition. Perhaps that was it. She saw his youthful face, so handsome. He had been well-educated, too. She smiled. Well-educated but not in Saul's school, despite all that they owed him.

Elias had never lived outside Amsterdam. Liberal, prosperous, tolerant, accepting of Jews. Amsterdam. "Our family and our people have flourished here. I came in rags and am now well-to-do and respected among Jews and non-Jews alike." And, she added to herself, I am even accorded more freedom than women usually experience elsewhere. How Saul must have hated that.

She reflected that Elias had never known the hatred and intolerance for Jews that crippled them elsewhere in Europe, especially in the Spanish Netherlands to the south, so close to Amsterdam. Even she, after more than fifty years, still woke sweating and disoriented from nightmares of her life before Saul rescued them. Her family had been fortunate to escape the dire poverty, hunger, and constant fear of discovery that brought with it torture and murder.

Greta returned with the teapot and cups. Isa poured out the tea as she considered Elias' plan. Perhaps he was right. Religious strife, wars, and a faltering economy were making life difficult in Holland. Uncertainty lurked in the air. Would England invade? France? Germany? What of Willem III? She sighed. The future here in Holland did not seem as rosy as it once did. Isa passed a cup to Elias and poured one for herself. Perhaps he would do better in Morocco.

She sat back and watched Elias, teacup in hand. "And these friends, how are they treated in Morocco?"

"Well enough," said Elias. "I have heard of nothing to fear."

That statement alone revealed his innocence. Isa set her plate on the low table in front of her. "Nevertheless, my dear, you have much to learn."

"Tante Isa, I am a grown man. . ."

Isa smiled. "Of course. my dear. I am not blind, but you have lived all your life in Holland. I can tell you that the rest of the world is not like Holland. The rest of the world provides much harsher lessons, especially for Jews." She leaned closer and spoke to him in her most solemn and stern voice. "When you leave Holland, you must guard your tongue. Do not speak of your beliefs or your philosophy. Do not parade as a Jew. You risk severe consequences if you do."

Greta appeared with another plate of pastries. Isa stopped what she was about to say. After Greta left, Elias helped himself to a sweet cake, holding it daintily as he sat back in the chair. He cleared his throat and crossed his legs.

"I am aware of our family's history," he said. "and I have heard the stories told by the Portuguese Jews at the synagogue. I know of the torture and murder of our people in Spain, Portugal, and their territories."

Isa shook her head. "Wherever you go as a Jew, you will be accused first of any crime that occurs, subjected to curfews and searches, robbed by governmental officials, watched for any infraction of the laws, and always you will be cursed as a Jew. You must know this and be cautious. Be wary of your traveling companions and everyone you meet."

Elias sipped his tea. "Really, Tante Isa, as bad as all that?" He chuckled.

"Worse," she said. She did not smile, nor did she chuckle or in any way soften the content of her words.

Elias sat in stunned silence.

Isa let the silence punctuate her words.

After a moment, Elias shrugged and broke the silence. "I understand, Tante Isa, and will heed your cautions." He reached for another small cake.

Isa watched him. *He does not understand, and he will not heed my words.* She leaned toward him. "Very well, then. This may be the last time we see each other."

As Elias started to protest, Isa held up her hand. "Perhaps we will see each other again, we cannot know. However that may be, you will be the last surviving member of our family. All that we have will be yours, but there is one piece I must give you now. I suspect it is of great value, and you are free to do with it what you will. I no longer have the heart for it."

She took her cane and hobbled slowly to the fireplace, stopping to regard the painting on the wall beside the chimney.

Elias set aside his plate and cup and jumped up. "That painting? But Tante Isa, that is by Rembrandt, and it is of our family friend, Rabbi Morteira. You must keep it safe on your wall."

"No, it is yours," Isa said flatly. "It holds no charm for me, only sadness. God only knows how few years are left to me, and you are my only surviving relative. If you are not here to claim it, someone else will take it."

Elias studied the painting. "Saul's family would want it, would they not?"

Isa turned away and hobbled back to her chair. She poured herself another cup of tea.

"I do not know his family. You may dispose of the painting however you wish." She felt a heavy weight lift from her shoulders. The painting would soon be gone. She need never look at it again. It brought back such a mix of feelings, guilt, remorse, love, sadness.

"Please take it with you. I think it must have some value, even now. Perhaps if you wait a few years it will be worth more. In this difficult time," she grimaced, "art is not a prized commodity in our country. The painting is quite well done, although the subject, I think, would not suit everyone's taste."

Elias laughed and broke the tension. "He is painted as a Moor. In Morocco they may find that painting most interesting. How did you obtain such a thing, Tante Isa?" He returned to his chair.

She stared up at the painting. "Our family commissioned it." She held up her hand to halt the questions springing to Elias' lips. "Before you were born. It was meant as a gift to Rabbi Morteira." The gratitude that had spawned the painting seemed so long ago. Her youthful adoration of the man who had rescued her family eclipsed by the personality and philosophy of the man he was, eroding the gratitude to dust. She knew his admiration for her had done the same. "He was. . .leaving. . . , and he wanted me, our family, to have it."

"The scarf and the lamp, those dishes in the painting, what do they mean?" asked Elias. He still gazed at the painting as if to study each detail.

"All Moorish." Isa sipped the tea. "And Spanish. Rembrandt had them scattered around his studio. We suggested he include them to symbolize our family and its connection to Spain and Portugal."

Elias looked at her. "I see."

"They are all common items in those countries. When you go to Morocco, no doubt you will see the same things in the shops."

Elias looked at Isa. "Am I to have your blessing then?"

"You are a young man. You may do as you please. I ask that you watch and beware, that you help others as you can, and that you remember who you are." She gazed at him, her eyes traveling from his head to his feet, as if to make every detail her own. She knew she would never see him again and that filled her soul with sadness.

Chapter 18 - Paris, 1999

Sara looked up at the shaded windows of the room over the curio shop. Ardon's office. Midnight and all was dark and quiet there. She still had a lot of reservations about this stunt. She'd hate to end up in a French jail. How would she ever explain it?

Down the street, she heard laughter from a couple of men and a woman exiting a bar, but this part of the promenade was deserted. No other pedestrians. Empty of traffic. They had snuck out of the hotel at nine to buy a few supplies and the black sweatshirts, knitted hats, and pants they wore for this dubious expedition.

She looked over at Josh and then down at her own outfit. A lot of people wore black and wouldn't give them a second look. But to Sara, they were dressed to be invisible in the shadows like movie cat burglars. She stood next to Josh, waiting and watching the darkened shop and the apartments above it.

She reached over and took Josh's hand. It felt cold and tense. She saw his furrowed brows and deep frown and knew he felt as scared as she did. A tenderness for him touched her heart. She caught herself moving closer to him but stopped. Would they always be just pals? Josh had never shown anything but friendliness toward her. How did she feel about him? She didn't know.

After twenty minutes of watching and seeing no activity in the building, Sara felt Josh squeeze her hand.

"Here goes," he whispered. She shivered.

She handed Josh a pair of black gloves and pulled a pair on her own hands.

Josh tugged the gloves up to his wrists. "Might as well be professional about it."

Sara followed Josh as they crept toward the shop. They both stopped and examined the old-fashioned wooden door. A large window had been cut into the top half, and a wooden grid in the window divided it into nine small panes of glass.

Feeling a sense of dread, Sara nudged Josh aside and cleared her throat, which seemed too tight to allow her to speak. She managed to whisper. "No lock pick, but I remembered the door window so I brought this." With trembling hands, she pulled a small hammer and a wide roll of duct tape out of her purse. She did not feel lighthearted, but she winked at Josh. "Duct tape is good for everything."

She covered a small glass pane near the lock with the tape, just like in the movies she'd watched, and then covered her glove with the tape to shield her fist as she broke the pane with the hammer. In the movies they'd just use a fist, but she didn't quite trust that. The tape kept the glass from shattering or falling to the floor. Sharp fragments hung down from the window, suspended by the tape. Sara reached through the window, glad for the gloves, and felt around for the chain. It hung loose. Either no one remained inside or they didn't bother with the chain. .

Sara reached for the doorknob, a standard knob with a lock that needed a key to open it on the outside but easily unlocked on the inside by turning the knob. She pushed the door open as she shook her head. Such simple locks for this store.

Sara swallowed and stepped aside to let Josh enter. They were committed now. They were really going to do this. "Your turn," she whispered, then jumped back, heart hammering, as a cat ran past her out onto the sidewalk.

Josh took a deep breath and glared back at the cat. "Damn. That cat will give us away." He closed the door.

Sara shook her head. "No. The broken pane will." She pulled off the tape and pieces of glass. Now that pane looked like the

others. Pretty much. If you didn't look closely. Or try to touch the
non-existent glass. She turned back to survey the shop, her nerves
so tightly wound that she knew she would shriek and run out into
the night at the slightest provocation. She listened. No sounds
except for the ticking antique clock in the corner.

Josh pulled a penlight out of his pocket, but Sara covered it with
her hand. "Don't need it here," she said, nodding at the street light
outside. "Enough light from that."

"You're right," he said, but he kept it ready in his hand. "Might
need it for the computer."

"Hurry up," she whispered.

"Don't worry. I don't like this any more than you do." Josh tiptoed to the stairs. "You stay down here. Keep an eye out."

Sara heard the tremor in his voice. He was trying to show a
brave front. "Stay to the sides of each step," she whispered, "maybe
you can avoid creaking."

"There's no one here." Josh set one tentative foot on the stairs.

"Maybe," Sara mumbled.

Josh tiptoed up the stairs to the dark hallway and looked back at
Sara. He waved a salute with crossed fingers, then disappeared into
the darkness as he walked to Ardon's office. Sara heard him try the
door followed by his soft curse. The door was locked. Then she
heard him chuckle. He must have found the key. Maybe over the
door frame. No high-tech security for these people. She heard the
door open and froze as it squeaked on rusty hinges.

Sara gritted her teeth. No one stirred. While she waited, she
pulled the glass off the tape and placed the shards onto a plate. She
kept the tape. She peered out the shop window to keep an eye on
the street. "Come on," she thought, willing Josh to hurry up. She
didn't know how long she could stand this.

She watched a man stroll down the other side of the street with
his dog, and then saw a beat policeman far down the promenade
but heading their way. He paused to peer into a bar a block down
the street. He chatted with someone inside. Maybe he'd go in. Sara
gripped the curtain and watched. He continued up the street,
peering through windows and doors as he proceeded toward the

shop. In another few minutes, he'd see the broken window for sure.

She tiptoed to the stairs. "Josh," she whispered as loud as she could. "Hurry up. We need to move!"

She heard nothing from Josh, but soft tapping noises floated down to her. How long was this going to take? She desperately wanted to flee, but she couldn't leave Josh. The policeman strolled toward the shop, each step bringing him closer. He would see the broken pane in the door.

To divert her thoughts from panic, she scanned the shop for something to cover that pane. Surely with all the junk in the place she could find a piece of wood that would cover the space without drawing attention. She spied a small wooden plaque with a Russian icon on one side. It was about the right size and the back was blank. She pulled out the roll of tape and held the plaque in place to cover the broken part of the window. She taped the plaque to the window frame with the blank side out. It would look like a normal patch-up waiting for a replacement.

She had no sooner finished the job when Josh appeared behind her. "Let's get out of here."

"Wait." Sara looked out onto the street, but the policeman had arrived at the store window. Sara was two feet away from staring into his eyes. She gasped and shrank back against Josh into the shadows. The policeman paused in front of the windows, then studied the door and tried the doorknob, but Sara had locked it after they'd broken in. He strolled on, shaking his head. They waited until he turned a corner and then Sara removed the makeshift window replacement, tipped the glass shards off the plate onto the sidewalk outside the door, and returned the plate to a shelf. "Maybe they'll think the cat did it," she said.

Josh reached for her hand, and they slipped out into the night. At the corner, they removed their gloves. Sara took Josh's gloves as well as her own and threw them into a nearby trash can. "I don't ever want to do that again," she said as she walked back to Josh.

"Did you get it?" she asked. He looked pleased with himself.

"Yep," he said, holding up the disk.

She clapped her hands and patted him on the back. He turned it into a hug and then, their eyes met and the hug became a kiss and then another one that lingered as they held each other tight.

"I was terrified," Sara whispered in Josh's ear, not wanting to leave his arms.

"So was I, but we did it, Sara." She felt his hands stroke her hair and her back. Bells rang in Sara's ears. She felt the frustrations and doubts of the past week melt away.

They walked back to the hotel, arm in arm. Sara used her key to open the massive door at the entrance. The lobby was deserted—even the reception desk, but the elevator made loud clanking noises as it descended to pick them up and then ascended to their floor, ending with a thud as it stopped. Dave was a heavy sleeper, but even if he woke up, he'd probably roll over and go back to sleep.

Sara tiptoed down the hall to her room, Josh behind her. To Sara's relief, they met no one. Their black outfits were not unusual, but the hour was late. They stopped at the door to Josh's room, looking at each other uncertainly. Sara still felt the warm glow of that kiss, but the exhilaration had ebbed, and now she was too tired, drained by the fear and tension of their midnight escapade. She wanted to stay close to Josh, but she could barely keep her eyes open.

She looked up at Josh and whispered, "I'm exhausted."

To Sara's relief, Josh said, "Me too."

"Tomorrow then?" asked Sara.

Josh bent down and kissed her. "Tomorrow."

Chapter 19 - Provenance, 1695

Fez, Morocco.

Elias ben Youli plucked a sprig of mint from a plant growing outside his door. Holding the mint to his nose and breathing in its crisp scent, he crossed the dusty street and stepped through a metal door into a walled enclosure. His face was as tanned as an Arab's, and he wore a white djellaba with vertical brown stripes. A white keffiyeh covered his head. No one would suspect he was a Dutchman and a Jew.

He looked past the pools of color—reds, oranges, yellows— formed by the huge vats of dye and gestured to a dark man in a similar white djellaba and keffiyeh watching the workmen. Piles of tanned leathers darkened the far corners.

The mint did little to overpower the intense stench that filled the air. Elias held his breath as long as he could while he summoned the man to follow him outside. Then he hurried down the street until he was far enough away to tolerate the stench. The man followed, a worried expression on his face.

"Is there trouble?" he asked when they stopped.

Elias put his hand on the man's shoulder. "No, Daniel, my friend. No trouble. I wish only to tell you that we expect two men and a woman to arrive tonight. They came from Gibraltar by fishing boat. Is there work for them at the vats?" He spoke in a mishmash of Spanish and Arabic tainted by the Dutch from his upbringing.

Daniel appeared to consider this. "Can any of them do sums? Our ledgers need constant attention. Or perhaps the new people could help in the shops."

"I will ask." Elias frowned. "Is there any other work for them?" He tossed the sprig into the rest of the debris that littered the road. A mule with bulging panniers, goaded along by its master, trudged towards them on the way to market.

Daniel shrugged. "We can make work for them. Perhaps the woman could join the others who cut and sew. We could train one of them to stamp patterns in the leather."

"Good." Elias gazed down the street. "I will ask the other merchants as well. Perhaps she weaves."

Daniel glanced back at the enclosure. Elias understood his concern. "You may go. I will talk to you when I know more about these people." Elias patted Daniel on the back. "You do good work at the tannery. I am pleased."

Daniel shrugged and returned through the metal enclosure to the vats inside.

The mule plodded past. Elias followed it into the marketplace. His shops did well here selling his leather goods, but not as well as his leather exports to Europe. They provided him with a visible income to satisfy the tax collectors as well as employment for his imports. He chuckled. Imports indeed. Human imports, refugees smuggled in along with the money and the trading goods, from Spain, Portugal and other lands that saw fit to persecute his people.

As he passed by their shops, Elias recognized with a smile and a brief word his workers, imports, friends, and neighbors. Jokes and laughter followed him down the narrow alleys. The shops dwindled as he reached a courtyard with a central fountain. He sat in the shade under the balconies to wait for the camels from Timbuktu.

They arrived at dusk. Elias stood in the shadows until he saw a swarthy man wearing a fez. Elias approached him. "As-salaam-alaikum, Achmed," he said. "May Allah be praised."

Achmed gestured to a small group waiting next to the camels. Two men and a woman hesitated, then slowly walked toward Elias. The woman hung back behind the men. She wore a black caftan,

and a black rectangular piece of cloth, a haik, covered her head and
shoulders and had been drawn across her face. The men wore white
djellabas and keffiyehs like the other men. They looked like Arabs
and would be mistaken for such unless they spoke. The leader of
this band bent to Elias, whispering. "Where shall we conduct our
business?"

"My house is not far," said Elias. "Follow me. My courtyard will
be safe enough." He began walking. Achmed followed with his
camel in tow. Both men watched warily for any undue interest in
them, while the three others who followed kept their heads down.

Elias unlatched the side gate and stepped aside to let them enter.
He cast an eye down the road checking for observers. Seeing none,
he closed the gate behind him and locked it. Achmed directed the
three refugees to sit in the shade of an orange tree by the central
fountain.

A servant approached Elias. He inclined his head toward the
three under the orange tree, then stared with a blank face at Elias.
Elias barely looked up from unlocking the storeroom door. "Yes,
serve them tea and refreshments."

Achmed pulled his camel over to the door of a reception area.
He began unloading the panniers strapped across the camel's back
and handed the contents in small sacks one by one to Elias. They
clanked as Elias carried them into the storeroom extending out one
side of the reception area.

Elias opened each sack, running his hands through the copper,
silver, and gold pieces, his profits from sales of his goods at the
market and, he chuckled, from his other. . .enterprises.

He pulled out his scales and placed them on the scarred wooden
desk. He then separated the contents of each sack by metal and
weighed each pile, noting the weight on a ledger sheet. Next he
counted the pieces. When he had finished, he totaled the sums and
whistled softly to himself. He peered up at Achmed, who was
watching every move. Elias swept a pile of coins off the counter
into a sack.

"For you, my friend."

The other man bowed. "May Allah be praised."

Elias answered the bow and the phrase. "May Allah be praised."
Together they replaced the empty paniers onto the mule. Elias
opened the gate and waved Achmed and his camel out, locking the
gate behind them. Elias returned to his office, retrieved a key hidden
under the floor boards, and used it to open his strong box. He
pushed aside the rolled canvas—that Rembrandt! He thought of his
family and Tante Isa and his days in Amsterdam. A civilized country. Prosperous with educated people. A wave of homesickness
passed over him. Bean soup. Herring. Those delicious cakes and
pastries. How he missed all of that. He placed the coins inside the
strong box, relocked it, and hid the key.

He left the storeroom in time to see his wife and son walking his
way. They were not smiling. He smelled trouble.

"Good evening, Ariela," said Elias. He reached over and cuffed
his son Jacob, now seventeen years old.

"I understand we are to have guests again tonight?" said Ariela,
arranging a scarf over her head and shoulders. Her cold tones could
not be mistaken. She looked with distaste at the three stragglers who
still waited under the orange tree.

Elias frowned at his feet. Why could she not understand? It was
but a minor inconvenience for her, but a life-saver for their guests,
dispossessed refugees, bereft of everything but their lives, which
were in jeopardy, too.

"They will be here only for one night. I will make other arrangements tomorrow," he said.

"They upset our lives, Father," said young Jacob. "I must hide
everything of value in the house. I do not trust them."

Elias walked with his wife and son back into the fine house he
had built for them. He called to the stout, red-cheeked woman who
served as the housekeeper.

"Ja, mijnheer?" The housekeeper arrived from the kitchen, wiping her hands on an apron. "What is it?"

"Hendrika," Elias smiled at her. "We have three guests tonight.
Will you make them comfortable?"

She curtseyed with a frown. "It will take a few moments,
mijnheer."

"Fine." Elias gestured toward the courtyard. "They wait there. Please inform them when the rooms are ready and get them food."

She bustled away, and Elias turned to speak to his wife, who had stood by, a disapproving expression on her face. Her words and Jacob's had depressed him.

They lived in a wealthy merchant's house behind a plain exterior. It did not draw attention to itself, but it had every comfort his money could provide. They had no right to complain.

"I myself was once one of them," he finally said to Ariela and Jacob. "My family had no possessions, no money, nothing, but we, too, were rescued by a stranger. I want only to help others who find themselves in similar situations."

"I have heard that story too many times," Jacob grumbled. "I simply wish they were taken somewhere else."

"You risk all of us with this foolishness," said Ariela.

"I will not argue with you," replied Elias, folding his arms. "This is what I must do."

Ariela and Jacob turned away. Elias watched them leave with misgivings. Perhaps Ariela was right. Perhaps it was time to leave this country. He had wealth enough, but where to go that was not a cauldron of intrigue and war? He no longer had ties to Holland. Stadtholder Willem III of the Netherlands was also king of England and together they had made an enemy of France. What would it be tomorrow? Would Spain be next to make an ally of Holland and then what would that mean for his people? Everything was unsettled in Europe. Wars everywhere.

Here he had prospered, here he would stay, and here he would help his people however he could. With that resolution, Elias followed Ariela and Jacob into the house to prepare for supper.

Chapter 20 - Paris, 1999

Sara whispered, "Goodnight," and moved on to her own room. She opened the door and walked in, but then she turned on the light and gasped. *Not again.*

The room was a shambles. Her suitcase had been dumped out on the bed, and the papers on the table were scattered across the floor. She ran next door to Josh's room and banged on his door.

"Come over here, you won't believe it," she said. She felt as if she'd been on a roller coaster of emotions all night. Coming back to this was such an anticlimax

She pulled Josh over to her room. "Look at this."

She peeked behind the door and around the room, fearing someone might still be hiding there, but the bed was too low to hide under and the bathroom door was open. No one concealed himself there. Whoever it was had emptied her toiletries bag in the basin. The invader must be long gone. She pushed her underwear back into the suitcase.

Now she was tired and in no mood to appreciate any humor, ironic or not.

Josh put his hands on his hips and surveyed the chaos then motioned her out to the hall. He closed the door behind them and leaned against the outside. "Could Dave have done this?" he whispered. "Looking for the key?"

"Dave!" Sara whispered back. She hadn't considered Dave at all.

"I'm thinking Ardon."

"Ardon?" Josh scratched his chin. "Ardon?" He chuckled and then he started laughing softly.

"Shhh. You'll wake Dave. What's so funny?" asked Sara.

"Ardon," said Josh, his laugh becoming a low chuckle. "Ardon."

Sara put her hands on her hips, feeling even more irritable. "I'm glad someone thinks this is funny."

"Sorry. Couldn't help it. Nervous energy, I guess. It's so damn ridiculous." Josh began laughing again, muting the sound with his hands over his mouth. "While we were breaking into his office, he came over and broke into your room. What irony."

"If it was him, he was taking a big chance," said Sara. "He must have watched us leave and found out our room numbers."

Josh pushed himself off the wall and paced the hall. "Other than Dave or Ardon, who else could it be?"

Sara looked around the room. "Whoever broke in didn't take anything." She put her hands on her hips. "I've been putting a hair on top of my clothes in the suitcase, but what's the point when they don't care if we know what they've done?"

"Just a minute," Josh said, opening the door to his room and slipping inside.

In a moment he was back. "Yep. He went through my things too. I thought my room looked different, but it's such a mess, I wasn't sure. Depending on who it was, he was probably looking for the painting itself, a clue to its whereabouts, or the key."

Josh followed Sara as she walked to the window at the far end of the hall. "I keep the key on a chain around my neck," she said, keeping her voice low.

Josh tugged his keychain out of his pocket. "Here's mine. Good thing I took it out of my suitcase."

Sara fingered her key. "We could put these keys into another safe deposit box, I guess."

Josh snorted. "Seems like overkill."

Sara dropped the key back under her blouse. "Ardon won't be able to tell we're the ones who broke into the curio shop, will he?" Sara clasped her hands together. "I'm hoping he'll think the cat broke the glass by accident. Worst case, maybe he'll think an ordinary burglar did it and was interrupted before he stole anything."

Josh brightened. "We stole nothing and left everything as we found it."

Sara frowned at him. "Excuse me, but we did break that window—and let the cat out."

"We wore gloves. Even if he did call the police, and he's shady enough I think he'd avoid that, there's nothing to link the burglary with us."

Another thought sent shivers down Sara's spine. "Our burglar didn't have to be Ardon or Dave." She swallowed. "It could have been whoever was following us in Gibraltar."

"I can't believe that. Not even the car rental place in Gibraltar knew we were dropping the car off in Madrid to catch a plane. Who else knows we're here?" Josh picked several papers off the floor as he talked. "We haven't seen anyone familiar, and I'm pretty sure no one's been following us."

"What about the man who asked for me at this hotel?"

Josh stood and frowned. "Let's hope he asks for us tomorrow, and we're here. We've got to find out who that person is."

"And what he wants." Sara walked back to her room. "I guess we don't need to call the police." She opened the door. "I'm bushed. I'll take care of this mess in the morning."

"Put the chain on," Josh whispered, giving her a quick kiss on the cheek. "See you tomorrow."

Sara watched him disappear into his own room before gently closing the door and pulling the chain across. She couldn't do anything about Ardon, but they might find a way to get rid of Dave, maybe something useful for him to do that would send him away. Far away.

She kept the bedside lamp on and watched the door chain as she drifted off to sleep, pushing aside the fear and reliving instead those wonderful moments with Josh.

Even with this diversion, she could not keep disturbing thoughts at bay. They had left Blank, the buzzard, and her son back in Gibraltar. Ardon and Dave threatened them here in Paris. Who else was tracking them and the Rembrandt? How dangerous was he? Or them. She turned over and buried her head under the pillow.

Chapter 21 - Provenance, 1695

Fez, Morocco.

Elias saddled his finest horse, a white Arabian he'd named Bloem, for the trip to Rabat and the slave auction there. Hidden under the grain in the saddle bags straddling the horse was a fortune in gold. Two trusted servants and his son accompanied him on this trip as they had the others. A few more trips like this one, and young Jacob would be able to negotiate this business as well as he. A good way to learn, Elias thought, and his son was gaining an understanding of humility and the rewards of benevolence as well. His mother was not so apt a pupil. Elias thought back to the argument that morning.

"Again you insist on bringing our son into such a desperate business?" she'd said as she did before every trip. "The road is dangerous. Who knows what brigands you might meet? They will murder you and our son and leave me a penniless widow."

Elias studied her with a grim smile. Mercifully, she did not weep. She never wept or fainted as he'd heard so many women did. Not ones in his experience. Ariela had grown up in Tangier, protected and nurtured in the courtyards and Kasbah of a wealthy, respectable family. As had he in Amsterdam, Elias reflected, but he remembered the stories Papa and Tante Isa had told him of how the family struggled to survive hunger and privation in the Spanish Netherlands. They had taught him to help others less fortunate.

And so he hoped to teach his son.

The road from Fez to Rabat was well-traveled, and Elias enjoyed the pleasant companionship of his son. As they neared Rabat, the road ran alongside a river into town. He slowed and stretched his arm out to pluck a date from one of the palm trees beside the road. The air seemed fresher and less dusty. He smelled the salt of the sea.

What would they find in the slave market in Rabat? He'd heard the pirates had captured a Dutch merchant ship with ten passengers. Through his trade connections in Rabat, he often heard the news before it traveled to other ports and towns. With the time needed to make ransom demands and then for family and friends to raise the money to meet these demands or governments to initiate tedious negotiations for release of the captives, Elias doubted that any of them had yet been freed or sold as yet.

Ahead he saw the cluster of buildings that signaled the outskirts of Rabat. Soon all other odors were eclipsed by the human sewage and garbage drawing flies in the gutters. The piles of animal dung, so ubiquitous in Europe, disappeared quickly in Morocco to be used for fuel and building. As they rode through the streets, small children yelled at them and men in doorways stared. Veiled women watched silently.

Elias and his son ignored them all and rode first to the household Elias had set up in Rabat. There, he untied the saddlebags and lifted them off the horses, storing the load behind a locked door off the courtyard.

As the servants began readying the house for guests, Elias and Jacob rode to the slave market near the docks. They saw the Dutch ship, stripped of sails, guns, and frippery, sitting like a naked baby, abandoned at the wharf. In front of the ship, in the middle of a town square, stood the captives, arms bound behind them.

Elias dismounted, tethered his horse, and walked up to them. Jacob followed him.

Twelve men, a boy, and three women. All dispirited and morose. One woman trembled so much she could barely stand and leaned against another. The smell of fear permeated the air around them. Elias had heard that the captives were merchants and their families traveling on personal errands.

"Those are the pirates?" Jacob asked. "They are uncommonly well dressed."

"They are indeed," said Elias, noting the fine gentlemen's breeches and waistcoats and cravats that the pirates wore almost in parody. One even shaded himself under a fringed parasol.

"It's easy to see where they got those clothes." Elias gestured toward the captives who stared down at their feet as they clutched the dirty and torn remnants they wore around their bodies.

The pirates were all descendants of Moriscos, Moors forced out of Spain by decree, much as the Jews had been forced to leave. Like the Jews, they had lost everything, but these men had turned to piracy to survive. The pirates carried pistols and waved them indiscriminately at the prisoners and the onlookers.

Elias tamped down his own fears as he approached the armed and fierce assembly of pirates. His face took on a dubious expression and he frowned at the prisoners. Speaking in Spanish, he asked a pirate who seemed to be the leader, "You have Dutch captives? Passengers, not crew?"

Another pirate came forward. "We have strong men, fine women. Good slaves." He snuck a sidelong look at Elias. "Perhaps you seek your family, no?" He tossed his head toward the prisoners. "What are they worth to you?"

Elias scanned the onlookers. Were there any other bidders to drive up the bidding? None had come forward. Perhaps there had been too many captives lately and the supply now exceeded the demand. He stepped closer to the prisoners and said in Dutch, "Which of you are Dutch passengers and crew?"

The women and seven men stuttered out confused responses in Dutch. The boy hid behind the women. Elias turned to his son. "Watch what I do here," he said in Hebrew so as not to be understood by anyone but his son. "I see no other bidders, so we'll try to win them at a lower price."

"Are they to come back with us?" asked Jacob, eyeing the disheveled assortment of women and men.

Elias' eyes roved across the captives as he assessed their potential. "We'll provide housing and food, even though they are not refugees. And give them the materials for contacting their families or anyone else who can assist them."

"Mama will not be pleased," commented Jacob.

"I know." Elias shrugged. "We'll put them to work in our factories and send them home as soon as possible." He smiled at his son. "All is not charity, Jacob. They will find ways to repay us many times over."

"What about the others," Jacob asked. "The ones who are not Dutch?"

"They are the ship's crew. I fear they must wait for the ransom, which I'm sure the ship's owners will arrange," said Elias. "I am concerned for my countrymen who may not have such resources."

"They are not my countrymen." Jacob folded his arms, feet apart, and surveyed the woebegone captives. "And they take our money. Mama says there will be no money for our own needs if you give it away to renegades and thieves."

"My dear Jacob." Elias saw the pirates eyeing him. He laughed and slapped Jacob on the back as if they shared a joke. "Laugh with me," he ordered Jacob. "The pirates watch us and are suspicious." Jacob laughed with his father as Elias said, "These captives are not renegades and thieves. They are people such as you and I who have met grievous misfortune. They hold important lessons for you, so you must listen as I bargain with this one." Elias turned away from his son and spoke again to the pirate in Spanish. "I wish to buy the Dutch captives."

The pirate grinned. "Make fine slaves. Strong. Work hard for you. Worth much."

Elias shrugged and feigned boredom. "I have no use for these people. I am simply here to help return them to their homes."

The pirate shook his head as if he questioned this assertion. Elias waited as the pirate pursed his lips, scanned the onlookers and called out for bidders. No one responded.

Elias hid his smile and glanced at his son who shrugged.

With no other bidders, the haggling took only a few moments

before a price was negotiated and accepted. Elias told Jacob to wait with the pirates while he obtained the money. Elias then rode his horse away from the onlookers, down a deserted alley and back to his house. He loaded the precise amount of gold and silver coins required and returned to the town square while keeping a wary eye about him. It was a nuisance to unload the gold at his house first, but a necessary precaution.

The agreed-upon amount of gold was handed over, the prisoners were untied, and Elias herded them toward his house. He walked alongside the captives, reassuring them as to his good intentions. Jacob trailed the group on his horse, pulling Bloem along behind him.

At the house, Jacob handed the horses over to a stable boy, and Elias led the group into the house. Elias spoke again in Hebrew to Jacob. "Watch how the servants parcel out the rooms and arrange for a meal," he said. "They are experienced in taking care of such guests. You can learn."

A houseman came forward and bowed to Elias before turning to the bedraggled group of captives. He gestured for them to follow him, but Jacob ignored his father's instructions and ran off to his own room. Elias walked into the courtyard to sit on the bench under an orange tree. He gazed at the small fish pond built in front of the bench and sighed. He wished at least someone in his family would appreciate all that he did to benefit the unfortunate. No one suffered from his generosity except in the time they spent complaining about it. He did God's work here. Why should it cause such discord within his own family?

In a few moments, Jacob interrupted his father's thoughts. "Our esteemed guests," Jacob said, a derisive tone in his voice, "do nothing but complain, Papa." He paced the floor, flailing his arms. "I need to walk about the town. This business is unaccountable to me. Absurd."

As he stepped out the door, he called back to Elias, "My mother is right."

Elias watched him walk out of the courtyard and into the street. Then Elias roused himself as if he had come to a decision. Joining the captives around the table in the dining room, he again accepted their thanks, tearfully given, assuring them that they should soon be on their way home.

Then he listened to the conversation for a sense of who these people were. Later, he spoke to each one alone, taking note of their family and their resources. He again reassured each one. "We will contact your family, tell them of your current condition, and ask for repayment if this is possible."

"But if it is not?" asked a man in shredded vest and britches. "We are respectable people, but none of us was prepared for this catastrophe."

"We will consider it a loan to be paid back when and if funds become available to you." Elias ran his eyes over each of the men as he spoke. He was giving them a license to steal or, at the least, to conveniently forget the repayment. That was one reason Ariela was so angry, but she tended to be avaricious. She did not need to know that the money he used to buy and free captives was inherited from his father whose dying wish was for his son to help others as they themselves had been helped.

And he had done this many times over.

Elias cleared his throat and raised his hand at the assembly to call for attention. "Remember that the money you repay will be used to help other victims of piracy and ill will." He raised his hand to forestall questions. "We will soon find passage for you on another ship."

Most of them groaned at the idea of boarding another ship that might be prey for pirates, but one of the men turned to them and pounded his fist on the table for attention. Then he glared at them as he said, "You know there is no other way to leave this accursed place." He turned to Elias. "We give you our most heartfelt gratitude for rescuing us from those brutes."

Elias bowed his head in response, waited a moment, then continued. "In the meantime," he said, "I will employ you in my factory, which will pay for your stay here and perhaps repay part of the loan." He heard more groans. He had heard them before, but he had also heard the heartfelt gratitude from those who had been without hope. Their appreciation was enough, he thought. It was enough. Once returned to their homes, some would repay his kindness with interest; some would not. Meanwhile, they worked for him in his factory and stores.

Ariela and Jacob would not starve because of his benevolence.

The next morning, sitting at breakfast with Jacob and the captives, Elias studied each man around the table as he referred to a list in his hand. He singled out the stout, red-faced man sitting to his right. "You are Mijnheer Erik deGroot, former council member in Utrecht?"

"Ja. Your information is correct," deGroot said cautiously.

"I would like the honor of speaking with you privately," Elias said. "Please follow me." Elias rose; deGroot did likewise and followed Elias into a small, sunlit room across the central courtyard.

Elias motioned deGroot to sit next to him on the cushioned bench against the wall. A servant brought them mint tea and withdrew. After they had saluted each other, Elias explained his proposition.

"I have a painting," Elias told deGroot, "that I fear is deteriorating in the dryness of this climate. It once held great meaning for my family, but, alas, no more. My son has no interest in it. My wife finds it depressing and old-fashioned. She refuses to hang it in our home. In truth, its somber colors and subject do nothing to enhance our living quarters. It is by Rembrandt van Rijn, perhaps you have heard of him?"

DeGroot thought a moment. "Perhaps," he said as he shook his head. "But I know nothing about art, mijnheer," he added.

"I believe the artist is an honored one and perhaps the painting is of value." Elias paused. Was he making a mistake? Should he wait a little longer? But he saw the deterioration. If he waited much longer, the painting would be of no value anyway. "I would like you to have it. Take it back to the United Provinces, hang it in your home or sell it for what you can get. You may find a buyer, perhaps in the Jewish community, who will treasure it."

"If it is a valuable painting, I am honored by your trust, mijnheer." DeGroot lifted his cup of tea in another salute. "Perhaps

I will keep it—as a memento of this fine adventure." He chuckled.

Elias laughed with him, but he was still uneasy about such an irreverent way of disposing of a valuable family heirloom. Tante Isa would not be pleased, but she was dead. Whatever the painting had meant to his family was dead too.

Chapter 22 - Paris, 1999

Sara spent a restless night and woke early, basking at first in remembering the warmth of Josh's kisses. Not just pals, then, she
thought with a smile. She lay in bed awhile, and her thoughts turned
to her ransacked room. Again she mulled over the possibilities.
Dave? Ardon? The person who had asked for her at the desk?
Someone else?

She finally rolled out of bed, dressed in jeans and a pink blouse
she knew flattered her, and took the elevator down to the breakfast
room. Dave joined her a few minutes later, wearing his jeans and
boots. Then Josh sauntered in, unkempt as usual in faded jeans and
torn T-shirt, yawning.

"You two look bushed," Dave said. He peered at her suspiciously. "What were you up to last night?" His eyes narrowed and
slid from Sara to Josh. "You didn't go out without me, did you?"

Sara was in no mood for conversation, not with Dave hanging
on every word. She waved aside his questions and sipped her tea as
she glanced at Josh. A slight smile crossed his face when he saw her
look. He winked. Flustered, Sara reached for the jam as a diversion.
"Couldn't get to sleep last night, that's all."

Dave looked suspiciously from Sara to Josh. "Don't leave me
out of whatever you're doing. Okay?"

His eyes turned to the breakfast buffet and roved across each
item. "So what's on for today?"

Sara saw that he'd had no trouble sleeping, but could he have been the one ransacking their rooms looking for the key? If so, he would have to know they'd gone out. She snuck a look at him. Cheery. No sign of guilt. Innocent questions. Probably went to bed, as he said.

Josh raised his head above his coffee cup. "Internet Cafe. I have files to check."

"Me, too," added Sara. "More surfing. Too boring for you, Dave."

After breakfast, Dave followed them to the local Internet Cafe. "So what are we looking for here?" he asked. "Anything I can do?"

Sara didn't reply. She took a computer and randomly surfed the Net as Dave watched. Josh sat across from her and did the same. It didn't take long before Dave yawned, looked at the wall clock, and backed toward the door.

"Let me know what you find out," he called to them as he walked off. "I'm here to help, but I'd rather go sightseeing today. Never been to Paris before."

Sara watched him leave, then squeezed Josh's arm in relief. Josh grinned at her as he inserted the disk. A moment later, they were both studying the entries on Ardon's database of Rembrandt paintings. Josh stopped at each entry as he scrolled down to the last one, listed as number 295.

"I had no idea Rembrandt was so prolific," said Sara.

"I don't think this is a complete list," said Josh, "probably a working spreadsheet for Ardon's own use. What's good about it is that he included three fields of interest to us. One notes previous owner or owners, the next shows the current owners and for some of these paintings that space is blank. What could that mean?"

"If the current owner isn't listed, I'd think those paintings might be of interest to us, too." Sara folded her arms on the table. "The last-known owners might also have been lost in the Holocaust. Gives us more people to track down and more possibilities for finding out who owns our Rembrandt."

Josh thought a moment. "I suppose. A bit convoluted, though. The other interesting field is the one that indicates a missing or lost painting, but none of the descriptions resemble our painting."

Sara felt discouraged. So much time had passed since her grandmother had buried it, and no listing anywhere of a Rembrandt painting that resembled theirs. Maybe it was a fraud. She sat back and frowned.

Josh drummed his fingers on the table and stared off at the opposite wall. Sara watched him. Was he feeling as dejected about this search as she was?

He sat up and reached for the keyboard. "Let's eliminate all those that are accounted for." He sorted the file and copied and pasted into a different file the Rembrandts listed as missing or with no current owner. This list was short—only eleven.

"Now let's see if anything resembles our painting." Sara read through the entries. "A couple are possibles, I guess." She felt disappointed. It was a stretch to consider the possibles as the actual Rembrandt they held. If it was a Rembrandt. If it wasn't a Rembrandt, then it wouldn't be on the list, would it? Her spirits drooped at the thought. Had any other Rembrandts been found that no one knew about?

She propped her chin on her hands. Josh sat back, one arm dangling over the back of the chair. "What now?"

"Exactly," a deep voice said behind her. "What now?" A fat hand holding a chewed cigar slapped down on the desk in front of Sara. She stared up into Ardon's face. Her jaw dropped open. She felt Josh grip her arm.

After an awkward moment of silence, Ardon maneuvered himself between Sara and Josh and set his fat ass onto the desk between them. He used the cigar to point to Josh's computer screen, where Ardon's database file was open and visible to all. Josh reached for the keyboard, but Ardon blocked that move, pinning Josh's hand flat on the desk under his own. "No you don't," he said. "I knew it. I could have you arrested for theft."

Josh pulled his hand free. "We could have you arrested for breaking and entering," he said, turning in his chair to face Ardon and folding his arms.

"Me? Breaking and entering what?" He plopped the cigar back in his mouth and narrowed his eyes, daring Josh to continue.

"Our hotel rooms last night," Josh said. "You trashed them. What were you looking for?

"Tut, tut," Ardon shot back. "Not me."

"Afraid so," said Josh, standing to look him in the eye.

Ardon chewed on his cigar. His eyes slid from Josh to Sara and back again. "Dear me, it seems we are at a stalemate." He leaned toward Josh. "I want to see that painting."

"And we want to return it to its rightful owner."

Ardon took out his cigar and studied it. "Such beneficence. I am impressed." He smiled at them with narrowed eyes. "But my innocents, what does that mean? It's all so subjective. Some say museums and only museums should be repositories for great art. In some places, ownership merely means possession. I have the painting, it is mine. You have the painting, it is yours. So simple, my friends, is it not? In some countries, if a painting is in your possession for as little as one year or in your possession at all, it is considered yours. End of story."

Sara pushed her chair away from him. "A scholar and true professional would help us properly identify it and tell us its background. The painting is not ours." She looked him in the eye. "Or yours."

"But so tempting, no? Worth so many millions of dollars." Sara was finding his oily voice almost hypnotic.

"I'm sorry, but if you have no further information for us, then I think we're done," said Josh. He sat down at the computer and turned his back.

"We are not done," said Ardon, "until you give me that disk."

Josh closed the file, retrieved the disk, and handed it to Ardon. He dropped it into his coat pocket.

Sara folded her arms and stared impassively at Ardon as he pushed himself off the desk. Then she looked past him as she saw Dave bustle in.

"Thought I'd tell you I signed up for a tour that ends late tonight. I won't be around for dinner." He eyed Ardon and stuck out his hand. "Pleased to see you again." He glanced from Sara to Josh, a question in his eyes. Sara shook her head.

Ardon stuck the cigar back in his mouth and bowed to Sara, ignoring Dave.

"Think it over, my friends. You know where to reach me. You could be wealthy beyond your wildest dreams." Ardon pulled out his wallet, opened it, and produced a card. "You have my phone number and you know where I work." His voice turned slimy. "I can be reached. . . easily. Call me." He swaggered out of the cafe, whistling.

"I gotta go, too," Dave said and hurried out after Ardon.

"Wealthy beyond your wildest dreams," Sara parroted. "He couldn't even come up with an original expression."

"He is right, of course," said Josh. "Even if that painting isn't a true Rembrandt, it's worth a lot of money."

"So what?" Sara continued to surf the Internet, looking for new leads. "It's still not ours."

Josh turned back to his own computer. "Wanted to make sure we're on the same page. Anyhow, while you two were sparring," he stopped and laughed at the expression on her face, "I was busy copying his files onto the hard drive of this computer. Now I'll copy the file onto a disk, delete the file on the drive, and we'll be back in business."

Sara reached over and shook his hand. "Excellent, Mr. Davila."

Chapter 23 - Provenance, 1729

Haarlem.

Pieter Smit stood beside the Leidsevaart canal and scanned the fields of tulips spread out before him. The reds and yellows of the blooms brightened this cloudy, chilly day. His pride swelled as he thought of the guilders they represented. Soon the visitors from Amsterdam would fill up his inn too, seeking respite from the summer stink of their canals. More guilders. He was a wealthy man, despite the filthy stockings, dirty brown breeches, and wooden clogs he wore on the farm.

He tramped down the dirt road alongside the canal to his house, the Rembrandt Inn. The name made him smile. All because of a painting, given to him in return for a favor. He wondered what had happened to the former council member from Utrecht. He was such a one for ill fortune, he was. The stories he told.

Pieter was not sure he believed much of what the man said. Captured by pirates; rescued by a Dutch Jew in Rabat, Morocco, of all places, who gave him a painting and a Rembrandt at that. He shook his head. Such things did not happen in real life. Then the man had become a merchant importing spices from Africa and his entire inventory was sunk on a ship scuttled near Gibraltar. Pieter could believe that particular story. Had not his own brother gone to sea and brought back such stories and worse? Pieter stopped and again cast his eyes across the fields. A farm could not be lost at sea.

.unless the dikes failed. Pieter had commiserated with the merchant and, rejoicing in a fine harvest, had the money to help the man by buying the painting. Even he had heard of Rembrandt. Pieter trudged up the walk to his house.

"So how are you now, this fine day?" asked his wife, Elsa, supervising the laundress who used a paddle to poke and stir the clothes she was washing in three copper tubs over hot fires.

Pieter only nodded to her as he tramped past, slipped out of his wooden clogs, and walked into the kitchen. He preferred not to run into guests when he'd been out in the fields. He reached into the pantry for a bottle of the local brew, glad the cook was outside gossiping with the women as they worked. He lifted the cloth on a bowl to smell the yeasty bread dough half-risen. His stomach growled, and he pinched off a bit of dough to taste. Then he picked up a stray carrot lying on the table and whittled it down with his teeth.

They had three guests for the night, so he'd be at the bar all evening serving the beer supplied by his friend Christiaan, the brewer. All was well, then.

Hours later, after dinner, only one guest remained in the dining room. Pieter eyed him suspiciously. Niels Anderson. Amsterdam. What did the man want? He had drunk only the one beer and now smoked a pipe and nursed a cup of tea. That was all right, they charged more for tea, but the man kept staring up at the Rembrandt painting, hung in the center of the wall opposite the fireplace. The lanterns did little to reveal its colors and details, yet the man continued to stare at it.

Pieter drew himself a beer and sat at the table opposite Anderson. "So you come from Amsterdam then?"

"Aye, I do." The man shifted his gaze from the painting to Pieter.

"I see you like the painting there." Pieter sat back, then he added, "You have heard of Rembrandt van Rijn, the famous painter from Amsterdam?"

"Ja, I know." The man puffed on his pipe.

"Meself, I prefer the paintings of Frans Hals, our local boy."

Pieter smiled to himself. That should impress this big barrel from the city. There was something disturbing about him and the way he kept looking at the painting.

"Perhaps you would see your way to selling the Rembrandt then?" asked the stranger, gesturing to it with his pipe.

The question took Pieter's breath away. Sell the painting? He turned to study it himself. He wasn't taken by the painting itself; the subject was no beauty. He grinned at the understatement. A pompous Amsterdam councilman, no doubt. It was the Rembrandt connection. Everyone knew the value of a Rembrandt painting. It gave his inn stature, made it better than the rest who only paraded their Delft tiles. His mouth twisted. So commonplace. No other inn he ever heard of displayed a genuine Rembrandt painting for guests.

"That painting is not for sale," Pieter said, thinking all the while that perhaps, if the price were high enough, then he would sell the Rembrandt and buy a Frans Hals. He'd heard that Hals was an even better painter than Rembrandt. And Hals was from Haarlem. Everyone hereabouts knew of him.

"I can offer you. . ." then Anderson named a price so high it staggered Pieter. It even made him forget to bargain. Could a mere painting be worth that much? He sat stunned as he debated what to do.

"Excuse me," he said as he pushed back his chair, picked up his glass, and walked through the door into the kitchen. His wife and the cook sat at a table, each sipping a glass of beer. They looked at him in surprise.

"So, are all the guests gone to bed then?" his wife asked.

Pieter grabbed a chair and straddled it. "Elsa, we are offered a sum for that Rembrandt beyond anything you have ever dreamt." He mentioned the sum.

Elsa laughed and winked at the cook. "Methinks my dear husband has drunk too much of our local brew." She reached over and patted his hand. "So? And do we sell him our souls as well for this fabulous sum?" She grinned at him. "Or perhaps this offer will disappear in the bright sunlight of tomorrow morning?"

"No. I am serious," said Pieter, shaking his head. "Our guest,

Niels Anderson, he looks at the painting all night. Now he sips his tea and offers me such a sum for the Rembrandt."

"The Rembrandt?" His wife sat back, frowning. "And such a sum?" She looked up at the ceiling a moment before turning to Pieter. "We would have to change the name of our inn," she said, ever practical. "No Rembrandt, no Rembrandt Inn."

"We could buy a Frans Hals for half that sum, and. . ." Pieter muttered to himself, "I prefer Frans Hals."

"I also. His paintings are so much more cheery," said Elsa. "And he lived here, in Haarlem, not in Amsterdam. We would be helping our own."

"I have never seen a painting by this Frans Hals," said the cook. "And that so-called Rembrandt is the dreariest thing I've ever come across—looks like a heathen to me. What kind of Christian was this Rembrandt?" She sniffed, a rigid Calvinist herself.

Elsa tapped her chin. "We could change the name to the Frans Hals Inn."

Pieter raised his glass to her. "We could then." His spirits rose as he considered what he might do with the princely sum offered for the Rembrandt. He glanced across the table at his wife. She had a faraway look in her eyes as if she, too, contemplated what she could buy with such a windfall.

"So we are agreed then?" Pieter rose.

"Would he offer more if we hesitated to part with such a valuable painting?" Elsa asked, and then noticed Pieter's expression. "I'm just supposing."

"I don't know," Pieter said, frowning. "I'm afraid to tempt fate. He may run from us, and I don't see us getting another such offer."

Elsa and the cook nodded.

"Take it," said Elsa.

Elsa and Pieter looked at each other for a moment, then Pieter stood. "So be it."

Chapter 24 - Paris, 1999

Sara glanced at her watch. Three hours had passed since Ardon left, and they'd continued to work on the computers, tracking down contact information on the organizations involved in returning art stolen by the Nazis. Sara was hungry.

"We're going about this all wrong," she said.

"How so?" Josh paused in writing down notes.

"I'm on a website listing resources for recovering art and other possessions looted by the Nazis. It says here that from 1933 to 1945, the end of World War II, the Nazis looted gold, Jewish bank accounts, art works, insurance, and non-monetary gold." Sara looked up. "That means they took the gold out of their victims' teeth." She shuddered. "In 1998. . . ," she looked up. "That was last year." She continued reading. ". . . investigators started researching the role of the Vatican, slave labor, alleged American and foreign bank misdeeds; looted archives and libraries; and Jewish communal and religious property."

"Yeah, well, they've also been investigating looted diamonds and securities, and the role of American corporations in their dealings with the Nazis." Josh sat back and stretched. "We're talking millions and millions of dollars worth of property stolen by the Nazis and their collaborators."

"My grandmother and your Uncle Samuel were heroes," Sara said. "They didn't even have to get involved at all in the war, since they lived in St. Thomas."

Josh got up to stand behind Sara and read the entry. "Says here that the U.S. National Archives has a huge database devoted to the problem of art stolen by the Nazis. It was created as part of U.S. investigations into cultural assets looted or otherwise lost during the war." He whistled. "Way cool."

Sara looked at him. "That means we'd have to go to Washington, D.C., to search through the documents. I'd hate to have to read through all of that."

Josh shook his head. "I had no idea there were so many."

"Impossible. Just impossible." Sara moved the cursor down the list of resources.

Josh frowned and rubbed his chin. "I guess it's good to know the information is available." He returned to his seat and continued searching.

Sara read through the list, seeking any bit of information that might be useful to them. She looked up with a start when Josh reached over and touched her arm.

"This might be easier." He pointed to the list of resources displayed on his computer screen. "The Commission for Looted Art in Europe," he read. "has been established to help individuals, families and institutions who were the victims of Nazi looting between 1933-1945. The CLAE will work to research, locate and recover your looted artworks." He looked up at Sara. "Then it gives an address in London, phone number, and e-mail address."

"Let's call them!" Sara said. "Someone may have put in a claim."

"I hope so," said Josh. "Make our job easy."

He continued reading. "They suggest writing down what you and your family may have been told, including your family's home and business addresses, details of when and where the works were obtained, and any exhibitions or publications in which they might have appeared during or before your family's ownership."

He stopped and turned to Sara. "They assume that people using their resources are looking for their own lost property. We've got the opposite problem. We have the property and we're trying to find the owner. We don't have most of the information they want."

"But they've got a good idea we could use, said Sara. "Looking up old programs or advertisements from, say, the thirties, to see if the painting was exhibited anywhere. Surely the owner's name would be included in a note of thanks if nothing else."

Sara continued to read over his shoulder. "The commission maintains two private searchable databases. One of them has information and documentation, but the other one," she drew a breath, "contains details of over 25,000 objects of all kinds-- paintings, drawings, antiquities, Judaica, and so on—identified as looted or missing from over fifteen countries."

"I suggest we call them right now," said Josh. "They search by Artist, Author or Maker, Object, and Provenance. This might tell us if anyone put in a claim for the painting."

Doubts surfaced in Sara's mind. "How could either of us tell if the claim was legitimate? We left at least one person back in Gibraltar who claims ownership; two others want it; someone has stolen Samuel's decoy; Ardon is interested and can probably cook up a claim with someone; Dave insists it's now my painting, and a mysterious person has asked for me at our hotel here in Paris."

She stopped, breathless. She would recognize any fake claims Dave might make, but all of a sudden, an odd assortment of people were interested in a painting that had been buried for sixty years.

Josh leaned back in his chair and folded his arms behind his head. "You're right," he said. "But that would be the organization's job to verify the claim." He stared off into space. "In fact, I guess we could select the organization we think would be the most careful and reliable and let them take over this job. Out of our hands then."

That idea depressed Sara. The common sense approach. On the other hand, what would any of the people claiming the painting do to get it away from her? She felt chills race down her back and acid burning her stomach. There may have already been one murder related to the painting.

She clenched her hands and shook herself to ward off these terrifying thoughts, then looked up to see Josh watching her.

"So what do you think," he asked, "shall we go back to the hotel and call the Commission?"

She rose, thankful to get out and walk. "Yes, but let's be careful what we say."

"I hate to think our rooms here are bugged, but they could be," said Josh, closing out his computer and picking up the disk.

Sara walked to the door. "It won't matter if they hear us make these calls."

Back in her hotel room, Sara wrote a brief script and handed it to Josh. He read through the script twice, picked up the phone, and tapped in the number. Sara waited as he was bounced from person to person, finally reaching one who began taking down the information.

After following the script to describe their request, he listened, then put his hand over the phone, and looked at Sara. "I'm on hold. Can you get a fax number?"

Sara found the courtesy book of hotel information and leafed through it searching for the number. She pointed to it as she gave the book to Josh. He gave a thumbs up, still on hold.

After another moment, he said thank you and then recited the fax number. He hung up and shrugged. "I'm not sure they'll be helpful. This is their first year in operation, so they're still setting up their database and collecting information. She said she'd fax us later today whatever they might have."

They waited. Sara felt tense and unsettled but hopeful that perhaps the commission would provide the answer. If she hadn't been so burdened with anxiety, she and Josh could have made much better use of all this empty time, but one look at him showed her that he was as tense as she was.

He pulled a couple of Cokes out of the room refrigerator and gave one to Sara. "The hotel receptionist will call us when they get the fax."

"With a key word like 'Rembrandt,' I should think the search will be straightforward, " Sara said. "How many lost Rembrandts can there be?"

She went back to the table to shuffle through the papers, seeking inspiration. Josh stopped pacing the floor and took the other chair at the table but drummed his fingers as he stared off into space. The waiting dragged on. Sara got up to stare out the window and then she took her turn pacing the floor. Two hours later, the phone rang. Sara answered it, thanked the caller, and grinned at Josh. "They've received the fax downstairs."

She and Josh raced each other to the elevator. They picked up the fax, returned to Sara's room, and sat side by side on the couch to read it. It was on letterhead stationery with the word "Results" in large bold letters. Below the word was a list of thirty or so entries in small type, each starting with Rembrandt, then his first name, then the title of a painting or etching that was reported missing.

"Look for anything that sounds close to what we have," Josh said, running his finger down the list. "It might be named something different from what we called it."

Sara read each entry slowly and considered it before moving to the next one. "Ardon's list isn't nearly as complete as this one," she said. "We were criminals for nothing."

"He probably developed the list for another reason." Josh stretched, and twisted in his chair waiting for Sara to finish. When she did, she looked at him.

"Nothing?" Josh said.

"Nothing." Sara opened another Coke and sipped it. "Don't you think it odd that no one has reported it missing?"

Josh shook his head. "Think of the circumstances. A Jew entrusted the painting to the resistance group your grandmother and Samuel belonged to. That person was terrified and desperate, in hiding, and seeking an escape route out of Nazi-occupied countries. Your grandmother buried the painting in 1941, if we are to believe that receipt, and at that time, the Nazis had taken over Austria, the Sudetenland, Poland, Netherlands, Belgium, Luxembourg. . . ." He paused and looked up at the ceiling, then counted the rest off on his fingers. "France, Denmark, Yugoslavia, Greece, and Norway."

A shiver ran down Sara's spine. "Horrible," she said, thinking of the devastation and lost lives. "In all that destruction, could the owner of the painting have left any descendants? Is there anyone left to claim the painting?"

Sara sat back, imagining the fear, the desperation. War brought out the worst in people. So many tried to turn it to their advantage, even friends and neighbors of the victims. "Maybe an acquaintance of the owner had his eyes on the painting. He knows it existed, knew its value, could be searching for it even now."

This whole adventure had been such a lark for her and yet behind it lay horror and tragedy. She thought of Josh. He was afraid that his parents or grandparents may have appropriated the art entrusted to them. Her own grandmother had kept the heartbreaking secret until her death. Samuel had suffered. Whoever owned the painting would inherit the terrible history of it.

They sat together on the couch in silence. Josh put his arm around her and drew her close. She turned her face to his. He kissed her. It was warm and comforting as it needed to be in that discouraging moment. She closed her eyes and snuggled closer, realizing how tense and tired she felt.

"I have an idea," Sara said at last.

"What?" Josh yawned, stretched, and sat up.

Sara couldn't help yawning herself. "I am exhausted. Too much happening too fast."

Josh smiled at her. "Me too. So what's your idea?"

"We should get a computer geek to scan Grandma's receipt and try to bring out the writing so we can read it." She rose and shuffled through the papers on the desk. "Here it is." She handed it to Josh.

"Good idea." He studied the receipt. "It's too faded to make out the name and address. Can barely read the date."

"That's been the problem all along," Sara said.

"We should also find other Rembrandt experts." He gave the receipt back to Sara. "Ardon was a lemon. Someone else must know about the painting. Someone legitimate who won't resort to theft or extortion."

"Yes. And while we're doing this, we need to keep it secret from Dave, Ardon. . ."

"And whoever has been following us around."

Chapter 25 - Provenance, 1729

Amsterdam.

Niels Anderson gloated all the way back to Amsterdam. Those fools. Those country bumpkins. He snickered, then laughed out loud as he remembered the look on the farmer's face. The 2500 guilders Anderson offered for the painting—a prince's ransom to be sure—pried the painting off the farmer's wall without any tiresome haggling or argument. They were afraid such a windfall would disappear. Greed. Worked every time.

Anderson ran his hand around the painting, worth four times, perhaps more, than he'd paid for it and now padded and wrapped in layers of thick wool for the journey to Amsterdam.

The coach pulled up to the marble steps of his three-story townhouse near the harbor. Anderson stepped down from the coach, then reached in to pick up the painting. His man-servant opened the front door to him while the coachman climbed on top of the coach to retrieve the portmanteau and the bundles tied there.

Anderson brandished the painting. "This is the best one yet, Maarten!" he said to his man-servant.

"Ja, mijnheer," said Maarten, taking the cloak and scarf. "It is a painting then?"

Anderson was already perusing the paneled walls of the foyer. "Not here, I think." He walked into the parlor as Maarten hurried to light the lamps. Anderson turned in a circle, admiring the effect of superb paintings and fine furnishings in his favorite room. Then he sat in his most comfortable chair, rested his chin on his fingertips, and studied each painting and its placement among the others on the walls. The paintings glowed in the soft lamplight.

"Light the fire, Maarten." Anderson said. *Two Rubens, one Vermeer, one Hals, and now*—he patted the wrapped painting beside his chair—*now I have a Rembrandt.* He unwrapped the painting, taking off one layer of wool at a time. He worked slowly, savoring the moment when he peeled away the last layer to reveal the dark tones and grim visage of Rabbi Saul Levi Morteira as a Moor.

No. Definitely not the foyer. The crisp and clear colors of the Vermeer would do well in the foyer—most impressive there. It would prepare visitors for the magnificence of his collection, although. . . . Truthfully, he saw now, if he had not known it was a Rembrandt, he would have preferred a painting that did not portray a powerful Jew.

He waved his hand. No matter. *I will place it to the right of the fireplace, near the window. That should brighten the tones a bit, and my visitors need never know the painting was anything more than a character study by Rembrandt, that supreme of all painters.* Anderson's eyes glittered in the lamplight, and his smile had the lust of possession in it.

Maarten touched a flame to the tinder in the fireplace and blew on it to send glowing embers up to help the cut branches catch fire and then the logs on top. Anderson watched him absently, listening to the crackling fire as he filled his pipe. "Maarten," he said, "I believe I will invite a few friends in for dinner to celebrate my new acquisition."

"Ja, I will tell the cook. What day is it to be?"

Anderson thought a moment. His old rival Garret Friedlander should be present. "I think three weeks should be sufficient time," he said. Thinking of Garret always brought up a vision of Marta. Lovely Marta. Perhaps not so lovely now after three kinderen. He snapped his fingers. *Marta should see my Rembrandt. She should see the success of the man she could have married.*

A cynical smile crossed his face as he thought of the latest market maneuver to undercut Garret. Garret faced trouble with the bank now. Anderson shrugged. *So unfortunate.*

Anderson took pen and paper and wrote out Garret's name, then added four other names of influential men in Amsterdam to the list. Five couples. He tapped the pen to his lips. Then he invited the widow Helsen to make twelve. A good number for dinner. He left the list on the desk for his secretary.

The invitations were duly sent out, and acceptances received. Anderson's hints about the plum he had acquired created a buzz of interest. Despite the elaborate preparations for the dinner and the excitement of unveiling a little-known Rembrandt, the evening was not a success.

Maarten ushered in Garret Friedlander, who was the first to arrive but he was alone. "My wife is ill," he said as he shook hands with Anderson. "She is unable to attend." Anderson's effusive welcome took on a sour note. Half the pleasure of the evening had faded.

The widow Helsen with watery eyes, red nose, and hacking cough, was ushered in next. "I have a nasty cold," she told Anderson, "but I could not miss such an exciting event." She tapped him with her fan and sneezed. "The town is abuzz with wonder." He quickly pawned her off on the other guests. The long-anticipated evening was becoming a disaster.

As the party went on, whenever Anderson stopped to chat with this guest or that, he saw Garret's worried eyes following him. That at least was a consolation. But even the congratulations and approval of the other guests as they viewed his art collection couldn't cast off the pall that weighed down his spirits.

To make matters worse, two days later Anderson received notice that one of his ships had been captured by North African pirates, and then ransacked and scuttled. Now the pirates demanded a ransom for the captain and the sailors. He groaned at the nuisance. "Better the pirates should have killed them all," he snarled to his secretary, "when they sunk my ship."

The wives of the captured captain and crew members visited Anderson before he thought to order his household staff to repel all visitors. Unaware of the ship's capture, Maarten brought the women into the parlor and then retreated to alert the cook to the need for refreshments. He left Anderson alone with them.

Anderson had never seen such weeping and wailing, yet their entreaties did not sway him. "I cannot help you," he told them coldly. "I have no funds to rescue those in my employ who behave recklessly and endanger themselves and others."

The captain's wife stared at him in disbelief. "My husband would not behave recklessly. He did all he could to save your ship and crew."

Anderson drew himself up. "Nevertheless, although I sympathize with you and the other ladies, I can do nothing to help. Paying the pirates' ransom will only impoverish me with no guarantee that the prisoners would be released. Such matters are the proper business of government, not unfortunate victims such as myself."

He called for Maarten. "Please see these women out." Then he walked out of the room.

"The fools," he said later to Maarten, "can't they see that I worry myself about this problem every day? I do not have the money to rescue the captain and crew."

Over tea that afternoon, Anderson considered the situation. He could afford the wrath of the captain and crew's families and friends and the sentimental fools of Amsterdam. The matter was of no real consequence and would soon be forgotten. The idea was absurd. He paced the floor, muttering. *How can I buy the paintings so necessary to my life if I have to pay ransoms for men foolish enough to be prey for pirates?*

He stuck out his chin and practiced his show of grievance. His ships had been lost, no doubt by the captain and crew's incompetence. That alone should absolve him from any responsibility toward them. That is the story he told those with the temerity to ask.

The matter, however, would not go away. It hounded him wherever he appeared in the city. The frowns of disapproval, the censure of the councilmen, the rebukes of the other merchants—he turned his back to them all.

The situation grew worse. Anderson thought of leaving town until the unfortunate business blew over as it inevitably would, but he needed to conserve his financial resources. At one point, he considered going out of business, hiding whatever stock remained in a warehouse out of town.

Yet he did not leave town or close his business. The sailors' families and friends continued to knock on his door, and he continued to turn them away, using Maarten to deliver the message that he was not at home.

Week after week, no ransom was paid and the gossip increased, along with stories of the extreme privation and suffering endured by the victims. If Anderson ventured out of the house, the ruffians in the street pelted him with rotten fruit and stones. He remained indoors, sending Maarten out on errands, and continued to ignore all entreaties, even the most desperate.

At last, the townspeople prevailed upon council members to raise the funds themselves to buy the captain and crew when they were auctioned off as slaves. These were not prosperous days and raising the funds took weeks. Relatives and friends fretted and complained and continued to send their pleas to Anderson to no avail.

Eventually, the town council was able to ransom the slaves, and the captain and sailors returned to Amsterdam. Maarten heard the news, saw the celebration in the streets, and returned home to tell Anderson.

"At last," Anderson said. "They have come to their senses and listened to me." He let a few days pass before he came out of hiding and acted as if he had a part in the rescue. He was met with cold stares or ignored in the streets. The men he had fed and entertained a few short months before now refused his invitations, often with no response at all, and did not send any invitations to him.

New problems emerged. He could not find men to work his ships. They stayed in port, the cargo rotted on the docks, and importers and exporters refused to patronize his business. The councilmen granted him no favors, and he continued to be shunned in the streets.

As more months passed, Anderson took to alleys and byways to avoid meeting anyone he knew. Especially Garret. Peering around corners, he would see Garret sauntering down the street, tall, cheerful, greeting everyone he met. Anderson would return home after a short walk, give Maarten his hat and coat, and with cold disdain, say, "Garret acts as if he owns Amsterdam." Most galling of all, Marta had regained her youthful bloom.

"Where are the friends who came to my dinners, who admired my paintings?" he moaned one day.

He cursed their folly. He didn't need them, but he did need their business. In the first few months, he brushed off the problem. "They'll soon forget the incident when they realize I can not be held responsible for such exorbitant ransoms." As he saw Maarten's raised eyebrows at this statement, he added, "The captain is responsible for mismanaging the ship. That much is perfectly clear."

A year passed. He could not afford to keep the cook. Then Maarten had to go.

Anderson took to drinking every night. At first two glasses, then three. As the weeks passed, his drinking increased until night after night he drank until he fell into a stupor. When he woke, he could not begin the day until he had a drink or two or three. As he drank, he stared at his paintings. Each one. Two Rubens, one Vermeer, one Hals, and one Rembrandt.

Gradually, the paintings disappeared. One Ruben, one Vermeer, one Hals, and one Rembrandt remained on his walls. Then one Vermeer, one Hals, and one Rembrandt. Then one Hals and one Rembrandt.

And then there was only the Rembrandt to keep the old drunk happy in the empty, frigid, broken house in Amsterdam. One fine spring day, a neighbor noticed a sickly sweet stench leaking out of the windows and doors. He climbed the cracked marble steps and peered in a window.

Two weeks later, the house and its contents were auctioned off. Garret Friedlander walked away with the Rembrandt.

"A fine gift for Marta," he said to his friends and held a dinner party to celebrate the acquisition.

Chapter 26 - Paris, 1999

Sara perused a local telephone book for photographers, but she was unfamiliar with the addresses and decided to ask at the desk downstairs. Josh was mapping out a Mètro route to the Louvre. The phone rang. Sara picked it up. The front desk.

"Bonjour, Mademoiselle, you have a visitor. He has been here before asking for you."

"Fine. I'll be right down." She looked at Josh. "Our visitor has returned."

At last they would find out who and why this stranger sought them out. He had to come from Ardon. Another thought occurred to her. Could Samuel have sent someone to help?

She and Josh took the elevator and walked to the front desk. The receptionist gestured toward the chairs in the lounge where a tall, lean man lounged. Sara walked over to him, Josh following behind. The man rose out of the chair and gazed at them with a toothy grin. He was dressed in a gray business suit, black overcoat thrown over his arm, and a hat in hand. "Bonjour. Mademoiselle Miller?"

"Bonjour. Yes, I'm Ms. Miller." She turned to Josh. "And this is Mr. Davila. How may we help you?"

"My name is Jean Roget." He bowed slightly to them both. "I believe you are in possession of an object stolen from my family." He spoke with a heavy French accent.

Sara gripped Josh's hand, her eyes traveling from Roget's ferret-

like face to his scuffed brown shoes. She should have been prepared
for such a bald statement, but she was not. Something about the
man made her pull back in distrust. His smile seemed false, a surface
gesture to please.

"Excuse me," she said. "I'm not sure I heard you right." Who
was he? How did he find out about them?

The man repeated his name. "I'm told you have my family's
painting. A Rembrandt." He extended his hand.

She shook it, glancing at Josh who stood back and studied the
man. "We're pleased to meet you," she said, a thousand questions in
her mind. Who told him that she and Josh had a painting? If Samuel
had found him, surely Samuel would have called her or Josh too.
And this man would have said so. This Jean Roget could be a
confederate of Ardon or Dave or even Blank and Smythe, and that
would mean Jean Roget, if that was his name, was a set up, given a
plausible story, and told where to find her and Josh. That fake smile.
The unctuous manner. The man had fraud written all over him.
After the strange characters they'd met on this journey, her guard
was up and she was biased against him. Yet, she admitted to
herself, she also didn't want their search to end this way.

"We need to find a private place to talk," said Josh. "Perhaps
my room. . .?"

Josh was right. The lobby was empty right now, but the clerk
and the concierge were all ears. "Let's go upstairs," Sara said,
exchanging skeptical looks with Josh.

"I'll follow you." Roget maintained his toothy grin but said
nothing else until they were seated around the coffee table in Josh's
room.

"Tell us about yourself," said Sara.

"Oui. I am a businessman here in Paris. My mother, she was
Jewish. Before the war, her family was prosperous. Prosperous
enough to buy fine pieces of art, including a certain Rembrandt.
When the Nazis occupied France, she and my father tried to leave
France for England but did not succeed." Roget shrugged. "I was
sent to relatives in England. A tragic affair. Terrible. They contacted
a resistance group—I believe your grandmother was part of that

group—that was able to smuggle out of France their more valuable possessions, including the Rembrandt painting." He stopped to assume a mournful expression.

"At the end of the war, they returned to their town to find everything destroyed. They did not know how to retrieve the art smuggled out of France. So it has been until this day, when by chance, speaking with my friend Dr. Ardon, I hear of your search." He finished and looked at them with an open face as if seeking approval.

Sara watched the man's expression as she assimilated his story. It sounded plausible. What exactly had they told Ardon? Could Ardon have briefed Roget on this story? Were they in this together?

"Can you tell us about the painting?" asked Josh. He leaned back in his chair, fiddling with a pencil, seemingly unimpressed.

Roget raised his hands, palms outward. "I am not sure exactly what the subject was," he said. "My parents are both gone now, and they only told me it was a Rembrandt painting of a man who is dressed, I believe, as a Moor."

Sara looked up from her notes. He did know about the painting. Ardon could have described it to him. Or Dave.

"I see," said Josh, glancing at Sara. "Do you have any documentation that would confirm your story?"

"The facts I've told you are proof enough that the painting is mine." Roget's voice turned angry and loud, but Sara was long used to Dave's tactics and wasn't about to be swayed by such bullying.

She folded her arms and spoke calmly. "Do you remember anything else?" she asked. "We need more than what you've told us. Some kind of papers. . ."

"I can't imagine why you need more documentation," Roget said. "I'll have to return home and search my files. A waste of time." A gleam appeared in his eye. "I should charge you with theft and bring the police into this."

Josh sat back with folded arms. "You do that."

"Until then," Sara added, handing Roget a pen and a sheet of hotel stationery, "perhaps you can write out your name, address, phone number, and whatever we need to contact you if necessary."

To check up on him, actually.

"All right." Roget dug into his breast pocket. "My card. I will expect to hear from you soon."

"Meanwhile, look for more documentation," said Sara. She rose and opened the door.

Roget stood, picked up his overcoat and hat, and frowned at them with brows drawn. "You'll be hearing from me." He stalked toward the door and paused. "Or my lawyer." He sailed out of the room. Sara quelled an urge to applaud.

She closed the door. "What a performance. Did he threaten us?"

Josh walked to the door and locked it. "Sounded like it."

"I don't like that guy, and I'm suspicious. Ardon coached him. What do you think?"

"I'm trying to remember exactly what we told Ardon," Josh said, leaning against the door with folded arms. "Ardon and Dave both know how we found the painting and what it looks like."

"We're dealing with three loose cannons," said Sara, biting her lip. "I'll bet Ardon dreamed this up. Or Dave."

"I wouldn't be surprised." Josh walked over to Sara, put his arms around her, and kissed her. "I've been wanting to do that."

"Me, too," she said, snuggling into his arms.

Later, they sat side by side on the couch with Josh's arm around Sara. She leaned back against him. "We've been too loose in talking about the Rembrandt," said Sara. "We've given dicey people all the information they'd need to make a claim. Roget even knew about my grandmother."

"What do you want to bet," said Josh, "that Roget comes back with more detail about the painting and the circumstances surrounding it. He might even bring fake documents ."

Sara laughed. "That he got from Ardon and maybe even Dave."

"If they are in cahoots, which I think they are."

Sara tapped her chin as she thought. "Dave left the Internet Cafe right after Ardon. In fact, I think he caught up with Ardon and walked with him up the street."

"Hatching this plot, no doubt. I'll bet Roget is an actor they roped into this scenario."

"I've got his business card." She picked it up and rubbed her thumb across the flat surface. "Plain black text on white card stock. Computer-generated. He could make one saying whatever he wanted whenever he needed one."

Josh roused himself and stretched. "Let's take a cab to the address on the card, just to see."

"Good idea." Sara picked up her coat. "From now on, we don't discuss the painting with anyone. Not Dave. Not Ardon. No one."

Chapter 27 - Provenance, 1759

Amsterdam.

Holding a square of oilcloth over her head, Marta Friedlander hurried to the port through pouring rain down muddy streets. This might be her last chance to touch her youngest son Johann before he left for Indonesia. She would not embarrass him with excessive affection, however she felt. The Dutch East Indies Company now claimed his allegiance, and she might never see him again. Life was uncertain and the sea especially so, but how could a mother ever be as persuasive as the lure of adventure and travel?

The demand for nutmeg, cloves, and Cubeb pepper that fed the Dutch East Indies Company had already claimed her oldest son, lost somewhere in the Indian Ocean. She had hoped Johann would remain at home and now prayed only that he would stay safe and return to a merchant's life here in Amsterdam. If only Garret were alive to add his arguments to hers, perhaps. . . .

She stepped around barrels and piles of heavy rope resting on the sodden planks of the wharf. The ship remained at the dock, but the deck swarmed with men wearing dark heavy coats and caps, all dashing about as their captain yelled commands. Marta searched each face for Johann and finally saw him near a mast. She waved a red handkerchief until at last he noticed her and blew her a kiss. She saw that they were casting off. She would have to be content with a distant kiss, but she could not help the tears that coursed down her face, mingling with the raindrops. Her heart felt heavy with grief and longing as she stood in the rain until the ship grew small in the distance, then she turned to trudge back to her house.

Her daughter Kirsten swung open the door as Marta approached. "Mama, you will die of the cold and the wet."

She threw the square of oilcloth aside as she pulled Marta in and shut the door. "Please, Mama, let me help you. You should not be out in such weather."

So tiresome, Marta thought. "I am not made of tissue," she said. "The oilcloth served its purpose perfectly."

She let Kirsten lead her to her bedroom where a maidservant waited with a blanket and dry clothes. The maid helped Marta change her clothes, then Marta arranged a yellow scarf around her neck to boost her spirits and pulled on gray mitts to warm her arms. Her dress was a simple green, pinned up to reveal a contrasting petticoat. She added a ruffled white cap to cover her damp hair. Then she returned to the parlor, where Kirsten stoked the fire, sending out a burst of flame and heat. The room was quite warm enough, but it could not assuage the chill in her heart.

"So he is off then?" asked Kirsten. Her dark blue dress, also pinned up to show the petticoat, was covered by a long white apron. "He always was a foolish boy."

Marta did not reply. She sat in the rocking chair, gently swaying to and fro, her eyes on the Rembrandt painting. Garret had been proud to own such an expensive work from a renowned master artist. She knew how he had acquired it, and it made her feel uncomfortable as if she were a vulture, feeding on the remains of the unfortunate.

Poor Niels. A sad end even if he was a vain, silly, selfish man. She had done well to refuse him all those years ago. She had known even as a frivolous young girl that Garret was the better man. Kind. Generous. Ah, well. Better not to think of those days. She tore her eyes away from the Rembrandt and saw Kirsten watching her.

"I am quite all right," Marta said. "You do not have to tend me. Your husband and children will miss you."

"They do. I must see to their dinner. You are all right, Mama?"

Kirsten asked. She rang the bell for the maidservant, who quickly appeared and curtsied.

"My cloak, please," said Kirsten, "and my hat. I will be leaving now."

"One moment," said Marta. "That painting there." She pointed to the Rembrandt. "I mean to sell it unless you would like it. Johan is not interested."

Kirsten walked over to the painting and studied it. "Quite gloomy, is it not?" She shook her head. "I never understood why Papa liked it so much."

"Nor did I," answered Marta. "So you do not want it?"

Kirsten bent to kiss Marta on the cheek, then stepped to the door. The maidservant draped the cloak over Kirsten's shoulders and helped her with the hat. "I think not, Mama. You must sell it and use the money for something special." She waved a good-bye as she stepped out, closing the door behind her.

The logs crackled and spit in the fireplace, and the rain beat steadily against the windows. The rocking chair creaked. Marta sat in the parlor as darkness cast its shadows across the room. She stared at the painting, wondering about the man who had posed as the Moor. A man once vibrant and alive, like Garret and her firstborn son, Joseph. All dead now.

Chapter 28 - Paris, 1999

Sara checked the address on Roget's business card as the cab inched along a trash-strewn street of shabby row houses near the infamous Pigalle area. They decided to take a cab rather than the Mètro after reading in Sara's guidebook that Pigalle was Paris' red light district with a proliferation of sex shops, bistros, and peep shows.

"Although," Josh said, grinning and putting his arm around Sara to pull her closer, "it might be interesting to visit, being tourists." He nuzzled her cheek.

"I'd rather not get my throat slit," said Sara, taking his hand, "walking down a side street to wherever Roget lives."

She peered at the house numbers on the row houses as the cab driver slowed down. "Here it is," she said, studying a weathered row house with warped and uneven wooden steps leading up to the front door. The house needed paint.

"Let's get out," said Josh, opening the door. Sara leaned over to pay the cab driver.

They walked up the steps to the house and entered the foyer. Four mailboxes were screwed to the wall next to the door buzzers. Numbers rather than names were attached to both the mailboxes and the buzzers.

Josh rang a door buzzer at random. Immediately, a female voice spoke over the intercom. "Bonjour?"

"Monsieur Jean Roget?" asked Sara.

"Non. Je ne connais pas."

"Parlez-vous anglais?"

"Oui, madam. There is no Jean Roget here."

"And not in the other apartments?"

"I have never heard that name," she said, "but I have not been here long."

"Merci beaucoup." Sara turned to Josh. "What do you think?"

He pressed the bell at the other apartments. No one was home at the others. He looked at Sara and shrugged. "Inconclusive, I guess."

"All right." Sara walked down the steps to the sidewalk. "We can take the Mètro back. We passed a station a block away."

"Roget balked on providing any kind of documentation, so let's assume the guy is a fraud and press on. If we're wrong, no harm done," Josh said.

"Why don't you contact the Louvre for another expert?" Sara rummaged through her purse to find the cardboard-backed envelope containing her grandmother's receipt. "I'll find a photographer's studio to see what they can do with the receipt." She waved the envelope. "They could scan it and then they're bound to have a photo restoration program that would bring out the lettering."

They returned to the hotel. Josh went on to his room. "I need to pick up a map before I head to the Louvre."

Sara stopped at the concierge's desk. "Bonjour."

The concierge looked up from the newspaper. "Bonjour, madam. Je peux vous aider?"

"Is there a photographer's studio nearby?" Sara asked.

The concierge frowned and thought a moment, her finger tapping her lips. "Oui, Madam." She spent a few moments with her Rolodex file, then with the telephone book, scribbled down an address, and walked with Sara to the door. "Tout droit," she said, waving down the street. "Le Studio. That way...a short promenade. À droite."

"Merci." Sara clutched her purse as she walked toward the studio. She veered away when someone came close but saw nothing suspicious. Still, it wouldn't do to have her purse stolen now.

Ardon and Roget, both unsavory characters, and Smythe's murder made her feel vulnerable and the idea that she might be kidnapped and held for ransom in exchange for the painting had begun to plague her thoughts and dreams, making her doubly cautious. She walked close to buildings and away from the curb. In the movies, a van would sweep in and carry the victim away. That could happen to her.

She entered the photographer's studio, a small shop with equipment strewn across the room and a small desk with a computer at one side. Sara stepped over the cables as the photographer, busy with lights and a reflective umbrella, turned around and saw her. "Bonjour, Madame. Un moment." He completed the adjustment and wiped his hands on his pants as he walked to the desk. "Oui, Madame?"

"Bonjour. Parlez-vous anglais?" Sara asked. This man seemed more mechanic than computer geek. Could he do what she wanted?

"Oui. Yes. What do you need?" He sounded impatient.

Sara took out the receipt and handed it to him. "Can you restore this receipt to make the writing legible?"

He peered at it and whistled. Then he sat down at the desk and studied it. He looked up at her. "I can do this. It is very old, this paper."

"Yes, and the writing is so faded we can't read it." Sara pretended not to see the questioning in his eyes. She didn't want to reveal any more than necessary, and this man certainly didn't need to know the story to do the job. They didn't want anyone else to worry about.

"Tsk, tsk," he said, holding the scrap of paper up to the light. "Ah, a mystery then. Perhaps this is the deed to a millionaire's estate? Perhaps an old will? Perhaps you will be wealthy woman if I fix this for you."

Sara shook her head. "Nothing like that. It's an old receipt. Found it in my grandmother's things when she died. I'm curious, that's all. No deed. No will. No mystery."

"Hmmm. Maybe so." He pulled a scanner out from under the desk, raised the flap and placed the receipt on it. He half-turned to

Sara. "This paper is fragile. I hope the light won't damage it."

He pressed a few keys on the keyboard, then rotated the computer screen so Sara could see it. "I'm scanning it, then I'll save it, and then we'll see what I can do." He suddenly noticed she was still standing, reached behind him, and pulled another chair around. "Sit," he said. "This may take awhile."

Chin in hand, he studied the image on the computer, then closed out the file and opened another. "I have a program that might do this. Good thing for you," he waggled a finger at her, "that I am also skilled graphic artist. I do many things."

"Certainly seems so," said Sara, looking around at the equipment scattered on the floor, hung on the walls, and filling shelves. She'd found the right person for this job.

Gradually, as the photographer worked the screen, the writing on the receipt grew darker and more legible. When it became too dark, the photographer backed up to a lighter version. The words became clearer until Sara could read the full receipt.

"That's it!" she said. "Print out that version."

"Voila! Perfecto, n'est-ce pas?" The photographer kissed his fingertips. "Moi, I do good work for you."

Sara smiled at him. "You certainly do." She took the print-out and the original and paid the photographer what he asked. "I would like you to delete that file while I'm here," she said. "Please don't tell anyone about it." She watched as he took care of the deletion. She knew he could retrieve the file should he want to, but why would he? Then she paid him an extra $100 for his help.

"This is for the last gift I received from my grandmother. It has great sentimental value—no other value, though," she assured him. "I appreciate your taking the time to help me, and I also would appreciate your not talking about it to anyone. I have relatives. . ." She let the photographer fill in what those nonexistent relatives might do.

"But mais oui, Madame." He walked with her to the door. "I know nothing, so I can tell nothing, n'est-ce pas? No worries."

No worries indeed.

Sara felt him watching her all the way back to the hotel.

Chapter 29 - Provenance, 1760

The Hague.

Marie Louise of Hesse-Kassel, regent to William V, Prince of Orange-Nassau and Stadtholder of the United Provinces, glided down the carpeted hall of Huis den Bosch, the royal residence in The Hague. She wore shoes of soft leather without heels. She wanted her walk to be silent.

She had been forced to dress formally to save time for this excursion in the midst of a full schedule of court appointments. Her full, floor-length skirt of silk brocade was stretched over wide hoops and her stomacher was trimmed with a column of graduated bows. Her hair was pinned up and covered by a fashionable towering headdress of lace and ribbons. A shawl covered her shoulders. The ensemble was heavy and awkward, and the swishing sound of her clothes annoyed her, but it could not be helped.

She had dismissed her maids and advisors, so she would be free to search throughout the palace, unfettered and unquestioned, during this time between appointments. She swept her eyes across the paintings that graced the walls on each side. All fine renderings, done by Dutch masters. None of them would do.

She held an inventory list in her hand, referring to it as she checked off painting after painting. She paused in front of an exuberant Franz Hals and smiled as she heard running steps behind her, then a swoosh. A fair-haired boy slid on the waxed wooden strip left bare on each side of the carpet and stopped at her feet.

"Grandmama!" yelled the boy, grinning up at her.

Marie Louise laughed and helped the boy up. "What kind of mischief have you been up to now then, sir!" she said.

He assumed a solemn expression. "I have not been up to any mischief, madam," he bowed. "But this!" He pulled a frog out of his pocket and wagged it in her face. "Do you like it? Grandmama, do you like it?" He giggled.

Hands on her hips, she put on her severest face. "Do I like it? I think. . ." She laughed. "It is a fine frog, William. I like it very much." She turned him around and gave him a pat on the bottom. "Now take it back outdoors and put it in the pond. Be sure you don't hurt it."

"Yes, Grandmama." William ran down the hall and disappeared out the door.

Marie Louise turned back to her task. She had visited each unoccupied room in the palace and found nothing that would not soon be missed. She tapped her fingers on her lips and thought. As much as she hated the idea, she would have to visit the attic storerooms. Gloomy places that hid rats and other vermin. This task was best done alone and now, with the servants engaged elsewhere, was the time to do it.

She stepped through the dining hall to the servants' staircase behind the kitchens, waiting and listening for the sounds of anyone coming her way. She heard no one and so proceeded, step by creaky step, up to the attic. It was immense and dark, although light drifted in through vents, cracks and small windows. How was she to find anything in here? Crates and boxes confronted her. None of them labeled. What on earth did they contain?

Her eyes gradually adjusted to the dim lighting. Behind the crates and boxes were pieces of furniture, most of it broken, scuffed, or torn. Old toys littered the floor. The sheer volume was astounding. Marie Louise looked around her, appalled at the waste. All of this litter should be repaired and given to the poor. She jotted a note on the paper she carried. She would see what could be done, but one ran across such pompous jackanapes at court who balked at every change that she doubted she'd be successful.

She stepped past the miscellaneous piles of junk, shaking her head at every step. Here and there, she recognized a piece she had forgotten or an old toy of her son's. The memories filled her with sadness. Her son would have loved going through these forgotten treasures.

The silence was unnerving. Each step sounded like a Goliath's. She shivered and looked back over her shoulder again and again, even though she knew no one had followed her. No one lurked in the shadows.

She stepped forward through the piles and then saw the long rack of forgotten paintings on the left. At last!

She pulled out each painting in turn, referred to her list, considered the painting, and returned it to the rack. Eventually, she came to Rabbi Saul Levi Morteira as a Moor, by Rembrandt van Rijn. She ran her hand across the painting to wipe off the dust and studied it. Morteira was not a handsome man, and it was not an attractive painting even though Rembrandt had painted it. Moreover, the subject was a Jew. How many people would buy such a painting?

She referred again to the note on the inventory list. Bought at auction, Amsterdam, 1731. It was bought almost thirty years ago, and it remained in the attic. As far as she knew, it had never hung in any of the Dutch Republic's royal residences. No one would miss it. Probably no one at the palace even knew it existed.

She carried it to the stairs, listened for steps or voices, heard none, and brought it down to her room where she hid it under her bed.

The next day she called for the carriage and waited until it arrived at the door before she emerged with the painting hidden under layers of wrapping paper. She asked to be driven to the home of Mijnheer Helsingcraft, patron to the arts, gallery owner, and auctioneer.

The carriage ride was short. The coachman carried the painting and waited with her at the door to be admitted. A maid answered the door and immediately curtseyed. "He waits for you," she said.

Marie Louise took the painting, dismissed the coachman, and was immediately shown into the parlor where Helsingcraft waited with another man. They both stood to greet Marie Louise.

Marie Louise smiled a greeting at Helsingcraft as he bowed, observing that he seemed ill at ease, fluttering his hands and darting his eyes everywhere but at her. Then she turned to greet the other man.

Unlike Helsingcraft, who was of medium stature, dark-haired, and quite pleasing in appearance, the other man was stout and bald with pig-like eyes and a frown on his face. Helsingcraft's simple wool coat and vest marked him as modest and unassuming. The other man wore a full, unpowdered wig, a blue coat trimmed with silver braid and a vest lavishly embroidered with silver and gold thread. Marie Louise recognized him as the minister of the treasury. She recalled the phrase she had used the day before: Pompous jackanapes.

She threw her shoulders back and lifted her chin. "Good morning, mijnheeren."

"Good morning, madam," said Helsingcraft. Marie Louise saw the warning in his eyes. "You know mijnheer Bocker, I believe."

She nodded at them both, wishing she could hide the painting behind her.

"Please, take a seat." Helsingcraft brought a chair forward and stood by as she sat. He took the chair across from her.

"I am surprised to see Mijnheer Bocker joining us for a private business matter," she said to Helsingcraft, anger sparking in her eyes.

"Am I not to visit my old friends?" Bocker asked, watching her as a snake eyes a mouse, a superior smile on his face. "Besides, I'm told you have business that concerns our country's assets. It is my duty to protect those assets."

Marie Louise felt her jaw drop open. How did he learn about the painting or her plans? She glanced at Helsingcraft. She had trusted him. He shrugged.

Bocker turned to Helsingcraft. "I beg of you to leave us alone for a few moments," he glanced at Marie Louise, "while we discuss important concerns of the state."

Helsingcraft sat up, startled. "You would like me to leave?"

"Only for a few moments, my friend." Bocker waved toward the door. "We will be brief, I assure you."

"As you wish." Helsingcraft bowed and stepped out of the room. Bocker walked to the door and closed it. He turned back to Marie Louise. "Now we are alone."

Marie Louise watched him with narrowed eyes. "I am here on business that does not concern you. I am astonished to find you here. What do you want?"

Bocker smiled and studied his fingernails before replying. "I know you bring to Mijnheer Helsingcraft one of our country's paintings, bought for the state, by the state. You wish to sell it to finance your old people's home. A most laudable idea."

"They need proper housing," said Marie Louise, lifting her jaw. This pretentious little windbag meant to thwart her plans. What did he want?

"Oh, I agree most assuredly," said Bocker, sitting back in his chair and watching her.

She waited.

"And so I permit you to sell the painting for your purpose and will say nothing of this act which could," he looked at her with menace in his eyes, "which could be construed as treason."

"Treason? Surely not, mijnheer." Marie Louise managed a laugh as fear curdled her stomach. Bocker was a little man with little dreams, but he had tremendous power.

"But of course, for this favor," Bocker tapped his fingers on the table beside him, "I will insist that you follow my orders in your position as regent to the stadtholder."

Marie Louise studied him. An evil man. She had never trusted him, and now he showed his true colors. He must not be put in a position to have power over her grandson. She would find other ways to finance the old people's home. She drew herself up and said in a haughty voice, "You are mistaken, mijnheer. I merely bring the painting to Mijnheer Helsingcraft for cleaning."

She tore the wrapper from the painting to uncover it. "It is a Rembrandt, you see. Its colors have become dark and dreary with age. I think it a pity to keep such a painting by one of our country's finest artists in storage, but I can not hang it in its present state. Do you not agree?" She did not wait for his reply. "I plan to display it in the great hall."

Marie Louise almost smiled as she saw Bocker think through his response in an effort to retrieve his advantage. "I have it on good authority that cleaning the painting is not your intention," he said finally.

"On whose authority?" she asked. Who had told him her plan? She had only raised it as a possibility to the regents of the old people's home. Would one of them have passed it on? She saw now that she had erred in trusting them.

He waved her question aside. "Come now. Our city needs another fine home for the elderly. That useless painting could bring a good price for such a beneficent purpose. I would be glad to support that enterprise." He paused and his tone again became menacing. "As a woman and a temporary, I say temporary, regent for the rightful king until he comes of age, you have no business interfering in affairs of state. I have the knowledge and experience to take the many onerous administrative tasks of your position, tasks that require skills you have yet to acquire, and place them in more capable hands."

Marie Louise took a deep breath and stood tall, chin up. "I think not. My grandson is not a chicken to be plucked. I will not place him under your control no matter how much knowledge and experience you have."

She rang the bell to summon a servant who arrived quickly, almost as if he had been listening at the door. "Your master may return now," said Marie Louise. "Mr. Bocker and I have nothing more to discuss."

A moment later, Helsingcraft walked back into the room. "Is all well?" he asked, looking at Marie Louise with a different question in his eyes.

"Of course," Marie Louise regained her seat. She picked up the painting and handed it to Helsingcraft. "I am sorry Mijnheer Bocker misunderstood my purpose in bringing this painting to you. I brought it merely to be cleaned," she cast a disdainful look at Bocker, "and not for any other purpose. Please deliver it to the palace when done. I know exactly where I am going to hang it." She arched an eyebrow as she smiled at Bocker. "It is a Rembrandt, you know."

As she walked toward the door, Bocker followed her. "Do not think you escape so easily."

"A proposition such as the one you made to me is tantamount to treason," she replied. "However, I will overlook it this time because of your excellent reputation as treasurer." She stopped to turn and look at him full in the face. "Any repeat of such threats to my authority will have instant reprisals. I hope that you understand me?"

Bocker frowned. His eyes threw darts, but after a moment, he bowed. "Perfectly."

Chapter 30 - Paris, 1999

Josh stopped by his room first to pick up a Paris map, then ran down the stairs to the hotel lobby, but as he passed through the lobby on his way out, a familiar voice called to him. He kept walking as if he hadn't heard it, but Ardon intercepted him at the hotel entrance.

"A moment, monsieur," Ardon said, reaching out to poke Josh in the chest, cigar in hand.

Josh brushed the arm aside and frowned at Ardon. "I'm in a hurry," Josh said. "What do you want."

"Come, come. You and I and Miss Sara too, of course, we have to work together, especially now that I have found the owner of that Rembrandt for you," said Ardon with his cigar dancing in the air. "I made a more thorough search and found the painting and correct owner listed in my files. You are obligated to return it to him."

Josh folded his arms. "I see," he said. "Your files suddenly provide such information. I am astonished. Exactly what proof do you have that this person is the correct owner?" His skepticism dripped from every word.

Ardon squinted at Josh with dislike. "You doubt me? I am offended. Let me remind you that I am a valued consultant for the Louvre and many other fine art museums. You and your friend came to me seeking my expertise and," Ardon put the unlit but chewed cigar in his mouth, "I gave it to you freely. You, sir, are in my debt."

"I am sure, and we appreciate your help. You must understand that we need proof of ownership. Perhaps you can substantiate this claim for us." Josh raised an eyebrow. "We need more than your word on such a valuable item."

Ardon removed the cigar. "My word is good, monsieur." He paused and his tone became threatening. "I am in touch with the true owner, and we will call in the police if you do not hand over the painting." His eyes narrowed, and he poked Josh in the chest with his finger. "You would not like to deal with the Paris police, my friend."

Josh pushed aside Ardon's hand. "Fine. You call the police. I'm sure they would insist on the same evidence of ownership that we do." He stepped forward, forcing Ardon back against the wall. "Now I have to go." Josh turned around and walked briskly out the door. *The nerve of the man. Bluff. That's all it was. Bluff.* Wait till he told Sara about this little interchange. Ardon's only accomplishment was to confirm their suspicion that Jean Roget was a phony, Ardon's plant.

Josh put Ardon's threats out of his mind, checked the Mètro stop for the Louvre, and headed out to find this famous museum. He was thrilled to be in Paris. After the Louvre, maybe he'd take a side trip to the Eiffel Tower. Had his parents ever been to France? He couldn't remember any time they had traveled to Europe or even to the United States, even though they lived in a U.S. territory. Art dealers who never went to Paris? Or New York? That seemed odd to Josh, now that he thought about it.

Guided tourist groups crowded the entrance to the Louvre. As Josh pushed his way through them, he heard smatterings of French, English, German, Spanish, and other languages he couldn't identify. Inside the museum, he was directed to a separate elevator for the administration offices on the top floor. He was glad to escape the crowds at the ticket counters.

He stepped out of the elevator into a lobby with a semi-circular desk against the far wall. A young, black receptionist looked up inquiringly from behind a computer monitor as he approached. Her name plate said "Hélène LaPierre." She took one look at him and didn't bother with French but after the requisite "Bonjour," spoke instead in heavily accented English. "How may I assist you?"

Were all Americans so easy to pigeonhole? He stepped over to the desk and looked down at Madame LaPierre. "I must speak to an expert on Rembrandt or on Dutch Renaissance painters."

"I see." She thought a moment, casually sorting through a Rolodex card file. "There are several who consult with us. All are quite busy right now, and they are not on staff, but we have experts here. Perhaps someone. . .?"

"I must see someone extremely knowledgeable about the work of Rembrandt. Do these experts live in Paris? Can you tell me how to contact them? A phone number?"

"Perhaps one of our adjunct consultants? There is one who lives here in Paris who might be available." She thumbed through the Rolodex. "Dr. Jean-Louis Ardon. I'll write down his contact information."

Josh shook his head. "No, no. He can't help us. Who else might be available?"

"Monsieur Ardon can't help you? La, but he is a fine man, is he not?" She smirked at Josh with a raised eyebrow before returning to the Rolodex. "However, we will see." She thumbed through the cards. "Most of these are out of town. But maybe. . ." She removed a card. This one, he lives in Amsterdam, but he maintains a gallery here in Paree. He may be there now. His name is Gregor Wilhelm." She scribbled down the address and phone number and handed Josh the slip of paper. "Perhaps he is here in Paris, and perhaps he can help you. He is very expert. But also, you understand, very expensive." She rubbed her fingers together.

"Merci beaucoup," Josh said. "May I give you my name and address? In case Monsieur Wilhelm is traveling and contacts you? I need to see him urgently. It's a very important matter. Also, I'd like to have your phone number. I mean the office phone number. Here. Just in case, I mean. I may have other questions."

He stopped and took a deep breath. He wasn't asking for a date, for Pete's sake. She gave him a card and wrote her name on the back of it.

"Just in case." She winked at him.

Josh returned to the hotel and knocked on the door of Sara's room. He listened for sounds from Dave's room but didn't hear any. He was still touring, no doubt. Josh smiled, glad that Dave was out of their hair for now.

Sara opened the door. "I got it!" she said, waving the receipt in one hand and a photocopy of the legible scan in the other.

Josh grinned, encircled her in a hug and kissed her. "Terrific! You were more successful than I was."

"This scan might be the answer," Sara said. "The photographer brought out the name of the person who gave the painting to the resistance."

"Awesome." Josh grabbed it. "You're right. I can make out the name. Double awesome. There's the address, too." He read it out loud. "Alain Bernheim, Rue de Bayard, Toulouse, France." He whistled. "We already knew the date, March 15, 1941."

"I wonder when the Nazis took him away," Sara said thoughtfully.

Josh waved the printout. "The first roundup in France of Jews to be sent to concentration camps was May 14, 1941. Another roundup took place on August 20, 1941, so he got rid of the painting in time."

"How can you remember all those dates?" said Sara in surprise.

"History major, remember?" He glanced at Sara. "Anyway, I looked it up a few days ago when I saw where our search was heading, This person must have been one of the victims. Was he married? Did he have kids?"

"Too bad we know nothing about him," Sara said. "We have to assume he was Jewish. The Nazis legitimized anti-Semitism, so he had probably lost his job. Then he was forced to abandon his home. Could he get out of France before the Nazis carted him away? He knew the Nazis would take everything."

"Toulouse is a university town." Josh rapped on the table. "He may have been a professor. The university might have records too.

This is our first big lead, Sara."

"Alain Bernheim. He may have known my grandmother," Sara said, a faraway look in her eyes. "Maybe he gave her the painting himself."

Josh waved the receipt. "We can go down to Toulouse and check out the street. One of the residents there might remember this person."

Sara stepped over to the telephone. "We can rent a car tomorrow and drive down there."

Josh dropped into an armchair. "Too far to drive there, do what we have to do, and get back in a day. A plane would be better."

"Okay. Plane. And we'll rent a car when we get there."

"Cool."

After Sara made the arrangements, Josh told her about Ardon's threats.

Sara frowned in distaste. "I can't believe he'd try something so. . .so sleazy," she said. "He must think he's dealing with idiots." She went over to Josh and kissed him. "You knew how to handle him and his threats."

"Yep. Don't mess with me." Josh pulled Sara into his lap and held her tight as he reported on his trip to the Louvre. "Sleazy as he is, Ardon actually is a consultant there."

Sara shook her head. "What a jerk."

"Yeah," said Josh, "but we're done with him. This Wilhelm might be more helpful. I'll call his gallery right now." He reached for the phone.

Wilhelm was attending a conference in Berlin, Germany, but was expected back in two days. "Would Monsieur like to make an appointment?"

Josh made the appointment as Sara watched with a smile.

"After our trip to Toulouse, we might not need him," she said.

"We can hope," Josh said and kissed her.

Chapter 31 - Provenance, 1795

The Hague.
Stadtholder William V of the Dutch Republic wrapped the brocade robe he wore over his vest, shirt, and breeches tightly around himself, seeking comfort even if for a moment. He paced back and forth in his private apartment in the palace, and then he called for his man-servant.

The servant rushed in carrying a cravat and the long curly brown wig William usually wore. While William fussed, the servant fitted the wig over William's head, removed the robe, tied the cravat, and helped him into a heavy wool greatcoat which boasted three short shoulder capes. Then he bowed and stood aside.

William waved him away but watched him leave the room with misgiving. If only this were a nightmare, and he could wake out of it. "What would my dear Grandmama think of such a disastrous turn of events?" he said to himself. "God have mercy on us all."

Whatever pride he had left, he placed in hoping that he had maintained a stoic royal presence despite the rampant fear and chaos around him.

There was no time to waste. Hampered by the wig and the coat, William clumsily stumbled out of his apartments. He turned back for one last look, then he marched down the hall to the great staircase. He paused before descending regally to the central reception area, holding his head high as if he still commanded the Dutch armies. In truth, he would have liked to curl up in his bed, his nightgown pulled tightly around him and his night cap tugged down over his head, shutting out the reality he faced.

History plays such cruel jokes, he thought, surveying the grandeur of the room. As Stadtholder of the Dutch Republic, he had sent aid to support the Americans in their revolution and to diminish the British. He had signed the papers himself. Then two years ago he had sent troops to support the monarchy in France. Such a waste and a mistake. So many of the royal families there were now gone. People he knew or had met. Once powerful. Murdered in the most gruesome ways. Heaven preserve those who survived.

He walked to a table along the wall and sat at the upholstered chair alongside, his elbow resting on the table. The French Republican Army was poised to attack his own country, and he and his family must flee. And irony of ironies, they must flee to England. Although. . .he tapped his chin, perhaps they could use history to their advantage. He remembered his ancestor, Willem III, also stadtholder of Holland. He had been crowned king of England as well, with his wife Mary. So many years ago, but it meant close ties with England, so perhaps all this was not so ironic then. From England, he could amass support and regroup his armies to reclaim his country.

He roused himself. He had no time for such musings. The servants had abandoned their usual duties to pack for the journey. They scampered around him as if he were of no consequence. He suspected they were right.

The ship waited in the harbor. The servants had boxed and crated the furnishings, clothing, and much of the furniture. They were now engaged in sending the crates on ahead to the ship. William himself had overseen the packing of the gold, silver, jewelry and precious objects into separate trunks. He personally knew the four armed guards designated to protect these valuable trunks. They were loyal and reliable Dutchmen.

The place looked ransacked. As it was. But William did not mean to rob the Dutch people. He meant only to protect their heritage. He left the barren grand reception room to take care of the last official duty left to him. The paintings. The sculptures. What should they take and what leave for the invading armies?

He had brought his dagger to slash the paintings they left behind but could not bear to destroy such beauty. He compromised, leaving paintings and sculpture by French artists in a heap on the floor. The French soldiers could not escape that message.

William proceeded through each room and down the main hallway, selecting paintings by Dutch artists to be wrapped, crated, and taken to the ship.

All except one. He paused in front of the dreary colors of Rabbi Saul Levi Morteira as a Moor, painted by Rembrandt van Rijn. It hung in the dark corner of a little-used reception room. Grandmama had disliked that painting. William wondered why, but it was not to his taste either even though he knew Rembrandt was Dutch and widely respected as an artist. William frowned as he studied the painting. The grim and unattractive visage of the subject did not please him either. The painting had no redeeming value except that Rembrandt had painted it.

He heard the clamor of running feet behind him. The servant who awaited William's decision stirred.

"The coachmen call for us," the servant said, wringing his hands. "Your sons are there waiting for you. We must go or we will not get to the port in time to escape capture."

William turned away from the painting, his decision made. "We have enough Rembrandts," he said, following the servant in the direction of the running feet. "Let the French have the rabbi."

He stopped at the pile of French paintings and then walked over them, stomping on each one with a grim sense of satisfaction.

Chapter 32 – Toulouse, 1999

At breakfast the next morning, Sara updated Dave on the receipt but gave him few details. It was wiser not to trust him, but with the painting's connection to their grandmother, Sara felt Dave should know something about what they'd uncovered. Then she added casually as if it weren't important, "We're flying down to Toulouse and renting a car today." Sara watched Dave over her tea cup.

Josh laid his menu aside. "This will give you a full day to tour Paris. So much to see and do here. You should have a good time."

Dave dropped his jaw in surprise. "But. . .but. . ." He cleared his throat, fluttered the menu in agitation, and tried again. "But I. . .I met a man who said he was the owner. Didn't you see him?"

Sara set down her cup and glanced at Josh. "We did meet someone who put forth such a claim."

"He sounded like the right one to me." Dave's eyes slid from Sara to Josh. "We can give the painting to him and ask him to at least repay our expenses. Then we. . .you'd be done and we could go home." He raised his hands, palms up. "Aren't you tired of all this traveling around?"

"Unlike you, I love traveling," said Sara. "I could do this forever." She saw Dave's face redden. He pushed his lips in and out in a pout. As she suspected, Dave was in on the plan to use a ringer to get the painting.

"And, Dave, we're looking for the legitimate owner," said Sara.

"That guy had no proof, and we didn't believe him."

"Obviously a fraud," added Josh, sending an amused wink to Sara.

"Obviously." She looked at Dave. "Don't try that again."

"What?" Dave raised his hands in front of him. "I never. . . ."

Sara shook her head as she perused the menu.

The server approached, pulling a pad out of his back pocket.

"Bonjour," Sara said. "S'il vous plait, un croissant."

Dave ignored the menu and the server. He spoke to Sara with flashing eyes. "Anyway, you might get in trouble with the law if you don't return it." Then he sat back, noticed the server and gave his order, followed by Josh.

"Au contraire," said Sara, looking at Dave, "The police would approve our careful approach. Anyway, we need strong documentation of ownership before we hand such a valuable object over. Giving the painting to the wrong person would push us out on a high, thin branch, making us liable for damages or for the value of it." Then she gave the knife an extra twist. "Finding the right owner could take years, couldn't it, Josh?"

Josh crossed his arms on the table. "Sure could," he said, smiling at Sara.

Dave spluttered, "You've got to be kidding." He took a sip of coffee and turned sad-dog eyes on Sara. "What was wrong with that guy? He looked okay to me."

"He sounded good, all right," said Josh, "but he told us nothing he couldn't have picked up from Ardon. . . ," Josh looked directly at Dave, "or you."

"Me! I would never. . . ." Dave choked on the coffee.

Sara raised an eyebrow. "I'm sure you would never try to cheat the real owner of the painting," she said to appease him, but she thought no such thing. "Certainly not, but we don't know that about Ardon."

"But Ardon's a consultant to art museums," Dave argued. "He must know what he's doing."

"But is he honest? A lot of people might want to get their hands on that Rembrandt, might even murder for it, as you know," Josh said deliberately, "so we have to be careful. We're on track now to find the true owner."

Dave was silent for a few moments, the frown growing on his face. "Maybe so," he said at last. "But you know whoever owned it has to be dead by now. Most people didn't survive the concentration camp. His family might have died too. You can fool around in Toulouse"—he pronounced it "Too-Lowse"—"if you want to, but I don't think you'll find anyone who even remembers that man. After sixty years, that painting should be ours."

He picked up his cup of coffee and waved it. "I don't know why you can't see that. All you're doing is wasting Grandma's money."

"I'm sorry you see it that way." She closed her mouth and raised her chin, hoping Josh would support her, but he only shrugged and studied his cup of coffee. He was leaving Dave to her.

Sara felt Dave staring at her. She could almost see his mind working. She ignored him.

Finally, he sighed. "I'm done with Paris. Doesn't anybody here ever pick up after their dog? I'm ready to go home."

Sara straightened the napkin in her lap. She didn't look up. "That would be the best idea, Dave," she said.

"But I might as well see how this all plays out." He took another sip of coffee. "I'll get my own ticket, and by the way, I'm bringing a guest." He waved at a woman in the lobby. "Here she comes now."

A twentyish woman in tight jeans and sweatshirt waved at Dave with a bright smile and loped their way.

"This is Genevieve," Dave said, taking her hand. "We met on the tour yesterday and really hit it off."

Sara opened her mouth in shocked surprise. Josh cocked an eyebrow at her. She knew they both thought the same thing. Was Genevieve a plant?

Sara quelled a rising anger, mustered a smile, and gestured to one of the chairs at the table. "Nice to meet you. Have a seat." She turned to Dave and managed a civil tone. "And how was the tour, she asked between clenched teeth."

Dave turned back from signaling the waiter for coffee. "What? Oh, the tour was fine. Even better after I met Genevieve." He smiled at her. "She filled me in on a lot of the historical details. Really made it more interesting."

Sara turned to Genevieve. "So you live here then? What do you do?"

Genevieve giggled. "Oui. I am a student at the university."

Dave looked up from the menu. "I told her about your little project."

Sara gaped at him in disbelief. "You told her what we're doing here?"

"Mais oui. So interesting, I think. You will tell me more?" Genevieve's guileless eyes shifted from Sara to Josh. She gave him a fetching smile. "It may be I can help, n'est-ce pas?"

Sara stared down at her plate as she absorbed this bit of news. Whoever this Genevieve was, Sara was going to assume she was a stooge of Ardon's and not to be trusted. "It's really not at all interesting," Sara said.

"Yep," added Josh. "Boring work on the computer."

"So now we're all going down to Toulouse," said Dave. "Care to join us? The trip's on me."

"Mais oui. How fun," said Genevieve, all bubbling enthusiasm.

"Excuse us," said Sara, rising. "Josh and I have to take care of a few things first." She headed for the elevator with Josh right behind her. As they rode up to their floor, Sara said through gritted teeth, "Let's get out of here fast."

"Good," said Josh. "I'll just pick up a few things and we can sneak out to a cab."

But they found Dave and Genevieve waiting for them in front of the hotel, holding a cab for them.

"You need to stay here," said Sara.

"Don't worry," said Dave. "We won't say a word. We just want to see Toulouse, that's all. We won't be any trouble at all."

"You'd better," said Sara, as she resignedly slid into the cab.

Later that day, they arrived in Toulouse and Josh drove the rented yellow Citroën into the ancient university city. Sara held a road map in one hand and a guidebook in the other, referring back and forth to each. "The Garonne River runs through Toulouse," she read from the guidebook. "The original part of the university is downtown right off the river bank. The university was established in 1229."

"So what?" mumbled Dave, his arm around Genevieve in the back seat.

"What do we see here?" asked Genevieve.

Sara ignored her. Using the roadmap, she directed Josh through the maze of unfamiliar streets to reach Rue de Bayard not too far from the university and a large synagogue. Josh drove slowly down the street as they read off house numbers and then stopped at the house number on the receipt.

Sara's spirits, buoyed by the feeling that at last they were working from concrete information for their search, plummeted when she saw the modern row houses ahead of her. None of them was more than thirty years old. The house they sought was as new as the rest of them. Kids' toys littered the porches and tiny yards. Young families.

She stared at the row house in dismay. Out of the corner of her eye she saw Dave's grin. Josh had stopped the car in the middle of the street and didn't say anything, didn't even turn off the engine.

"I'll go knock on the door," Sara said at last.

"Go ahead," said Josh. "I'll park."

"Take your time," said Dave with a snicker while Genevieve surveyed the neighborhood appraisingly.

"I've had about enough of you and your attitude," said Josh. "Knock it off or get out and go home."

Sara didn't wait to hear what Dave said to that, but she was grateful that Josh told Dave off. They were both fed up with Dave. She walked up the steps to the door and knocked. She heard a baby crying inside. She knocked again. The door opened and a harried young woman, patting a baby whose chin hung on her shoulder, frowned at her. "Je ne need anything. No solicitors, s'il vous plaît."

"Bonjour. Parlez-vous anglais?" Sara asked. "Je ne selling anything. I'm looking for someone who used to live here."

"Oui?" The tired face turned interested. "Thank God. You're American. I'm so tired of trying to speak French." She looked beyond Sara, and her expression changed. "I only have a minute, and I probably can't help you. What's the name?"

Sara realized at once that the woman had seen Josh and Dave in the waiting car. Too bad they hadn't parked around the corner out of sight. Sara would bet this lonely mother might have invited her in for a cup of coffee and a little gossip and maybe more information.

"Hard to be so far away from home and with a baby, too," Sara said with an engaging smile. "I'm pretty homesick myself."

The woman looked back at Sara. "Tell me about it."

"I'm trying to find a man named Alain Bernheim who used to live here many years ago—before World War II," began Sara.

"But these houses are twenty-five, thirty years old. We've only lived here two years." The woman prepared to close the door.

"Is anyone in the neighborhood old enough to remember the way this street used to be?"

"I'm sorry," the woman said, still patting the baby's back. "I hope this person was no one close to your family? The street was bombed in the war, you know. People killed or taken away. The Jews, I mean. No one left." She bestowed a compassionate look on Sara. "I'm sorry."

Sara turned away. "Thank you for telling me."

She returned to the car. "Dead end here." She felt too disappointed to say any more.

Genevieve looked at her. "But Dave tells me this Monsieur Ardon has discovered the owner of the painting. Coming here is such foolishness, I think." She crossed her arms and stared at the shops passing by.

Nobody bothered to reply.

They drove to the university and found the library. "The university must have records of the faculty, past and present," said Josh. "We'll try the library first."

Josh and Sara walked in and found the reference desk.

"Let me have the keys, said Dave, "so we can wait in the car if we want."

Josh looked at Sara.

"Come on," said Dave. "We're not going anywhere."

"All right," Sara said doubtfully. "But stay right there."

Dave waved them on.

The reference librarian, a tall, thin man with graying sideburns, rested his head on one hand while the other maneuvered a mouse as he stared at a computer screen, boredom written across his face. Sara waited for him to look up from the screen. Eventually, he noticed her and cocked an eyebrow. "Bonjour." he said. "Je peux vous aider?"

"Bonjour. Parlez-vous anglais?" Sara asked.

"Ah, vous etes Americains, n'est-ce pas?" he asked, then stopped and shook his head. "Excusez-moi, mademoiselle." He cast a curious glance from Sara to Josh. "How may I help you?"

Sara explained their search, leaving out any mention of the Rembrandt. The story sounded thin and hopeless even to her, but she was beginning to feel more confident. They now had a name.

"He may have been a faculty member at this university, but he was lost in World War II," she said. "We must find him for important reasons. He lived in Toulouse and was probably an educated man." *Surely if he owned a Rembrandt, he had to be educated.* "We want to know if he survived the war, and if he had descendants."

"Ah, Alain Bernheim. Oui. Un instant." He maneuvered the mouse and tapped on the keys as he stared intently at the computer.

Sara waited for another disappointment, the faint confidence she had felt a moment ago dissipated, leaving her feeling depressed and enervated. Where could they go after this? There were no more clues to follow. Perhaps they could donate the painting to a Jewish art museum or university. Probably not this one with its early history of anti-Semitism. She reached for Josh's hand and squeezed it. He squeezed back.

Behind the librarian, students sat at tables surrounded by stacks of books. All hard at work. No one had come in after her and Josh, and no one seemed at all interested in them, which was a relief. If anyone had been following them, they would be obvious here.

From time to time, the librarian stood back to observe them when he wasn't shaking his head and frowning. "The problem, you see," he said, "is that records of our Jewish faculty were expunged

during the Occupation." He shrugged. "Et voila, we work to restore
the damage, n'est-ce pas? But sometimes. . . ." He peered closer at
the screen. "Voila. Alain Bernheim. Oui." He turned the screen
around so they could read it.

Sara could not believe her good luck. There was the name, the
same name that was on the receipt. She nudged Josh. Did he feel as
excited as she? Perhaps they had reached the end of their search.
She read further.

"I see a birth date and the dates for his tenure here," she said,
looking up at the librarian. "But no date for his death. It simply
notes that he died. Are they sure of that? Without a date, it sounds
tentative."

"Oui. Quel tragic. But he was a Jew, you understand? He was
arrested by the Nazis and taken. . . ." He ran a finger across his
throat. Sara got the message. Then he snapped his fingers. "His
daughter, she survived. Of course. Now I remember her. She
married well and dedicated a memorial scholarship in her father's
name. Let me see now. . ."

He took the screen back and worked the keyboard. "Voila! The
Alain Bernheim Scholarship. Ah yes, here's the announcement.
'Established in the name of Alain Bernheim, victim of the Nazi
Holocaust, by his loving daughter, Celeste Vilar."

Sara gripped Josh's arm. They were almost there now. They may
have actually found the owner of the Rembrandt. "How can we
contact his daughter?" asked Sara.

"The people who issue the scholarship," said Josh, "they must
know how to reach her."

The librarian nodded. "I would think so. I will print out the information I have on Bernheim and the submission information for
the scholarship." He pressed a button and a moment later, reached
over to retrieve the pages from the printer. "Voila! And good luck."

"Thank you, thank you," said Sara.

"Merci beaucoup," added Josh, grinning at Sara.

Sara felt like skipping in glee out of the library. They had found
the owner of the Rembrandt and had only to make a few phone
calls to find out how to deliver the painting. This job was almost

over. Then the dismaying question emerged again. What would she do when the job was done?

Sara mulled over this problem as they walked out the door toward the car. What did she want to do? What kind of job would she want after this? And Josh, what about Josh? She was so engrossed in her thoughts that Josh's sudden stop startled her.

"Uh oh, Sara," said Josh.

Sara looked up at him. He pointed to the car. Or where the car should have been. She gaped at the empty space ahead of her.

The yellow Citroën was missing. And so was Dave. On the sidewalk were their backpacks.

Chapter 33 - Provenance, 1810

Pavilion Welgelegen in Haarlem.

Lodewijk Bonaparte, King of Holland, formerly Louis Bonaparte, sat alone at a table in the throne room, chin in hand, pondering the map of Europe laid out before him. Depression shrouded his soul as his eyes moved from country to country across the map. He ran a finger around the starched linen cravat to loosen it from the red double-breasted cut-across coat he wore. He usually displayed quite a dashing figure with the square coat tails that sloped down in back and his snug white breeches tucked into black Hessian boots. But today he was not interested in such frivolous things.

He rapped the table once and stood, stretching and shaking his legs. Napoleon, his older brother, had conquered most of Europe, and he was now wealthy and alternately loved and feared. It was upon Napoleon's request that he, Louis, no, not Louis but Lodewijk, had accepted proudly the responsibility of ruling this industrious nation. Holland. A land he had come to love. He had ruled well here, he thought. His eyes dropped to the latest redrawn map of Europe.

"Napoleon." Louis put all his rage into that name. "The most powerful man in Europe and a monster." Louis fumed at the latest news from France. His own brother planned to invade Holland and force him to abdicate after only four years as king. Had he not performed correctly as a king should? The people of Holland loved him, their King Lodewijk. How dare Napoleon force his own brother off the throne. The rage he felt tasted bitter in his mouth.

Louis stared at the abdication papers in front of him. He had been forced to sign them, and he had named his eldest surviving son to succeed him, for what good that may do any of them.

He had done his best to excel as the king of the Dutch, even changing his birth name of Louis to the Dutch Lodewijk, and he had toiled long hours to learn the Dutch language. All he had done as king had been correct and to the benefit of the Dutch people. He had even personally and to good effect overseen relief efforts for the two major tragedies of his reign. He bent his head in remembrance of all those who had died when a cargo ship loaded with gunpowder exploded in Leiden. And then, a year ago, a disastrous flood had caused major damage in the country. *Now these people, my people, call me Lodewijk the Good. Is this not excellent for a king?*

Of course it was, but one cannot be loyal to two masters. This he had learned to brutal effect. Being a kind and effective king for the Dutch people did not protect him from the overbearing demands of his brother, Napoleon, Emperor of France. Louis had seen first hand the hardship caused to the Dutch people when Napoleon forced him as king to fleece the Dutch businessmen who had invested in France. The loans that these businessmen had made to France in good faith were arbitrarily reduced by two-thirds, not by repayment but by fiat! *And I, Louis, he banged his fist on the table, had been forced to agree to that bit of thievery to please my brother.*

To regain the esteem of the Dutch, he had protected their interests by refusing Napoleon's demand that Dutch troops be sent to join the French in Napoleon's invasion of Russia. *Quelle idée!* Louis had been correct in refusing the troops. If Napoleon had not been so swollen with his own success, he would have seen the insanity of using Dutch troops in a French cause and the folly of invading Russia.

What happened next was even more insane. Napoleon accused him of putting Dutch interests above those of France. *But of course! Am I not king of the Dutch?* He was glad to see French forces leave Holland for Russia, even though Napoleon ignored Louis' objections and took with him such a huge number of Dutch troops that Holland was left with only nine thousand soldiers to protect its borders. No one thought to look across the North Sea where England was amassing its armies for an invasion.

The English took advantage where they found it, and Holland's vulnerability made it an attractive target. Louis had felt powerless to prevent the coming catastrophe.

The English attacked his country with an army of forty thousand troops. How could nine thousand men succeed against forty thousand! Fortunately, Napoleon saw his mistake and was even now sending eighty thousand militiamen to repel the English and rearm the country. Holland would be protected, but it then became clear that there was another objective, ordered by his own brother, the great Napoleon. Louis lifted a nostril in a sneer. He, Louis, Lodewijk, King of Holland, was to be deposed.

Louis looked up as a messenger approached and bowed.

"The mail pouch from France, your majesty." The messenger laid the pouch on the table.

"Where is my secretary?" Louis asked.

The messenger cleared his throat and dipped his knee. "He has fled. Napoleon's army has assembled at the border."

"I see." Louis drummed his fingers on the table. "All right. You may go then."

Louis opened the pouch and withdrew a letter from the spy he had sent with Hortense, his abominable wife. According to the letter, she had left the Palace Het Loo in Apeldoorn to take the waters in Plombières. Next he supposed she would return to her mother's estate in France. As much as they both wished for a divorce, such was not to be granted, and yet they were so poorly matched. He hoped never to see her again, but he loved his sons. He would fight to keep them.

Perhaps he would have done better if he had found a congenial place to live. The Hague, Rotterdam, other towns. He had lived in them all. He even rebuilt Amsterdam's town hall as a palace, but it did not suit him.

He walked over to the golden throne, mounted the steps and

surveyed the huge room, imagining it filled with his subjects. Then he sat on the throne, leaning on one elbow, until the late afternoon sun flowed through the western windows and left sunlit patterns on the floor.

"This will not do," he said at last. He stood and stretched. A maidservant passing by the open door paused and curtseyed. "May I bring you tea and biscuits, your majesty?"

He swept past her. "In the library, please."

She curtseyed again and left. He walked to the library, planning his escape. He could not return to France, but he would see that Hortense and the boys were provided for. He did not expect his son to remain on the throne for long. He pulled his favorite chair, stuffed and covered so it was quite comfortable, toward the hearth. A fire had been laid but not lit since the day was so warm. Still, he liked sitting there. The maid appeared, bringing in the tea and pastries. "Where are the stewards?" he asked.

She curtseyed. "I will ask them to come to you."

He reached for the tea. "Good."

As he munched on a crumb cake, three men entered the library, hats in hand, and bowed.

"We must leave here," Louis said. "I wish you to pack for me." He stood and walked past them out into the hall. "Follow me. I will point out the items to pack and where they are to go." He ambled down the hall, looking at the paintings that hung inches apart on both sides, grateful that he had known these stewards for several years; they were French. He trusted them.

He stopped walking and turned around to gaze at them with a benign smile. "We have been guests of the Dutch for four years. They have been most gracious in their acceptance of us, have they not?"

The men bowed.

"We have returned their hospitality as well and are pleased to call them our friends." Louis gazed at one of the stewards in particular, knowing that this steward had married a Dutch woman and would remain in Holland when the others left.

"Our leader, the Emperor Napoleon, now calls on us to return to France." Louis paused, feeling the sacrifice of his pride, before continuing. "I do not wish to be called a thief or worse when I leave, so we will not ransack the palace."

One man stepped forward. "So the rumors are true? That you no longer wear the crown?"

Louis frowned. "My brother has asked me to abdicate." He shrugged. "Since he has mounted armies to attack if I do not, I am forced to comply with his wishes. You may return to France or stay here, but I must find residence elsewhere."

He smiled at the shocked looks on the faces of the three men. "My wife Hortense resides in Malmaison, outside Paris, with her mother, the former Empress Josephine. I ask that one of you accompany my possessions to Malmaison for my wife's use."

Two stewards looked at each other before coming forward. "We will return to France, and take your trunks in exchange for the passage."

"That will be arranged." Louis continued down the hall, the other men walking alongside now. The shock had changed to pity.

Louis barely glanced at the paintings of Pieter de Hooch, Jan Steen, and the other Dutch masters that graced the palace walls. He walked into a gloomy reception room and pointed to a dark, dreary painting hidden behind the door. "That is the painting I covet. It is by Rembrandt—quite a well-known artist. . . ," he said in an aside to the men, "but I think the Dutch will not miss it, hidden as it is. It is not a favorite. My wife will find a Rembrandt easy to sell, I think. The money from the sale should support my family in France."

One of the stewards spoke up. "You do not return to France with us?"

Louis sighed, his hands clasped behind him. "I think not. My brother and I. . .do not agree. I wish to avoid further contact with him. Austria has offered me asylum. Perhaps I will move there. I am still undecided."

He smiled at the stewards. "You may remove the painting now and pack it with your own possessions. You must be on your way by morning."

Chapter 34 - Toulouse, 1999

Sara gaped at the vacant space where she had parked the car. She stamped her foot. "Damn it! We should have known he'd try something like this!" *How dare he.*

Josh frowned, shook his head, and waved at their backpacks on the sidewalk. "At least he unloaded these."

"Thoughtful of him," said Sara. "He wants the painting no matter what he has to do to get it. My key is still on the chain around my neck. Where is yours?"

"I hid it. Sandwiched between two bars of soap I squeezed together. In my suitcase. In my room in Paris." He stared down the street as if looking for the stolen car. "Suitcase would be the first place he'd look, but maybe he wouldn't notice the soap."

"I think Genevieve is Ardon's plant."

"So do I," said Josh. "In fact, she may have forced Dave to do this."

"Forced him? How?" Sara knew from experience that Dave wouldn't do what he didn't want to do. "She'd have to be very persuasive."

She sat down on the library steps. "What are we going to do? We can't let him get away with this." Her brother had taken the rental car. That changed everything. She felt as if she had never really known him before. Memories flashed through her mind of all those times growing up when he had bulldozed over her own wishes and their mother's. They had been too forgiving, and now here was the result.

No matter how strongly he felt he was right, that they should sell the painting and keep the money, he had totally disregarded her feelings and broken the law, for she had rented the car with her money in her name. That made him a car thief, and now he was heading back to the hotel to steal the painting as well. He had only to look back on his past history in their family to know he could do what he wanted with impunity.

"He's got a head start on us." Josh sat down next to Sara on the steps. "A fine kettle of fish this is."

Sitting on the sidewalk steps, elbows on her knees, chin in her hands, Sara stared out over the university campus. Leaving their backpacks on the sidewalk showed that Dave had no plans that included them. He was probably on the way to the airport, then they'd get the next flight back to Paris and try to find the key.

Sara turned to Josh with a smile. "Some good might come out of this, you know."

"How's that?" asked Josh, leaning back against the hard concrete of the step.

"He's my brother, and I've tried to be considerate of him. It's what I've always done. I know he struggles with his job and his finances, but that's no excuse for this." Sara drew circles with her finger on the step.

Josh laughed. "You've got that right. We should report a stolen car to the police."

"I don't think we have the time," said Sara. "We'd have to fill out forms. I'll bet he drove it to the airport and turned it in." She stood and brushed off the seat of her pants. "He can't get into the safe deposit box even with the key. He'd have to prove his identity and sign in at the bank, and he doesn't know which bank."

"We've given him enough time," Josh said, standing and stretching his arms. "Let's get to the airport."

They grabbed their backpacks and walked down the steps to the campus sidewalk leading toward a busy road.

"We need a cab," Sara said, shading her eyes with a hand and looking down the road. Josh started jogging. "Maybe we can get the same flight."

Sara jogged alongside. Dave probably had turned in the car at the Toulouse airport and was even now waiting to board. Anger pushed up her adrenaline. For a few minutes, she outpaced Josh, and they arrived at the main road together. She checked her watch. "He's had a thirty-minute head start to get back to the airport. We can probably make it to the same plane."

A cab got them to the airport in record time, and they raced to the ticket counter.

"As of now," Sara held up her watch, "all bets are off. Dave's on his own and we're out of here. I no longer feel any obligation toward him."

"Good." Josh grabbed her hand and squeezed it. "Good."

Sara heard the undercurrent of exasperation in his voice. He had probably felt frustrated at the allowances she was in the habit of making for her brother. "When he arrives in Paris, he has to get to the hotel, then he has to break into your room, search for your key, find it, and make his way to Gibraltar. And that will be tedious. He'll have to fly to London and then Gibraltar or fly to Madrid and drive to Gibraltar. Plenty of time for us to catch up even if we miss the next plane."

Josh began to grin. "If he tries to drive straight to Gibraltar, which I doubt he'd do since it's a long drive, the police might pick him up and he'll have to explain about the car. If that doesn't happen, the Spanish customs guards will drag out his wait to get into Gibraltar. They always do that."

Sara looked at Josh. "They do? Why?"

Josh shrugged. "Because the citizens of Gibraltar insist on remaining British. Spain has other ideas."

"Okay." Sara shook her head. "He'll probably get a plane, though, unless. . ." her face brightened, "he's running out of money and decides to drive the car on my credit card."

"After this episode," said Josh, "I wouldn't put anything past him."

Flights to Paris ran every hour. Sara scanned the passengers around her, but didn't see Dave. He was probably at the gate, or he took the previous flight. They bought tickets for the next flight and reached the plane as it was boarding. Sara scrutinized the passengers and spotted Dave and Genevieve about twenty seats behind her. Neither one looked up at them.

Sara buckled her seat belt. "He's back there," she said. "That simplifies things."

Sara settled back and folded her arms. "It sure does. We'll get back to the hotel the same time he does." She settled back comfortably. "We're close to the owner of the Rembrandt. We'll pack up and get out of that hotel. Dave is on his own now."

Josh looked at her. "You're sure?"

Sara frowned, her lips tightened. "He didn't play fair."

Josh leaned back and stretched out his legs. "Yeah."

Two hours later, they arrived in Paris. Sara and Josh pushed their way through the crowds ahead of Dave, hailed a cab, and promised the driver fifty Euros for a fast trip to their hotel. The driver earned the fifty Euros.

"We're way ahead of Dave," said Sara as they raced to their rooms.

As they exited the elevator on their floor, Sara reeled at the pronounced stench of a cigar permeating the hall. She hurried to her room to get away from it, opened the door cautiously, and looked in.

The reek was even stronger here, but nothing, not even the papers stacked on the table, seemed disturbed. She stepped into the room cautiously, then she heard a sound in the bathroom and her stomach turned over. The bathroom door was not quite closed. She stared at it, trying to remember how she'd left it. Was someone hiding in there? She hefted her purse and looked around for a better weapon as she backed toward the hall door.

Before she reached it, the bathroom door opened, and a burly man she had never seen before walked out, gun in one hand, cigar in the other. He was short, bowlegged, and bald and wore jeans and a navy blue sweater over a dress shirt.

"Bonjour, Mademoiselle Miller," he said, in amusement.

Sara shrieked in shock, then turned it into a loud scream to alert Josh. The man darted forward and slapped her. Hard. "Shut up!" He held the gun to her head and was no longer amused.

Sara backed away from him as he lowered the gun. She rubbed her face where he'd slapped her. That hurt. She was tired, fed up with Dave, and now this. She felt too irritated to be afraid. "Who are you? How did you get in my room? What do you want?"

"Must we? You waste time. Where is it?" He aimed the gun at her again, this time as if he meant it. The words were English with a heavy French accent.

"What do you want?" she asked, taking a deep breath and slowing her speech to buy time and control her fear. "I don't have any idea what you're talking about."

"I find myself interested in art." The man smirked and stuck the cigar in his mouth.

"I'm sure we're all interested in art." Spin it out, get him talking. She hoped Josh heard her scream. Were these walls soundproofed? The man sat down on her bed. "You know what I talk about. You speak to me now please where it is."

"You shoot me, you'll never find out anything," Sara said with as much bravado as she could muster. "That is even if I knew what you are talking about."

"I do not have to shoot to kill you, but I hurt you very, very bad." The man leaned against the bed pillows. "Where is it?"

She concentrated on remembering details—his ears, nose, chin. It kept her focused. She didn't want to tip him off to Josh or Dave's presence on this hall, but surely he knew about them already. "Who are you?"

The man waved the gun. "You may call me Pierre. Not my real name. Give me the painting, and never you see me again."

She folded her arms and looked at him squarely. "I told you. I don't know about any painting," she said. How could she alert Josh? She didn't want him running in here to be caught. What kind of noise could she make? At that moment, she heard the door knob rattle as a key was inserted in the lock and slowly turned.

She looked at the door. Was that Josh? She kept her face deadpan. She had never had much luck with ESP, but with her mind and all her energy, she willed Josh to stay away.

But despite her silent urging, the door opened. Sara held her breath, then released it as Dave barged in.

"You!" he sputtered as he saw her. "What are you doing here?" He saw the man, stopped and pointed at him. "What's he doing here?" Then he noticed the gun. "What. . .?" He put his hands up. "What's going on?"

"What are you doing here?" Sara shouted. Surely Josh would hear that. Dave hadn't closed the hall door.

Genevieve had followed Dave but was hidden behind him as she entered.

"Shut up!" The man waved his gun from Sara to Dave. "So this is your boyfriend."

Her boyfriend. Sara realized that Pierre knew she traveled with a man but didn't know who that was. He must not know a second man, her brother, had joined them. If only Genevieve would keep her mouth shut.

Sara found it hard to believe so many people were after a painting lost for sixty years. Maybe the Gibraltar contingent were one set of thieves, possibly connected to whoever stole the decoy from Samuel. Ardon and Roget were a different contingent. Was Pierre working with them or was he on his own, a third contingent? How did Pierre find out about the Rembrandt if he wasn't connected to Ardon?

Dave started to correct the gunman, but Sara stumbled against him and pinched him hard. Genevieve took advantage of the distraction to retreat out the door and disappear. Would she bring help?

Pierre sat on the bed, still holding the gun on them. "Where is the painting?" he repeated.

"We don't have it here," blurted Dave.

"I don't know about any painting." Sara spoke as loudly as she dared. "You keep asking me about it, and I've told you again and again that we don't have any paintings."

The man glared at them. "Nice try. I ask you again before things get ugly. Where is it?"

Before things got ugly? He wouldn't shoot them in the hotel, would he? People would hear and why would he until he got what he wanted? Was he planning to torture them? Then people would hear her screams. Her stomach pumped acid, and her legs felt as if they would collapse. *I have to keep him talking.*

"Why would you want it?" asked Dave. "It's probably only a copy."

"Copy? I think not. I myself have seen it. It was praised by experts. That painting should have been mine," the man snarled. "I'm the descendant it should go to. By rights."

Not a hired thug then, thought Sara. Who was he? "So you were related to the owner?"

The man's face reddened. "Phah. He was nothing but a Jew. All he had was too much education and too much money. My grandfather work for trash like that to put meat on table."

He shook his fist in the air. "But he saw painting on wall in Jew's house. He know what it worth. A painting like that hang on wall in Jew's house. Better we have it to keep our family warm and fed."

"You would have sold it, you mean," Sara said to keep him talking. She didn't dare look at Dave. He now seemed frozen and speechless. Terrified probably. Sara's fear had morphed into curiosity about this man who called himself Pierre and about his motives—and his connections.

Pierre waved the gun from Sara to Dave and back again. "It do no good hanging on wall. Dark, ugly thing."

Sara seized on this. "Dark, dirty? Probably take thousands of dollars to fix up such a thing to sell." She examined her fingernails. "That is, if there were such a painting."

The man snorted. "You think I'm stupid? My father saw university people come in, they admire, congratulate that Jew. They call it genuine Rembrandt. They would know." He spit on the floor and rubbed it into the carpet with his shoe. "A Jew had no business owning anything. We soon took care of him. That painting is mine."

The man's talk chilled her. He meant the Nazis had taken care of Bernheim. Concentration camp. Now that she had him talking, Sara took the risk of sitting in the desk chair. Dave didn't move. Sara sent silent reassurance his way. He seemed petrified.

"Why should it be yours?" she asked Pierre, gently to avoid more anger, as if she simply wanted to understand.

Pierre was willing to explain. "We know storm troopers pick Bernheim up in couple of days. My father, he wait, until that Jew and his family gone. But one day, my father, he go through the house and the painting, she is not there. She is gone along with the silver and everything, everything that should have been ours, everything gone." He sat upright on the bed and pounded his fist on the covers. "Nothing left, you see? We got nothing. Nothing! And it should all have been ours." He brooded, frowning down at the gun now resting in his lap. "My father tell me the story, and we search for painting ever since. The silver they would have melted down, but the painting not so easy to disguise or sell."

The gunman was immersed in his grievance. He wasn't looking at her. Could she make a run for it now? She sat poised, ready to move, but Dave still stared blankly ahead in shock, and he blocked the door.

The phone rang. Sara jumped. Dave shook himself. The man narrowed his eyes, looking from the phone to Sara and back again.

"I should answer it," Sara said. "If I don't, the clerk downstairs may come up here to check on me. She knows I'm here."

"All right." He waved the gun toward the phone. "No funny business."

Sara walked to the phone. *It could only be Josh. Surely it would be Josh.*

"Hello?" she said, her voice quavering.

"Have you got someone in your room?" It was Josh. *What had taken him so long?* Sara felt her legs go weak at the relief.

"Yes, Josh is here," she said. *Would he get that?*

The man pointed his gun at her and mouthed, "Hang up now."

There was a pause before Josh replied. "Okay. Go downstairs. You and Dave first with him last," Josh said. "He'll want to play it that way, so act as if it doesn't matter."

"Thank you," Sara said and hung up. She turned to the man. "Just the front desk." *She had to get him out of this room.*

The man rose. "I tire of nonsense. Where is painting?"

"You'll need the keys—one's in the hotel safe, and then we'll have to leave here and go to the airport."

Dave seemed to wake up. "Sara, are you crazy? That painting's worth millions," he blurted.

The man waved the gun at Dave's nose "You shut up."

"I've got the other key here." Sara walked to her suitcase, found the key ring with her apartment and car keys from home, brought it out, and dangled it. The ring also held an ornate luggage key. That should work. She removed it from the key ring and paused. "Before we go, how did you find us?" she asked, as she put the other keys between her fingers pointing out like miniature knife blades. A simple weapon if whatever Josh had in mind didn't work.

The man laughed. "It was, how you say, duck soup. You go to Ardon and then your friend here go to Louvre. I figure painting show up, and they are experts. A logical choice. I contact them many years ago. I tell them about painting, how I own it and offered a huge reward if it was found." He laughed. "A reward you no pay can be very handsome, yes, very handsome." He spotted the luggage key in her hand. "Give me that." He tore it out of her hand, but he kept the gun on her so she didn't dare use the makeshift weapon in her other hand. She winced and made a show of pain, so the key would appear more valuable but kept her weapon hand hidden behind her.

Grudgingly as if she hated giving in, she said, "All right, then let's go."

She walked out of the room, bumping the door to make noise and clumping her shoes in the hall. Dave followed her with the man taking up the rear. Whatever Josh was planning had better work. She swallowed and kept her pace slow.

As they passed Josh's room, the door slammed open, and a sheet was thrown over the man's head. In the confusion, Sara pushed him into Josh's room and Josh slid his foot behind the man to trip him. He fell to the floor. Dave sprang into action and rolled the man to wind him into the sheet.

Josh grabbed his backpack and pulled the door shut. Sara ran into her own room, tossed everything into the suitcase, threw her backpack over her shoulder and ran out.

"Let's go," Josh said. Dave hesitated but then ran to his room and came out with his suitcase. They raced down the stairs, out of the hotel, and hailed a cab.

"Let's get away from here," said Sara in relief. "Too much riff-raff."

She tumbled into the cab after Josh. Dave took the front seat. "We need another hotel." Josh kept an eye out the back of the cab. "Don't see him. He's probably still untangling himself from the sheet."

"Great rescue, by the way." Sara settled back into the seat.

"Yeah, but now he's got the key." Dave whined from the front seat, folding his arms and pouting as he stared ahead. "We'll never get that Rembrandt now."

"So you'd rather have been tortured or killed?" Sara asked.

"You know what I mean." Dave frowned at her. "Our chance to get big money. We could sell that painting for millions."

"It's...not...ours," said Sara through gritted teeth once again.

Dave refused to look at Sara. "You gave him the key."

"What's this about a key?" asked Josh, looking at Sara.

"I gave that man an old luggage key." She waved a hand. "And he took it."

Dave gaped like a fish. "You've still got the right key?"

"Of course."

Dave stared at her through narrowed eyes. "Where?"

Sara folded her arms and shook her head. "After that stunt you pulled in Toulouse, do you think I'm going to tell you?"

"Aw, Sis, . . ."

She held up a hand. "Enough. Go home, Dave." Then she added savagely, "And take Genevieve with you."

Chapter 35 - Provenance, 1815

Chateau de Malmaison, Rueil-Malmaison.
Hortense Bonaparte laid aside the piece she was composing for piano to appreciate the warm breezes wafting through the windows. It was scented with the fragrance of two hundred and fifty roses.

"Such a lovely place," Hortense whispered to herself. How she missed her mother.

Her mother Rose, the Empress Josephine, had cultivated those roses for la belle France, just as she had developed nearly two hundred new plants in the chateau's greenhouse. She had been quite an experienced botanist, a legacy no doubt from her plantation upbringing in Martinique.

Hortense heard hoof beats pounding down the road, coming to a galloping halt with loud whinnies at the door. She sprang up from the piano. They must bring news of Napoleon!

The last report had come from Waterloo, where Napoleon was amassing his troops to face the British. She had prayed long and hard for his success and as "Empress Hortense" had rallied what support for her stepfather she could. Napoleon must succeed.

She waited, hands clasped, as the servant brought the messenger to her. When she saw his face, she almost fainted. Her body turned cold with fear. "Is he. . .?"

The messenger knelt at her feet, then rose, hat in hand. "All is lost, madam." He swallowed and continued. "The British troops far outnumbered Napoleon's, and he has left the field. He plans to come here before returning to Paris to abdicate in favor of his son. We wait now to find out what they will do with him. I came quickly to prepare you."

"Merci," said Hortense absently. Napoleon had lost, and she had spent all her credibility on his behalf. She was undone. His enemies—now her enemies—were in power. There would be no help from any quarter.

She left the messenger and walked out the French doors into the gardens, fresh and green in early summer. She thought of her mother's tender ministrations to her plants that brought such joy to all who lived and visited here. Hortense loved this place as much as her mother had. To see it no more would be insupportable.

An overwhelming sadness filled her spirit. She had not felt so depressed since her eldest son had died in Holland. All that seemed so long ago. Even Tsar Alexander, who rallied behind her when she sought refuge here, would not support her now. No one would. What was she to do?

What would happen to her dear stepfather Napoleon? He was coming to see her, the messenger said. He might arrive at any moment!

Hortense rushed back indoors to summon the cook and the housemaids. "The Emperor Napoleon and his men are on their way here! They are to be welcomed however they come. We will prepare a feast and make the rooms ready for him."

The cook curtseyed as did the maids. They scurried off, several for the bedrooms, several for the kitchen. Hortense watched them go. They do not know yet of his defeat, she thought, but then she realized that they were even now feeding the messenger in the kitchen. Of course he would tell them everything.

Nevertheless, she planned to treat Napoleon as the emperor he was. She would always respect and love him as her stepfather.

But even as she prepared to welcome Napoleon, she must herself make ready to flee. She sat down first to write a letter to her lover, Charles de Flahaut. He must know of this disastrous turn of events. She sealed the letter, rang for the maid, and asked her to post it immediately.

She must have money. She flew down the halls, seeking treasures that might be sold quickly. She knew one that she would be glad to be rid of. That awful Rembrandt painting, dreary as it was. Moreover, it was a gift from that wretched man—she could not make herself say his name—her husband. Her mouth curved in disgust. She'd sell that first, and it should bring a good price. She found the painting and removed it from the wall.

All the rest of the day, she added treasures to the pile.

Then she announced to her remaining son the decision to leave France. "But where do we go?" he asked.

"Switzerland," she answered, a secret smile on her lips. Moving to Switzerland took care of one other awkward little problem. She was pregnant with Charles' child.

She had not seen her husband in years, and this would be all the vindication he needed for his insane rages, his jealousies, and the torment he had inflicted on her in their abominable marriage.

In Switzerland, she could manage this little surprise in secrecy. No one would know. And once arrangements were made for the baby, she could lead the sophisticated life of literature, music, and culture for which she longed.

Chapter 36 – Paris, 1999

Their cab pulled up to the entrance of a large hotel near the airport, far from the other hotel. Sara paid for the cab and walked in, noting the number of doormen, the valet parking attendant, the concierge, a long reception counter with several clerks, and other guests milling about, all most benign and ordinary. The more people around the more comfortably anonymous and secure she felt.

Dave followed her into the lobby and frowned as he tallied up the opulent furnishings. "This hotel is too expensive," he grumbled.

"Go home then," Sara said.

"I'm going to call Samuel." Josh checked his watch.

"That man, Pierre, is probably long gone," said Dave. "In a couple of hours, I'll go back and reclaim the rest of my stuff."

Sara shivered. "Fine. I'll give you my key and you can pick up whatever I left and check out too. I'm never going back there. But," she glared at Dave, "don't try any more funny stuff."

"What funny stuff?" Dave said, glaring back at her. "I've tried to help you despite your pigheaded refusal to see reason. I wash my hands of the whole business."

"No more car stealing? No more portrait stealing, either? How nice," said Sara. "And try not to take up with any strange women or lead any of those crooks back here." She turned her back on him and headed toward the cafe. "I'll buy whatever else I need this afternoon. Right now I'm going to get a cup of hot tea and relax before we check in. We almost lost our lives back there."

Josh waved as he walked toward the phones. "I'll meet you after I call Samuel."

Fifteen minutes later, Josh joined Sara in the cafe, a light, airy room with soft, unobtrusive music. Two latecomers were finishing up lunch, but otherwise the cafe was deserted except for the server and a cashier. The peach and aqua color scheme and soft lighting soothed Sara's spirits, although she still felt rattled at the close call with Pierre. Twice a gun had been pointed at her, once in Gibraltar and once a short while ago. She had survived both times, but how long would her luck hold?

"Coffee," Josh said to the server as she hovered at Sara's table. He seated himself and muttered, "Trouble," to Sara.

"More trouble?" Sara's stomach turned. She set down her tea cup. She had begun to relax, but the one word from Josh brought all the terror back. "What kind of trouble?"

Josh scanned the room as he talked in a low voice. "Samuel didn't say where he was, but he talked to a neighbor at his condo in St. Thomas a couple of days ago. She said a man representing himself as an agent from a Nazi loot investigation team showed up at her apartment asking for Samuel. The man was thin and bald. She thought at first he was a salesman, looked like one in his business suit, she said, but she didn't know anything to tell him. He asked a lot of questions about Samuel."

"Blank," said Sara.

Josh leaned back, stretching his legs out in front of him.

Sara put her head in her hands. "I don't believe this," she said. "People are chasing us in Gibraltar, Paris, and now St. Thomas. How can this be happening?"

"Incredible," agreed Josh.

"I suppose the pension concierge in Gibraltar or her son or a friend of hers was following Samuel, too," Sara said, "but they lost us when we rented a car and drove up to Madrid."

"Then we flew to Paris," said Josh. "But we, uh, activated Pierre by contacting Ardon in Paris who knew Pierre was looking for a painting like ours. Ardon and maybe Dave set up the fraud with that loser, so we actually triggered the Paris incidents."

"I guess Ardon wanted to deal with a client less volatile than Pierre," Sara said.

"Probably. And Samuel may have taken the decoy bit too seriously and laid a trail that put him in danger."

Sara shook her head. "Unbelievable."

"A lot of money involved," added Josh.

Sara paused as another thought occurred to her. "Why now? Almost sixty years later, all of these people crawl out of the walls to claim the painting."

"Someone may have been watching Samuel and. . ." Josh sat back, sipped his coffee, and raised an eyebrow at Sara. "And possibly your grandmother."

"What? My grandmother?" Sara gaped at Josh. "They were after my grandmother too?"

"Your grandmother and Samuel were survivors of the resistance group," Josh said. "If anyone was paying attention to the group, they might have known or suspected what was going on."

"Seems so farfetched. All that happened a long time ago."

She stared down at her hands, remembering the call from her mother. Her grandmother had been killed by a hit and run driver, hadn't she? Why would anyone deliberately kill her? They wouldn't get the painting that way. "I don't believe it," she said. "My grandmother was too secretive. No one ever visited her, and no one in Martinsburg knew her past, not even her family."

"Seems farfetched to me too," Josh said. "They'd have to find her first, and she'd buried her past, married, and changed her name."

"Right." Sara pursed her lips. "Then she lived with us after our grandfather died. Our house was never broken into, which I think they'd do if they were looking for a clue to the painting's whereabouts."

"Did they ever find the hit and run driver?" asked Josh.

"No," said Sara, "so I suppose there could have been a nefarious plot my grandmother was involved in." She shook her head. "Except I don't think so."

Josh drummed his fingers on the table. "Do you suppose any of this is more of Dave's work? Putting out lines of his own to find a buyer? Where is he anyhow?"

"I saw him check in. He's probably taking a nap." Sara looked through the glass door of the cafe into the lobby and the hotel entrance. "He was going back to the other hotel later, but I haven't seen him go out."

Josh took another sip of coffee.

Sara appreciated the lack of response. It was one thing for her to criticize her brother. She didn't want to defend him against Josh or anyone else. She changed the subject.

"The most logical answer is that Samuel talked too much and the wrong people heard it."

"Makes sense," said Josh.

"Also, we're assuming Blank was the one asking about Samuel in St. Thomas," Sara said. "But what if it was someone else? And if so, what Nazi loot investigation team? From where?"

"Yeah. It all sounds fishy to me, too." Josh rapped his knuckles on the table. "Wouldn't you think that whoever is after the painting would kidnap Samuel and torture him for it?"

Sara felt a twinge of fear. "If that's on their mind, what's to keep them from kidnapping us? I'd give them my key in a minute if they resorted to torture." She reached for her tea but stopped as she saw her hand was shaking. "Do we have a fresh set of villains after us?"

Josh shook his head. "I don't know. Samuel thinks Ms. Pickford was paid to report on him."

"She probably liked the money. A concierge at a pension in Gibraltar wouldn't earn too much. Her son heard the story too, and he attacked us. I think he killed Smythe."

They were still in danger. Sara surveyed the cafe. All appeared peaceful and normal. The late diners had left, and the server and cashier were both staring idly at her and Josh, the only customers.

Were the server and cashier wondering how they could get hold of the painting? Get a grip, Sara told herself, then realized Josh was still talking.

"They knew who Samuel was. They knew of his war activities.

They knew he helped smuggle Jewish valuables out of occupied countries." Josh rapped his knuckles on the table. "And they knew a valuable painting—maybe a lot of valuable paintings—was missing."

"I suppose they heard stories from their fathers about stolen or hidden paintings," Sara said, sipping her tea. "Even stories about Samuel and the others in his group, then tracked them down, befriended them and tried to get Samuel or the others to talk about their wartime activities."

"Or someone else besides Pierre in Bernheim's circle of non-Jewish friends and servants," said Josh. "They might wonder what happened to a Rembrandt."

"Was Smythe murdered because of the painting?" Sara put her trembling hands around the tea cup to feel its warmth. "Blank could have killed him, or it might have been an unrelated street killing. We should find out what's happening with the murder investigation in Gibraltar."

"I don't believe Blank would kill Smythe and still hang around the hotel watching us." Sara thought a moment. "Ardon knows the painting is in Gibraltar."

"Let's hope we've derailed him."

Sara shivered. "So what are we going to do about this situation? Do you suppose they've planted bugs on us?"

Josh shrugged. "I don't know. If they did, we should check our clothes, but we probably left the bugs back at the other hotel."

Sara thought a moment. "There must be millions of dollars worth of Nazi loot still unclaimed or lost, hidden in attics or cellars or caves . . ."

"Quite an incentive for a modern-day treasure hunter." Josh sat back and grinned. "Enterprising, these treasure hunters."

Sara didn't feel amused. "Newspapers print stories now and then about the discoveries of Nazi loot." She paused to sip her tea. "And also about the lawsuits concerning who owns it."

Josh stared into his coffee cup, shaking his head. "Don't forget Ardon could have sent out e-mails to his network of experts and resources when Pierre first contacted him. Would be a natural thing to do, I guess, to ask your colleagues if they knew of a Rembrandt matching a given description. He could have alerted a lot of people, some legitimate and honest, and considering the kind of man Ardon is, some not so."

"No one followed us in here." She frowned. "I don't like it that Dave is going back to the other hotel, and it's compromised."

"I'm sorry, Sara," said Josh, "but your brother wants the money and he'd probably make a deal with whoever offered the most. That is, if he got his hands on the painting."

Sara pushed back her cup and stood. "I know. Let's get out of here."

Josh glanced around the cafe. "Yeah."

Sara left money on the table to cover the check and a tip, and walked out.

"I checked my suitcase." Josh said as he walked toward the bell captain. "You make the plane reservations."

"To where?" Sara asked, already knowing the answer.

Josh stopped, came back to hug her and whispered in her ear. "Madrid. Then we'll rent a car and head for. . ."

Sara grinned and whispered back, "Gibraltar, here we come."

Chapter 37 - Paris, 1874

Paris.

Jean Pierpont Thibault, formerly of Alsace, now a resident of Paris, paced the living room of his Parisian townhouse. Soon, he thought with grim humor, he would enjoy a sea voyage to New Caledonia at government expense, and all because he had built, in good conscience, of course, his own empire on the stocks and barrels of new weaponry.

The problem was that the machine gun he had invented and sold to the French government for the Franco-Prussian war had malfunctioned—through no fault of his. The manufacturer built the thing with a faulty trigger mechanism. And France lost the war.

To make matters worse, his name was connected to the Communard radicals during the war through the flimsiest of accusations. And from a serving girl, no less, at the brasserie he frequented, but she had the ear—and everything else, it seemed—of Adolphe Thiers, leader of the Third Republic, and that along with the machine gun fiasco was enough to declare him persona non grata.

Now he had to look forward to a miserable sea voyage and even more miserable life as a prisoner in that godforsaken island in the South Pacific. He sighed. *Quel dommage.*

His entire household was to be dismantled and the servants dispersed. Fortunately, he was a bachelor, so there would be no heirs squabbling over the spoils. Unless a bastard came forward. He laughed again at the absurdity of it all.

He could take precious little with him. The expensive Persian carpets, the furniture fit for royalty, the draperies, the paintings. . . . He stopped taking inventory. The paintings. He stepped into the large parlor of his town house and paused to admire as he always did the Courbet, the Manet, and the small Goya on his walls. Perhaps he'd pack those for the trip to New Caledonia. They would be such a comfort in whatever living condition he found himself. He grimaced. A grass hut, most likely. But. . .the native women. . .a smile fluttered across his face. . . the native women were most permissive, he'd heard.

A flash of memory, usually suppressed with a shudder, crossed his mind of eating rats during the mercifully short year the Communards were in power. Perhaps he owed the rats something, he thought. They kept him from starving.

He lingered to admire and savor each painting before passing on to the next. After the Goya, he came to the Rembrandt. Rabbi Saul Levi Morteira as a Moor. The name Rembrandt had drawn him to the painting from the first time his father brought it home. He was a small boy at the time, but he had heard stories of the beautiful and accomplished Hortense Bonaparte. His mother had been incensed at the purchase. He had wondered about her reaction, but as he became a man, he understood the jealousy that lay at the root of her anger.

His father had taken him to visit Malmaison. Even now, the scent of roses drew him back into memories of the lush greenery surrounding the grand house. And the pineapples. Luscious fruit from the greenhouses. Perhaps New Caledonia would have pineapples. A smile flitted across his face. Then the trip would be worthwhile.

He stared at the Rembrandt, lost in his memories. He heard a servant behind him and ignored him, focusing on the painting. It was not particularly beautiful even though it was a Rembrandt. The subject was Jewish. Did he have any Jewish acquaintances? Perhaps he could give it to a synagogue. Would a gallery want it?

He shook his head. An economic depression had France in its

grip. Money was tight. Unemployment was high. No one would want a painting of such a dubious subject.

He lifted the painting off the hook and set it against the wall by the front door. He would simply have to dispose of it.

The next evening, he donned his top hat, frock coat, and gloves and picked up his walking cane for a trip to the nearby saloon. As he walked down the hall to the door, he spotted the Rembrandt, still propped up against the wall. On a whim, he picked it up and carried it with him.

A chill wind bit his cheeks, and fog obscured the street lights. Late fall. Winter coming, but this year, Jean thought with a queasiness curdling his stomach, he would not see the winter. Perhaps he would never see winter again. He shrugged. Perhaps moving to New Caledonia would be a good thing after all.

He heard laughter and the tinkling of a piano bursting out of the saloon's open doors. He walked in and paused, peering through the haze of tobacco smoke to find his friends, then he spotted them at a round table in the rear. He doffed his coat and hat, leaving them with the attendants, and wound through the rowdy group of men at the door to take a seat with his friends.

"Ah, bonsoir, Pierre and Jacques. Good. And you have secured our table." Jean waved his cigar at each man.

"Bonsoir. What have you got there?" asked Pierre, a red-faced, portly man, cigar in hand, his vest stretched tightly across his bulging stomach.

Jean looked down at the painting. Now he thought of the perfect thing to do with it. A kind of parting salutation. "This, mes amis, is a fine painting by that most famous and celebrated artist, Rembrandt." He lifted it up onto the table.

"Go on, not a Rembrandt," said the other man, Jacques, tall and thin, wearing a fitted coat, cravat, and waving a cigarette. He peered at the painting and raised an eyebrow. "It does say Rembrandt." He pointed to the signature.

Jean laughed. "Of course. My father bought it from Empress Hortense, stepdaughter of Napoleon Bonaparte, the first."

"So what are you doing, bringing it here?" asked Pierre.

"Gentlemen," said Jean, "as you know, I have been requested by the government to travel to New Caledonia."

The other men erupted. "Hiss! Hiss!" they shouted.

"I agree," said Jean, "but there it is."

"What does that have to do with the painting?" asked Jacques. "It's a valuable piece."

"Indeed it is," Jean agreed. "But I have grown weary of it and see no reason to subject it to a long sea voyage."

"So what is your plan?" asked Pierre, tapping the ash from his cigar onto the floor.

"We will play cards, and the winner will become the proud owner of this prize." Jean grinned at the other two men.

Pierre shuddered. "My wife will not be pleased with such a thing," he said. Then he leaned forward with a wink. "But my mistress, now, she shall have it. She will be most delighted, I think."

The other man laughed. "A fitting owner for it. For my part, I would hold it for sale when times become more prosperous."

Jean signaled a waiter. "A beer," he said, "and cards, s'il vous plaît."

"Oui, Monsieur."

"More beers all around," said Jacques.

"Oui." The waiter departed, returning a moment later with a deck of cards.

The play began.

At the end of the evening, the three men were soused, the painting had changed hands five times, and Pierre was the final winner. He peered at the painting through bleary eyeballs. "Maybe my wife will like it after all."

Chapter 38 - Gibraltar, 1999

"Dave is checking us out of the other hotel," said Sara. "Dave thinks we checked in here. Let's get out of here."

"Good." Josh hustled Sara into a cab. "Airport," he said, then turned to Sara. "Dave will think we're out shopping and hang around waiting for us."

"Going back to retrieve his things will give us a few extra hours anyway. Let's hope he's ditched Genevieve."

She peered out the rear window to see a cab swerve over to the hotel entrance and pick up a passenger. She watched as it followed them through the streets and onto the highway to the airport. She didn't get a good look at the passenger, but no one but Dave knew they were at that hotel. They were simply other hotel guests going to the airport. She turned to see Josh smiling at her.

"I'm getting paranoid," she said.

Josh turned to look out the back window. "Considering all that's happened, you're right to be paranoid. Now we're leaving one wasps' nest to step into another."

"True," Sara said, reaching for his hand. "Our advantage is that no one knows we're going back to Gibraltar."

Josh had the money ready to pay for the cab as it pulled to the curb. The cab that had followed them swept by, but too fast for Sara to get more than a glimpse of the person inside.

Josh pushed her forward and gave her his passport. "Run inside and get the tickets. I'll be right behind you."

As Sara bought two tickets for the next plane to Madrid, she looked behind her at Josh who was watching everyone who came their way. She scanned the crowd herself but saw no one she recognized. She picked up their boarding passes, relieved that there had been no problems and no awkward questions.

They walked to the gate hand in hand. "Did you see anyone?" she asked.

"No," answered Josh. "Doesn't mean they weren't there."

"I know, but probably we've lost them." For the first time in days, Sara felt lighthearted, as if a heavy weight had rolled off her spirit. No one knew they were going back to Gibraltar, and once there, they had only to contact the Bernheim scholarship people, retrieve the Rembrandt, and deliver it to the rightful owners. After that. . . .

Her spirits plummeted. They still had to confront Josh's parents. What if they were thieves? What would Josh do then? He would be devastated and, she suddenly realized, she would be too. She didn't think her relationship with Josh, still tenuous, could survive such a blow. Her eyes flitted to him, but he stared straight ahead, intent on reaching the gate.

Whatever happened, she still needed to find a job. So far, she had focused on what she was not going to do, but what was she to do? Vague notions of travel, research, floated in her head, but how could she work those ideas into a career?

Sara stopped at a souvenir kiosk and bought a scarf, a large T-shirt, and a couple of heavy navy blue sweaters. She handed the T-shirt and the larger sweater to Josh, then paused at the ladies' rest room. "I'm going in, but when I come out, I'll be wearing this scarf and sweater. You change into the t-shirt and sweater. Carry your jacket on your arm. I'll do that too."

They met again a few minutes later, slightly changed in appearance. Josh also walked with a limp. "I put a wad of paper towel in my right shoe. Changes my gait."

"Good disguise." Sara nodded in approval. "You seem like a different person."

A couple of hours later, they had landed in Madrid and rented a car. Sara checked her watch. "It's a six-hour drive to Gibraltar. Let's spend the night here and leave early in the morning."

They checked into the airport Hilton, and that evening, they sat at the computer in the Hilton's business office for guests.

"Here it is, the Bernheim Scholarship," said Sara. "She read through the submission requirements, muttering to herself. "Administered by the Bernheim Foundation, established 1975 by Celeste Vilar in memory of her father, Alain Bernheim, distinguished professor of history, Toulouse University, 1930-1938." Sara's eyes blurred. Such a terrible tragedy. How had Celeste Vilar survive? How old had she been when her family was taken by the Nazis? She thought of her own grandmother, another victim, who had lived the rest of her life in camouflage, disguising who she really was in a pervasive distrust.

"Excuse me," Sara said, "I can't do this." She walked to the ladies' lounge because she didn't want to start bawling in front of Josh in that office.

She sat in the lounge with its comfortable chairs and artificial palms for half an hour, sniffling into a tissue, remembering her grandmother, thinking of the path she had taken to fulfill her grandmother's bequest. She had met Josh and learned her family's history along the way. She and Josh made a good team, but so many changes in such a short time. She felt so sad and tired.

She took a deep breath. "I'm exhausted," she said to herself. "I need a good night's sleep free from worry." No one else lingered in the ladies' room. She sat back and said a quiet prayer to her grandmother. "We're almost there, Grandma. We'll have returned the Rembrandt to its proper owner. Your final challenge will be completed, and you can rest in peace."

Sara walked back to the business office. Josh was talking on his cell phone. "Just a minute," he said. He smiled up at Sara as she plopped down in the other chair. "Would you like to speak to Celeste's son?" he asked, handing her the phone.

Chapter 39 - Provenance, 1930

Paris.
Alain Bernheim hunched in his coat and pulled down his hat against the bitter cold wind sweeping through the streets of Paris. Sheets of newspaper blew down the street ahead of him, and he stepped around the piles dogs had left on the sidewalk as he cursed this nuisance.

He hurried along the street, heading toward his parents' home in the Marais section of Paris. He had become immersed in reading at his neighborhood bookstore, and now he was late for his own birthday celebration. His whole family would be waiting for him. Mama and Papa, his sister Ruth, Uncle Jacob and Aunt Aliza and the three maiden aunts, Rachel, Harriet, and Judith. He smiled as he wondered what outrageous gift the three aunts would give him. They had a reputation all right, but their love shone through the silliness.

Alain crossed the street, waved at Pierre Goldman, the butcher in the shop under his parents' apartment. He climbed the stairs and burst into the living room. "Voila!" he shouted. "The conquering hero returns."

He startled them. He saw them all, frozen in place, as they stared, then the tableau fell apart.

"Alain, you crazy boy," his mother said, coming forward to fold him into her plump arms. He smelled the garlic like spring grass.

His father took a cigar out of his mouth. He wore his only suit and a tie for this celebration. "That's my son," he said to the others. "The college graduate."

"And more, Papa!" The fact that he held a doctorate degree failed to register with his family, still in awe that he had gone to the university at all.

"Happy birthday, Alain," said his sister, standing with her hands behind her back. The heavy gray sweater thrown over her shoulders and buttoned at the top only partly covered the short, flat-chested flapper dress she wore. He gave her a hug. "How lucky am I," he said, "to have such a beautiful sister."

She smiled and stared down at her feet.

Uncle Jacob pounded him on the back. "You make the family so proud. University graduate!"

Aunt Aliza hugged him, and the three aunts in their shawls and long dresses tittered.

Alain laughed, happy to be with all of them. His family. "I have good news," he said. "I have a job!"

"A job," his mother breathed.

His father cocked an eyebrow. "A job?"

"I've been appointed to the faculty of Toulouse University." Alain couldn't restrain the glee he felt saying those words.

His mother looked down at her hands, clasped together holding her apron. "Toulouse. But that is so far. . ." She glanced at her husband. "And not so friendly a place. . .for us, I mean."

Alain put an arm around her. "Not so far, Mama. I can come back by train anytime."

His father clapped him on the back. "He has a good job, Mama. A university job. This is my boy." He choked up and turned his back to the assemblage.

Uncle Jacob pumped Alain's hand, and the three aunts came forward like three blackbirds and trilled, "Congratulations!"

"Mama." His father had regained control of himself. "Bring out the wine. We must celebrate!"

She hurried into the kitchen.

"Happy birthday, too," said Aunt Aliza. "I make you a fine tart with cream and fruit." She kissed her fingers. "Superb! You will like it."

Alain kissed her on the cheek. "Merci beaucoup, Aunt Aliza."

His mother returned with a tray of glasses and a bottle of red wine. She handed the corkscrew to his father.

"C'est bon!" he said, inserting the corkscrew and pulling the cork out with a pop. He poured wine into each glass and handed them to Alain to be passed on to the others.

After each person had a glass in hand, he raised his. "To a fine young man," he saluted Alain, "who will go far. I guarantee it. L'Chaim!"

"L'Chaim," the others said. His father touched his glass to Alain's and drank, his eyes full of pride.

"Now, we would like to give Alain our own special gift," said Aunt Harriet. The three aunts tittered.

"One moment," said Aunt Judith. She left the room and quickly returned with a large, thin box wrapped in plain manila paper. Alain smiled. No fancy decorative paper for them, but they had wound a blue ribbon around the box and placed a blue bow on top.

"Sit down," said Aunt Harriet. Then the three aunts together brought it to Alain and stood close while he opened it, excitement and anticipation lending a glow to their faces.

"You'll never guess where we found it," said Aunt Judith. "We paid hardly anything for it at all."

"Shhh," said Aunt Harriet. "Don't tell him that."

"Why not? It's true, isn't it?" Judith grinned at Alain. "Anyway, you'll like it, being a university graduate. It is a fine gift for a professor."

Alain gingerly took off the bow and unwound the ribbon. He felt the rectangular raised shape of a frame inside the box. Could this package contain a painting? He almost groaned at the thought. He imagined what the aunts would think was a nice painting, all flowers and fruit, but they meant well, and he would do his best to appreciate their gift.

He tore off the wrapper and lifted the box lid. What he saw

staggered him. It was not, as he expected, an amateur rendition of flowers or a landscape. Nor was it by any of the modern painters whose works were the buzz of the university crowd. Artists like Cezanne, Picasso, Braque, or even Man Ray or Duchamp.

This painting was a Rembrandt. The artist had signed it at the bottom. Was it a fraud? It must be. Alain looked up at the aunts. He must show his appreciation, but he couldn't imagine that it was a genuine Rembrandt. "It is a Rembrandt!" He held it up so everyone could see. "I am stunned. What a wonderful, wonderful gift." He managed to keep the doubt out of his voice.

Aunt Judith nudged Aunt Rachel. "See? I told you he would like it."

"I do. It is stupendous," Alain said. "Where did you find it?"

"Estate sale," said Aunt Rachel. "In a rack with other paintings. We liked this one the best, didn't we?" Judith and Harriet chorused, "We did."

"They had the same price for all of the paintings. We don't think they knew anything about what they had." Aunt Judith pointed to the name at the bottom of the painting. "Rembrandt signed it. See that?"

Alain nodded as he studied the painting. He saw why they were able to buy the painting for so little. The subject was a Moor. He turned it over to see another drawing of the same man and a title, Saul Levi Morteira as Abraham—he'd have to research to find out who this Saul Levi Morteira was. The painting itself was rather dreary. The style of painting, too. Such realistic treatment was out of vogue. Not like a Picasso or a Man Ray. He looked up to see the aunts watching him expectantly.

Alain stood up and hugged each of them. "I will treasure this gift. It is worth far more than you can imagine." And he would find out where exactly they bought it and what its story was.

"Dinner is ready," his mother said.

***

Later that evening, Alain pried out of his aunts the location of the estate sale and name of the company that had organized it. Early the next morning, he visited the site of the sale, a vacant town home in a fashionable and expensive street in the eighth arrondissement. He walked by the house several times, climbed the stoop and peered through the window in the door. All the furnishings had been trucked away, but several piles of trash occupied the corners in the hall. Otherwise, the house seemed to have been well maintained.

Seeing nothing further to be gained by perusing the house, he walked the mile over to the management company that had organized the estate sale. A secretary reading a book in front of her typewriter glanced up as he entered.

"Bonjour, Monsieur?" she said. "Je peux vous aider?"

Alain took a deep breath. He didn't want to seem anxious or too interested. "I am inquiring about the house on la Rue de Surene. Your company held an estate sale there recently."

"Oui. You should speak to Madame Farette." The secretary picked up the phone, pressed a button, and waited. "A gentleman is inquiring about the DuBois sale." She listened, staring at Alain and twirling a strand of hair, and then she replaced the phone. "Madame Farette will be out in a moment. Please take a seat." She gestured to the two upholstered chairs against the wall behind a coffee table.

Alain didn't take a seat. He paced the room instead.

Madame Farette appeared almost immediately. "Bonjour. How may I help you, monsieur?" she asked.

Alain turned to greet her. She seemed pleasant enough. Not hard to deal with, as he had imagined. He smiled. They shook hands. She invited him into her office and gestured for him to take a chair while she sat behind a mammoth walnut desk.

He cleared his throat. "I'd like to know more about the family who lived in the house. Is there a relative I can contact?"

Her eyes narrowed as if she were sizing him up. "But why, monsieur? You cannot return any items you bought at the sale."

Alain shook his head. "No, no. I have no wish to do that, but my aunts bought a painting there, and I would like to know more about it, where the owners got it, how long they've had it, that kind of thing."

She pursed her lips. "I see. You want to know the provenance of the painting. You must think it a good one." She raised an eyebrow and grinned at him. "Oui?"

He laughed and sat back as if to deprecate the idea. "I have no idea. I'm curious about it, you see."

"But of course." She picked up the phone, dialed a number, and waited, tapping a finger on the desktop. "Bonjour, Monsieur Thomas? I have a person here in my office who would like to speak with you about a painting he purchased at your estate sale. May I send him over?" She watched Alain as she listened.

Alain caught the name Thomas. He waited.

Madame Farette put down the phone and scribbled a note on a scrap of paper. She handed it to Alain. "The heir to the property," she said. "He will see you now at that address."

Alain stood. "Thank you," he said, hat in hand and clutching the scrap of paper. "This means a lot to me."

"De rien," she said, standing to shake hands and wave him out of her office.

Alain walked briskly to the address, only a few blocks away, and stopped in front of an elegant hotel. Who could this person be to afford such a place in these economically unstable times?

Monsieur Thomas lived in chaos on the third floor. He greeted Alain cheerfully and motioned him in. Thomas seemed quite young, perhaps in his twenties, and looked as if he had hurried to dress. His black trousers were half-buttoned and his white ruffled shirt was open at the neck. His suspenders hung down over his pants.

Alain entered the apartment in wonder as he navigated the narrow path to the couch. He could only characterize the objects that filled the floor and furniture as junk. Broken toys, cheap trinkets, stained bolts of fabric, piles of newspapers, magazines, and books.

"I know, I know," said Thomas, clearing a place on the couch. "All junk I've got to get rid of." He gestured for Alain to sit on the couch while he eased himself onto a bare spot of chair. "What can I do for you?"

Alain tried to keep his distaste off his face, but how did anyone live like this? He turned his attention to Thomas. "My aunts bought a painting at your estate sale. . ."

Thomas held up his hand. "Wait a moment. It can't be returned.

No money back."

Alain laughed. "No, no. Nothing like that. I'd simply like to know more about it. How long was it in your family?"

Thomas sat back in the chair, steepled his fingers, and smiled at Alain. "I can't believe my family left anything valuable, but perhaps you think so?"

"Oh no," Alain hastened to say. He didn't want to haggle over it now. "I wondered, that's all. It seems very old."

"I see." Thomas raised an eyebrow, clearly not believing him. "Which one was it."

Alain cleared his throat. "It's a painting of. . ." Alain hesitated. "It seems to be a painting of a rabbi by, uh, Rembrandt." Even saying the name seemed preposterous in the clear light of day.

"A Rembrandt? You're saying a Rembrandt was in that stack of paintings I sold?" Thomas clapped a hand to his forehead, but only in jest. "Fancy that," he said and chuckled.

"It's signed by a Rembrandt and it appears quite well done and very old. Whoever did paint it is very good." Alain rolled his hat around in his hands, wishing he hadn't bothered to find a provenance for a fake Rembrandt.

Thomas looked at Alain. "I'd hate to dash your hopes, old man, but the story in my family is that my grandfather won it in a card game and that was many years ago. Nobody liked it. Piled in the attic with the rest of the junk no one wanted." He sighed. "No one likes to throw anything away in my family, you see." He sat back in the chair and crossed his legs. "Not because we were thrifty." He shook his head, an ironic smile on his face. "Oh no. We had money then, again thanks to my grandfather. No one could be bothered with mundane matters. That was left to the servants." He snorted. "Wonder we weren't robbed blind."

To Alain, hoarding was as natural as wearing a hat. His family had lived for years in poverty and used, reused, and reused again. Even when times were good, nothing was thrown away. He pitied the helpless young man. "Perhaps your family could have sold it then, if they didn't want it."

This idea warranted a heavy sigh. "But of course, if we knew it was there or had any value." He pulled out a handkerchief, waved it, and blew his nose. Then he looked over at Alain. "A Rembrandt, you said?"

"It's signed with that name," Alain said cautiously.

"Fancy that." He shrugged and scratched his chin.

Alain waited.

Thomas flicked his handkerchief again and grinned. "Nope. Don't see any way I can get it back. It's yours now."

"Thank you," said Alain, walking toward the door. Thomas followed.

"Good luck to you, sir," Thomas said as they shook hands.

Chapter 40 - Gibraltar, 1999

Sara froze as she stared at the phone. Would she like to speak to Celeste's son? Alain Bernheim's grandson? A thousand thoughts crossed her mind. Was their journey really almost over? Was it only a matter now of flying to wherever this man lived and giving him the Rembrandt? Job done? After the terror and the tedium of the search, could it really be that easy?

As she took the phone, she realized her hands were shaking.

She heard a deep, well-modulated voice, a lecturer's voice. "You are Sara Miller?"

"I am," said Sara, already reassured by the confident tone.

"My name is Alain Vilar." He cleared his throat. "Mr. Davila has told me that it was your grandmother who saved my family's Rembrandt? I hardly know what to say. My mother told me about it, but I thought it had been lost forever. How can I thank you enough for returning a piece of my family's history?"

He spoke slowly as if she didn't understand English. Sara stumbled a reply and then asked. "Where do you live, Mr. Vilar?"

"I teach here in Jacksonville, Florida. In the United States. I understand you are in Gibraltar. Do you know where Florida is?"

Joy welled up in her heart. How fitting. Jacksonville, Florida, where she had begun the quest, a few miles north of there in Yulee, Florida. "Yes," she said, "I know where that is."

"How will you get the painting to me? Should I come to you?

Would shipping it be at all feasible?" He hesitated. "I'm afraid I'm so flabbergasted I don't know what I'm saying or even what to think."

"That's all right," Sara said. "Does Josh have your address?" She looked over at Josh. He nodded. "Bringing it to you would be most fitting. We will let you know when we can deliver it." Closure was what she wanted. A successful end to an exciting adventure. She had to give this painting to its rightful owner, face to face.

"That's fine then. Wait until I tell my wife—and my children."

No, no, no. Fear raced up and down her spine. "Please, Mr. Vilar, not yet. Let us deliver it first, and you find a place for safekeeping. Then you may tell everyone you wish."

There was a long pause. "I see," he said. "It is a valuable painting, I suppose."

"Yes," said Sara, "it is." She hesitated, then added, "and there are dangerous people who will do anything to get it."

For a long moment, Alain said nothing. Sara thought he had hung up, but then he spoke, his voice firm. "Dangerous people, evil people, murdered my grandfather. They will not get the painting."

"Good," said Sara. "You must be careful." She signed off, and Josh slapped her on the back.

"We found him!" he said. "We actually found the owner of the painting!"

They grinned at each other, then Josh pulled her into a long kiss that evaporated all the frustrations and misunderstandings and anger that had crept into their relationship since they'd begun this search.

Sara looked up at Josh and smiled. They did make a good team. She liked Josh very much. Perhaps she even loved him, but right now all this emotion had drained her. She felt exhausted and yet she knew their job was not over yet.

"It's late and I'm hungry," she said, "but let's get our food here in the hotel—I don't want to risk going out tonight. We don't need to meet anyone else after the painting."

Josh stood and headed for the door. "I agree. Low profile it is."

***

They left Madrid at seven the next morning. The drive took six hours plus a tedious wait at the Spanish border. Shortly after three, they arrived in Gibraltar, turned in the rental car, and then took a cab to the Hilton Hotel and registered for the night. Two rooms, as usual.

"I need a good night's sleep," she'd told Josh, "and two rooms splits us up, making it harder for someone to attack us." Sara felt too nervous and unsettled to add another dimension to her already high stress level. She was all too aware that they'd had to show their passports and use their real names at the hotel desk. Was anyone watching? They must know the Rembrandt was hidden in Gibraltar and that she or Josh would be back to retrieve it.

"This is what I think we should do," said Sara, as they walked into her room. "First, we reserve seats tonight on a plane leaving Gibraltar around noon tomorrow. They only go to England, so we'll transfer there for a flight to Jacksonville." She pulled off her sweater and took a chair by the window.

"Cool." Josh folded his arms and leaned against the wall. "That will give us enough time to get the Rembrandt and then take a cab to the airport for the flight out."

"Right. And not much time for anyone to learn we're here."

Sara looked at her watch. "I'm heading out to pick up a few things, since I left everything in Paris."

Josh pushed himself off the wall. "Be quick, then come back. I'm staying put and reading a book. I'll call Samuel too. We'll catch dinner later here at the hotel."

The next morning, they sat in the bank lobby, waiting for a teller to let them into the vault. Sara's hands gripped her purse, and she bit her lip out of nervousness. Feeling the need to appear sober, adult, and dignified, she wore a dress and stockings with low heels. She carried her jacket over her arm. As usual, Josh had no such inclination. He slouched in the chair beside her, wearing the airport T-shirt covered by the navy sweater and torn jeans, a shopping bag beside him. He'd thrown his jacket on the chair next to him. Only a few customers loitered nearby, filling out slips at a tall desk.

The teller beckoned, led them into the vault, and used Sara's key and the bank key to open the safety deposit box. She waited while Sara pulled out the long metal container inside.

"I'll wait for you outside," the teller said.

Sara opened the container and withdrew the package. Josh returned the container to the safety deposit box. He reached into the shopping bag and pulled out a garishly colored box that had once held a toy train. Sara placed the painting in the toy box, closed it, and put it in the shopping bag. They closed the safe deposit box account and walked out. "Thank you," Sara said to the teller as they passed her.

Feeling as if a dozen eyes stared at her back, Sara walked out the door with Josh and onto the sidewalk. They hailed a cab lurking down the street. It swerved over to them and stopped. The front door opened, and a man stepped outside. Pickford. Sara gripped Josh's arm, then gasped as she saw the gun Pickford held under a newspaper, but the sarcastic side of her mind wanted to laugh. What a cliché.

"In the cab. Now." He gestured toward the back door, pushing her into the car with his free hand.

Sara fell into the cab, yelling "Run!"

Pickford lifted his fist as if to hit her but instead turned back to Josh and aimed the gun at him. "In," he said as he jerked his head at the car.

"Run!" Sara said again. "Don't worry about me! Get out of here!"

She saw Josh darting glances around the street seeking help, but she felt too angry and affronted by these crooks to be afraid of them. They were not going to get the painting. Not after all that her grandmother and Samuel and she and Josh had done to rescue it for the rightful owner. What could she do? She tried the door on the other side but it was locked. She rummaged through the door pockets for a weapon but found only a map and a dirty tissue.

Pickford grabbed Josh's arm and swung him into the car. "I said in," he growled. Josh landed on the floor with the shopping bag on top of him. Pickford grabbed at the bag, but Josh held it tight.

Josh crawled up onto the seat with the shopping bag between

his knees. Pickford took the front passenger seat and swiveled to hold his gun on them, swinging the gun from Sara to Josh.

"Go!" Pickford yelled to the driver.

Sara looked at the driver for the first time and saw that it was the buzzard, wearing a man's jacket with her hair pushed up under a man's hat. A cigarette dangled from her lips. A thin disguise but probably effective.

"Safety belt," Josh whispered to Sara.

Right. Always buckle your safety belt. Click and drive. She watched Josh buckle his too. Such a mundane thing and probably useless, considering these thugs had guns and probably no plans for Sara or Josh to see the future. Neither of the Pickfords in front wore safety belts. For what that was worth, Sara thought as she furiously searched for anything she could use as a weapon. These crooks were not going to get away with this.

"That's fine, then," said Pickford. "We're going for a little ride."

Another cliché. Sara watched the boats sailing on the Mediterranean as the cab that imprisoned them sped down the coastal highway. She pulled out the map she'd found in the pocket behind the front seat and fanned herself with it. Could she possibly use it as a weapon? Could she signal a passing car? A police car? Cars passed by too fast on this two-lane road for that. She surreptitiously tried the door handle again, but it remained locked. Even if it weren't locked, the car was going too fast to leap out.

The man watching her from the front seat snickered.

Could she grab the gun out of his hand? The buzzard kept her eyes on the road to drive. As Sara debated grabbing the gun, the cab slowed and turned left onto a narrow, unpaved mountain road. This is it, she thought, glancing at Josh. His hand closed over hers and squeezed.

"What the hell. . . ." The gun in Pickford's hand wavered as he stared out the rear window.

A car had turned in behind them. Sara looked around and gasped as the other car speeded toward them and rammed their cab in the rear. Hard. Sending it into a pile of construction gravel. The two in the front seat slammed into the front windshield, fracturing it into long cracks. Sara's head hit the upholstered back of the seat in front and then bounced back. She held her head, dazed.

"Out!" whispered Josh, unbuckling his belt. Sara turned to Josh, caught on and did the same. The driver had hit her head on the steering wheel and lay against the wheel, moaning with eyes shut and blood streaming from a head wound. Pickford was spitting out bloody teeth and feeling the blood gushing from his forehead, but the gun had flown out of his hands and through the car window.

Sara flung the map at him and grabbed the shopping bag. She and Josh unlocked and opened the doors, thankfully not wedged shut in the crash, leapt out of the cab and ran to the car behind that had unaccountably rammed the cab. They had to hope that whoever drove it was their friend. She didn't know how badly the Pickfords were hurt, and she wasn't anxious to find out. She'd call an ambulance when they got back into town or, preferably, the airport.

The driver of the rescue car flung open the passenger-side door. "Get in!" a familiar voice yelled.

Dave. Dave? *Was it possible?*

Sara had never felt so glad to see her brother. From now on, she would always consider him a hero. Josh scrambled into the back seat as Sara took the front. Dave backed up, turned around, and bounced them down the dirt road and back onto the highway.

"Airport!" said Sara.

"Airport it is." Dave pressed on the accelerator. They raced back down the highway toward town. Sara kept her eyes on the road behind them, crossing her fingers that the car they'd left behind was too damaged to move. Both the buzzard and her son had been badly banged up.

As they neared the congested area, Dave slowed down and Sara saw a cab far behind, but then she saw another and another. None of them looked damaged.

"Let us off at the terminal," Sara shouted. Once through Security, she'd feel safer.

Dave shook his head. "Uh uh. Not letting you out of my sight."

"Dave!" Sara shrieked. "We were almost killed back there. They could be right behind us."

"We'll be sitting ducks at the rental car turn-in," added Josh.

"Yeah, well, you all were going to dump me." Dave looked back at Sara. "Good thing I saw you leave." He stared ahead as he drove.

"What did you expect?" said Josh.

Sara glared at Dave. "You stole our car."

Dave didn't respond, but he kept his eyes on the rearview mirror. "I'm sure they're not behind us."

"Let us off at the terminal," Sara repeated.

"Okay," Dave said, "but Josh stays with me."

"But. . . ," Sara sputtered.

"It's all right, Sara." Josh was staring at the cars behind them, too. "I doubt they were able to turn around and follow us. Even if they could, they can't be too close and probably won't see you get out. We'll join you as soon as we can."

"Sure." Dave turned into the airport road. Dave looked at Sara with a grin. "Glad I bought the full rental car insurance."

He swooped into the departure lane, pulled to the curb, and Sara leaped out.

"Get the boarding passes!" Josh yelled.

"And a ticket for me!" added Dave.

Sara disappeared into the terminal and Dave drove away.

Chapter 41 – Jacksonville, 1999

"They might give us a reward," Dave grumbled. He frowned at the houses they passed on a shaded residential street near Jacksonville University. "Still time to change your mind."

Sara ignored him and continued to drive down the street. They had left Pierre and Ardon in Paris. Blank had disappeared, and the Pickfords remained in Gibraltar, possibly injured. None of them knew where she and Josh were now. She had begun to breathe more easily. She would soon hand the painting and all its attendant worries on to someone else. Their job would be done.

Sara studied the houses they were passing. "Alain's grandson must be doing quite well," she said. The neighborhood seemed affluent. The dusty live oak trees spreading across the street were as green as the shrubbery and grass landscaping on the broad lawns. The weather felt cool on this late fall afternoon in north Florida.

Sara slowed as Josh read the house numbers out loud and then came to the house number they wanted. She parked the rental car in front. Her stomach fluttered, and she felt. . .proud. She looked past Josh to gaze at the sidewalk that led across a well-nourished lawn to a ranch-style home. "This is it," she said. "I can hardly believe it." She smiled at Josh.

He reached over and squeezed her hand. "Here goes." He opened the door on his side. "Mission almost accomplished."

The painting, still in the toy train box in the shopping bag, lay next to Dave on the back seat. He picked up the bag, shaking his head, but Sara held her hand out for it, frowning at him. He may have rescued them, Sara thought, but she didn't trust him and was not going to risk him running off with the painting. He handed it over to her and followed Sara and Josh up the sidewalk to the front door, mumbling to himself.

The door opened immediately as if the couple inside had been watching for them. "Ms. Miller? Mr. Davila?"

Their smiles answered the broad smile on the man in front of them. He looked to be in his forties, and he wore a blue short-sleeved shirt, khaki pants, and running shoes.

"I am Alain Vilar." He put his arm around a woman standing next to him. She also wore running shoes and khaki slacks but with a flowered blouse. "This is my wife, Gail." He looked doubtfully at Dave, standing behind Sara.

Sara introduced Dave, and they all followed Alain Vilar into the cool, paneled living room.

"Please sit," said Gail. "I'll be back in a moment." She returned with glasses of lemonade and chocolate chip cookies, which she handed around. "Now where is this painting we didn't know we had?"

Sara handed Alain the shopping bag.

He laughed as he took it. "So much in so little," he quipped. He looked up at them. "I have never seen it, you see. I only know of it from my mother, but it pained her to talk about those days. The betrayals, the horror. . . ." He shook his head as he gazed at the package. "Is it damaged?"

"It is very old. . ." began Sara.

"I don't think you should open the package," Josh broke in. "Take it to a painting restorer and let him repair and frame it for you."

Alain still gazed at the package. "You're right, of course. Still, maybe just a peek." He pulled the rolled-up painting out of the bag and unwrapped the package. He held the rolled painting in both hands.

Gail placed a restraining hand on his arm. "He's right. You can wait if it will prevent further damage. . . ."

"And," said Sara, "until you can get it to a restorer, keep it in a bank vault."

Dave shuddered. "Yeah. Bank vault. That's what you need."

"Absolutely," added Josh, "immediately. Too many people find this painting of interest."

Gail's eyes flitted from Sara to Dave to Josh. "Tell us the story," she said.

Chapter 42 - Jacksonville, 1999

Sara drove the rental car back to the Jacksonville airport. She didn't feel like conversation. A lump of sadness weighed in her heart. They had succeeded in returning the Rembrandt to the rightful owner. She should feel happy but depression loomed over her spirits because Josh sat blank-faced and unresponsive, staring out the window. Dave dozed in the back seat.

What would happen next? Josh hadn't initiated, and she had deliberately postponed any talk of what they would do after they delivered the Rembrandt. Was this to be the end of their adventure together? Would they simply say good-bye and part? The thought depressed her.

She had grown so close to Josh, and she thought he felt the same about her. Was she going to return home to her old life? And what would she do there? She was not going back to a boring, routine job. She still had more than $10,000 left of her grandmother's bequest. What could she do with that? She glanced at Josh. How could she continue this adventure?

She remembered the way they'd met, first in a quiet living room in West Virginia, then later in a colonial mansion museum in southwest Florida. She had followed him to Cedar Key and met him again in St. Thomas. Together they had traveled to Gibraltar for the end of one adventure and the start of another. Both adventures concluded successfully. Her grandmother would be proud. So why did she feel so sad? She swallowed to control the tears she refused to shed. She would not have Josh feeling sorry for her, and she would not manipulate him with tears into declaring more than he felt.

They arrived at the airport and parked the rental car. Sara picked up the paperwork to close out the rental, stepped out of the car, and then turned to Dave as he pulled his suitcase and carry-on out of the car trunk. "You can go on home now. I may take a few days to relax while I'm here."

"I'll come with you," Dave said. "Your treat, right?"

Sara shook her head. She wanted time to speak to Josh alone, whatever happened. Dave needed to leave. "I think you should go home and check on Mom. You're on your own now. You need to get back to work."

For once Dave didn't wheedle. "Yeah. I'm tired of traveling. Don't have any leave left anyway. And what's the point?" He cast her a reproachful look. "You gave away the Rembrandt." Then he laughed and hugged her. "Take care. See you when you get back."

She watched him board the airport shuttle. Then she walked into the car rental office. Her heart felt heavy as she joined Josh for the next shuttle to the airport. She waited for him to say good-bye, mustering up a smile to make it easier, but he had taken her hand.

"Sara." He was looking into her eyes, but he wasn't smiling. Sara's stomach turned over. What was he going to say? Would this be the end? Would they ever see each other again? She waited for the doom. She felt his grip on her hand tighten.

"We haven't finished the job," he said.

Sara's ears buzzed. Of all the things Josh could have said, this was not what she had expected. "We haven't?" she said in a weak, girlish voice. She cleared her throat and made her voice sound strong and in control. "We haven't?"

"Please, I would like you to come home with me," he added. "To St. Thomas." He cleared his throat and Sara saw how nervous he was. She almost smiled.

"After all we've been through together, you deserve to learn the truth from my parents with me." His voice was deadly serious.

"Especially. . ."

"Especially what?" asked Sara. She felt a tremor of. . .of what? Curiosity? Fear? Excitement? She searched his face and met his eyes. She had hoped to see softness and, perhaps, love, anything that would say how much he wanted her to stay. What she saw was apology.

"I'm sorry, you know, for behaving like such an ass." The words rushed out. He wouldn't look at her, casting his eyes beyond her. "You're probably thinking you'd like to go on home and get rid of me. . ."

Sara couldn't believe what she was hearing. "After all this time of being together? You think I don't like you?" she asked in a thin high voice.

"I haven't been the best company. . ." Josh stared down at his feet and mumbled the words.

"Josh, I like you. We've been a great team." Sara took a deep breath. "I don't want to leave you. Of course, I'll go to St. Thomas with you."

At last he looked at her and a grin slowly appeared. He put his arms around her and swung her around, then he kissed her. The kiss lasted a long time. Sara's fears dissolved in understanding.

"Yes," she said. "That's more like it." She stepped away from his embrace and hooked her arm through his. "Let's go find out what your family did with the paintings they helped rescue."

They boarded the shuttle, sitting close together, and together they walked arm in arm into the terminal. "Tell us the worst," Sara said. "We can handle it."

Chapter 43 - St. Thomas, 1999

They arrived in St. Thomas early in the afternoon and took a cab into Charlotte Amalie to the art gallery belonging to Josh's parents. As they walked in, his mother, Sarah, ran forward to hug Josh and then Sara. Benjamin, Josh's father, followed behind his wife, a huge grin on his face.

"My prodigal son returns," he said, winking at Sara. He wrapped Josh in a big bear hug and then drew Sara into it. "We've been expecting you."

"We returned the Rembrandt," said Josh, extricating himself from the hug.

"And we want to hear all about it," Josh's mother said, "but first you must relax, have refreshments with us."

"Samuel reappeared as soon as he heard you'd found the owner of the Rembrandt," said Benjamin. "He has arranged an important executive meeting for this afternoon." The smile left his face, but Sara saw him wink at his wife and wondered what that meant. "It's a big deal, he says." Benjamin laughed.

Sara's eyes flitted from Sarah to Benjamin, trying to peer beneath the surface. They didn't appear afraid or ashamed or upset, but how much had Josh told them? Did Benjamin think this was a silly game Josh was playing? Had he dismissed the meeting as the foolishness of an old man and nothing to worry about? Possibly he had no idea what they were going to ask.

Josh put his arm around Sara. She felt the tension in his body and saw the grim set to his mouth. Confronting his parents was going to be hard for him. She hoped for a good outcome. They walked into the living room where Josh's mother Sarah had laid out sandwiches and fruit. Sara felt too uncomfortable to eat much. Josh had taken a sandwich, but it lay on his plate untouched while he pushed his lips in and out and stared at the floor. Only his parents seemed unconcerned and kept up a light conversation of local news.

Sara was glad when the meal ended and composed herself for the ordeal ahead as Benjamin led them to the conference room in the back of the gallery. Like the showroom, it was paneled in light pine, but no pictures graced the walls. Instead, three tall filing cabinets were jammed against one wall, a large steel safe faced them on the opposite wall, and boxes of paper and office supplies were piled against the wall along the side walls. Sara noticed a large, locked closet behind the boxes.

"Have a seat," said Benjamin. "I've brought in snacks, a bottle of wine, glasses. . ."

Josh's mother smiled at them. "We have to wait for Samuel." She walked out to the gallery. Sara saw no hint of worry in her face. If anything, Sarah seemed amused.

A few minutes later, Samuel joined them. He looked at Josh. "You brought all those papers I gave you in Gibraltar?"

"Of course," said Josh.

"Good. Good." Samuel looked up to take a glass of wine from Benjamin, who handed glasses to Josh and Sara as well, then Josh's mother returned with a notebook. They all sat down at the conference table.

"So now," said Benjamin, holding up his glass in a toast, "welcome back. We congratulate you on finishing the job you set out to do."

"Thank you," said Sara, too nervous to acknowledge the toast as she placed Samuel's papers and her own notes and computer printouts on the table in front of her. On top was her grandmother's receipt that had begun the search.

"We're not quite finished though," added Josh. He cleared his throat. Sara saw how uncomfortable he was. He also had not lifted his glass. This was going to be tough.

"We need to clean up the details," said Sara, reaching over to hold Josh's hand.

"We want to make sure that all the paintings that came to our family for safekeeping during World War II were returned to the proper owners." Josh rushed the words and gulped. He kept his eyes down at the table.

Benjamin stared at him. His wife frowned. Samuel sat back and observed. The room felt as if time had stopped.

Oh no, Sara thought, they're guilty. They did steal those paintings. That's how they became wealthy. She stole a look at Josh and squeezed his hand. *This is terrible. It's much worse than I thought it would be. Josh will never get over this, even though he had nothing to do with their bad decisions.* Sara couldn't bear to look at them now. She hated to hear what was coming next.

Benjamin sighed. In a sad and solemn voice he said, "I can see we made a mistake." He cocked an eyebrow at his wife. "But how were we to know?"

Despite her concern about Josh, Sara felt irritated at the cavalier attitude Benjamin was taking. Sarah too. Despite their somber demeanor, they seemed secretly amused. Didn't they understand how serious Josh was? They could be charged with theft.

Josh's mother turned to him, reaching over the table to pat his hand. "You weren't going into the business," she said. "You showed no interest in the gallery. Ever."

Josh pulled his hand back. "What happened to all the rescued paintings?" He frowned at them and folded his arms.

"You think we kept them? Sold them for ourselves?" asked Benjamin, leaning toward Josh with narrowed eyes. "Is that it?"

Samuel sat back and watched, his face unreadable. Sara wished she were anywhere but here.

"I don't know," said Josh. "Our family is wealthy. How did we get that wealth?"

Benjamin put his elbows on the table and steepled his hands.

"Our boy has grown up, Sarah," he said and chuckled.

Sarah grinned at Josh. "I see."

"Your grandparents, my boy," said Benjamin, "they're the ones who started this gallery. Their families had grown wealthy in the sugar and rum trade. When they were young, they moved to Paris for a few years and bought many paintings cheaply—paintings by Picasso, Mondrian, Braque, Modigliani, before they became popular. They brought the paintings back here. Eventually, they opened this gallery, which I now own. I had thought you, Josh, would take it over when I retire, but you showed no interest. Couldn't be bothered to learn about it, so. . . ," Benjamin leaned back, "I left you alone to find your own way."

"How could you think we would ever take advantage of another person's misfortune?" asked Josh's mother. "As soon as we had proper identification, we returned every one of those paintings to the rightful owners." She laid a hand on Benjamin's arm. "Except for three that no one has claimed."

"Those are in storage here," Benjamin pointed to the safe, "and each one has its provenance." He stopped and glanced at Josh. "Samuel told us all about the Rembrandt, but he said there was no provenance. Is that true?"

Josh looked at Sara. She shook her head. "We never thought of such a thing," she said.

"I see," said Benjamin. "And yet you know it as a Rembrandt?"

"It was signed," said Josh.

Benjamin sighed. "Perhaps it is; perhaps not. The owners will probably get a few bucks for it, if they sell."

Josh folded his arms and stretched out his legs. "Whether it is or not, whether its provenance is known or not, that's not our concern. We returned the painting to its rightful owner. That is what we set out to do and that's what we did."

Sara leaned forward. "We don't know anything about a provenance. There certainly wasn't one with it."

Benjamin shrugged. "I supppose the painting has been through many owners over the centuries. The provenance papers could have been lost. As for the three remaining paintings, we have contacted a

Nazi loot investigation team about them and eventually expect to find the proper owners."

"This is a legitimate team?" Samuel asked. Sara remembered the imposter who showed up at Samuel's condo.

"Of course," said Sarah. "We confirmed the team's credentials." As Sara listened, the joy bloomed inside her along with the smile on her face. She squeezed Josh's hand and looked at him. He seemed stunned. He didn't speak for a moment, then he grinned at his father. "I guess it's time I learned the business," he said at last.

Sara got up and hugged everyone around the family. "We never really thought your family had taken them," Sara said. "But we were worried. Josh didn't know anything about the paintings sent to you. We had all those receipts and no information on what had happened to the paintings. We wanted to finish that chapter."

"Of course," said Josh's mother. "I quite understand. "You two were so serious," she laughed, "we had to have a little fun with you."

Josh shook his head. "You have no idea. . ."

Benjamin picked up the wine bottle. "I'm glad my boy asked. First time he's shown any interest in the business." He grinned at everyone. "More wine?"

"I hope you'll let me help find the owners of those three remaining paintings," added Sara. She smiled at Josh. "After all, I've got experience."

***

That evening, Josh put his arm around Sara's shoulders as they walked down the beach. The warm breezes rustled the palm fronds overhead and carried with them the scents of jasmine and oleander.

Dave was back at work in his boring insurance job in Martinsburg, West Virginia. It was winter there. Gray slush from an early snowfall covered the sidewalks and streets. Her mother now filled her days with volunteer activities, and all was well with her family.

"Do you suppose," said Sara, "that Abe Carilla's Modigliani is in your parents' safe?"

"Let's take a look tomorrow." Josh stopped and turned to look at Sara. "I don't want you to go home, Sara."

She swallowed and risked looking into his eyes. "I like being here with you, Josh." She hesitated. "What do you think you'll do now?"

"What I said. Learn the family business." He chuckled, then laughed out loud.

Sara smiled. Josh seemed more centered and confident than she'd ever seen him. "I loved our search together," said Sara. "That's the kind of thing I want to do. Do you suppose there's a job like that for me in your family's business?"

He looked down at her with a smile. "We'll make one. I'll tell Dad to put you on salary. We'll learn the business together."

He took her hand and together they strolled back under a full moon toward the gallery.

Epilogue, 2000

Sara stood behind the cash register in the Davila Art Gallery while Josh hung a newly acquired painting. She watched him with pride in his cheerful, hard-working manner. He no longer played the melancholy, lackadaisical grad student gone bad.

She looked around the light, airy gallery. It was a pleasure to work here, even though she had much to learn and had not as yet begun her search for the rightful owners of the remaining paintings.

The door opened, and a man and a woman entered. They were dark silhouette against the bright sunshine outside. Unlike most visitors to the gallery, they didn't begin browsing the paintings but walked directly toward her. "Hello, Sara," said the woman.

After a stunned moment of surprise, Sara said, "Gail!" She walked forward to greet them. "And Alain! How wonderful to see you!"

Just then, Josh emerged from the back room.

"Great to see you too," said Gail, hugging Sara. "And there's Josh. We came by to talk with both of you."

"We're on a cruise," explained Alain.

Josh greeted them with a smile, shaking Alain's hand and nodding at Gail.

"We'd like to take you to lunch," said Alain. "We want to talk with you about the Rembrandt."

"Did you have it restored?" asked Sara. "Have you hung it yet?" Alain laughed. "That's what we wanted to talk to you about." "I'll ask Dad to watch the store. He's in back." Josh disappeared into the back room and returned in a moment. "I'm ready." Josh led them to the door. "Nice place down the street."

They walked to a small cafe and found a table outside in the shade where the ocean breeze felt cool and fresh. "So nice to see you again," said Sara. "How's the painting?"

"Let's order first," interrupted Josh as the waiter hovered. They perused the menus and gave their orders quickly. Sara sensed excitement in the air.

"We have a proposition for you," Gail said, smiling at them. "We think you'll like it."

"Proposition?" said Sara, glancing at Josh.

"After hearing your adventures, we didn't think we could provide proper security for a Rembrandt—and we didn't want to worry about it." Alain grinned at them. "We sold the painting to the local art museum in Jacksonville. There was a problem about the provenance, but it is a fine painting of a notable Jewish subject, and it comes with a fascinating story. Even without the provenance, we knew several wealthy backers who put up the money, and they're planning to include it in a special exhibit about the Holocaust.

"So we feel we owe you more than a debt of gratitude," added Gail.

Sara demurred. "We were glad to find you. My grandmother's bequest paid the expenses. I did it for her."

Gail reached forward to pat Sara's hand. "We know that, but we don't feel right not letting you share in our good fortune. So. . ." She pulled two envelopes out of her purse.

Alain took the envelopes. "We're giving you each twenty-five thousand dollars as your part of the payment we received for the Rembrandt." He handed one to Sara and one to Josh.

Sara sat stunned. So many thoughts crossed her mind at once. She didn't want this kind of reward, but then she realized that with twenty-five thousand dollars, she would be able to continue her travels to find the owners of the other paintings without depleting the gallery's reserves. She looked at Josh.

"I know what you're thinking," he said with a smile and put his hand on hers.

She smiled back at him. "Yes," she said with joy in her heart, "our journey is not over."

ℬibliography

Benbassa, Esther. *The Jews of France: A History from Antiquity to the Present.* Princeton University Press, Princeton, NJ, 1999.

Bruce, Evangeline. *Napoleon & Josephine: An Improbable Marriage.* Scribner, NY, 1995.

Cummings, Valerie. *The Visual History of Costume Accessories.* Costume & Fashion Press, New York. 1998.

Forrest, Alan. *Napoleon: The Legacy and Image: A Biography.* St. Martin's Press, New York, 2011.

Goldstein, Rebecca. *Betraying Spinoza: The Renegade Jew Who Gave Us Modernity.* Schoeken Books, New York, 2006.

Israel, Jonathan I. *The Dutch Republic: Its Rise, Greatness, and Fall, 1477-1806.* Clarendon Press, Oxford. 1995.

Israel, Jonathan I. *Radical Enlightenment: Philosophy and the Making of Modernity 1650-1750.* Oxford University Press. New York, 2001.

Levinton, Melissa, Consultant Editor. *What People Wore When.* St. Martin's Griffin. New York. 2008.

McGuire, Leslie. *Napoleon.* Chelsea House Publishers. New York, 1986.

Mee, Jr., Charles L. *Rembrandt's Portrait: A Biography.* Simon & Schuster. New York, 1988.

Nadler, Steven. *Rembrandt's Jews.* University of Chicago Press, Chicago, 2003.

Saperstein, Marc. *Exile in Amsterdam*. Hebrew Union College Press, Cincinnati. 2005.

Schreiber, Mordecai, Editor. *The Shengold Jewish Encyclopedia*. Shengold Books, Rockville, MD. 1998.

Other Books by Eileen Haavik McIntire

Shadow of the Rock

"Chapters move quickly in a mixture of danger, excitement, and pure enjoyment." *–Foreword Reviews.*

"A riveting tale of time and humanity, highly recommended." *-Midwest Book Review.*

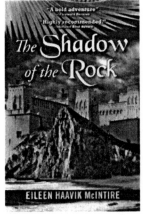

Two women, 200 years apart, seek their past and their future on journeys that will link the old world with the new and change the map of Florida.

Setting sail for America in 1781, Rachel Levy and her father Moses are captured by Barbary pirates and brought to Morocco for sale. The loathsome vizier forces Moses into slavery as his assistant and compels Rachel to choose between himself and the king's harem. Without money or resources Rachel and Moses must use their wits to find a way to freedom.

Two hundred years later in West Virginia, Sara Miller's grandmother Ruth is killed, and Sara discovers Ruth's buried past, long hidden by the terror of the Holocaust. Ruth's bequest sends Sara on a journey that will uncover Ruth's mystery and the link to their ancestor, Rachel Levy.

Available as a paperback and e-book on Amazon.com and Smashwords.com

Print ISBN: 9780983404903. $17.95

The 90s Club Series
By Eileen Haavik McIntire

What would Nancy Drew be like at 90? We suspect she might be like Nancy Dickenson, founder of the 90s Club at Whisperwood Retirement Village. If you read Nancy Drew as a kid, the titles might be familiar and you'll probably enjoy the buried references to the Nancy Drew stories.

The 90s Club & the Hidden Staircase

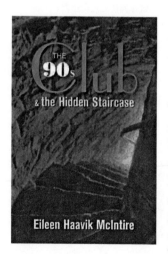

"With plenty of humor and its own original tale...a must for readers of cozy mysteries."
- *Midwest Book Review*

The 90s Club at Whisperwood Retirement Village discovers a simmering brew of thefts, murders, and exploitation bubbling beneath its luxurious lifestyle. Nancy Dickenson and fellow club members pile up clues like tricks in a bridge game to uncover the culprits—and almost lose their lives. The menace grows into a bloody climax and even Nancy's suspiciously wild kitty cat Malone takes part, turning the murderer's confidence into terror.
Available as paper back and e-book on Amazon.com and Smashwords.com.   Print: 9780983404934. $17.95

The 90s Club & the Whispering Statue

"A fun read. . . . nostalgia and. . . social commentary, wrapped up in an engaging mystery novel."
- *Foreword Reviews*

Nancy Dickenson and the 90s Club at Whisperwood Retirement Village head south to Fort Lauderdale to rescue one friend and find another. Four attempts to murder Nancy's long-time confidant Peter Stamboul have failed, but in the placid lifestyle of his retirement condo, who would want to kill Peter and why? Adventurous young Jessica Cantwell takes a job as crew on a boat, but when the captain is murdered, she disappears. Once again, murder and mayhem stalk Nancy and fellow 90s Club members Louise and George as they race to save Peter and Jessica's lives and ultimately their own. Print: 9780983404972. $17.95

The 90s Club & the Secret of the Old Clock

"An impressively well crafted and thoroughly entertaining mystery that plays fair with the reader from beginning to end,"
-Midwest Book Review

Nancy and the 90s Club pursue a killer and crooks at Whisperwood Retirement Village, but the killer is no fool and attacks first. This time, the killer swears, Nancy will not escape. Available as paper back and e-book on Amazon.com and Smashwords.com. 9780961451905. $15.95

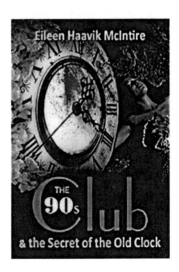

Summit Crossroads Press

**also publishes parenting books
by Dr. Roger McIntire
and the First-Person History Series.**

Teenagers & Parents:
12 Steps to a Better Relationship
By Dr. Roger McIntire

The long-awaited revised and updated edition of *Teenagers and Parents: 12 Steps to Better Relationship* by award-winning author Dr. Roger McIntire comes on sale September 15, 2016.

Ten years in the making, this new edition adds discussions of teen addictions to computers, cell phones, and social media, while providing the daily advice that present-day parents need.

This practical guide is written from the viewpoint of a behavior analyst with numerous examples and conversations of family

**TEENAGERS
&
PARENTS**

12 Steps To
A Better Relationship

New in This Fifth Edition: Dealing with Your Teenager's
Cell Phones, Computers and Social Media.

Dr. Roger McIntire

life from the author's counseling experiences and home life with three daughters. La Leche League called the first edition, "Reassuring and enjoyable." Parents have called Dr. McIntire's books "life-savers" in helping them build better relationships with their children.

Dr. McIntire is professor emeritus of psychology (ret.) at the University of Maryland. He served 33 years as teacher, associate dean of undergraduates and research director.

Raising Good Kids in Tough Times: 7 Crucial Habits for Parent Success
By Dr. Roger McIntire

"These are the habits parents need for confidence and the ones that can help in moments of trouble." – Dr. Donald Pumroy, Founder of Assn for Behavior Change; Prof. Emeritus, Univ. of MD.

This practical guide for parents of children two to 12 provides the strategies needed to be ready and confident when these questions come up:

❖ All the kids are going, why can't I?
   (See Habit 4 about values and character)
❖ Mom, how can I make good grades?
   (See Habit 2 about handling school problems)
❖ Mom (Dad), can we talk?
   (See Habit 1 about hints on talking and listening)
❖ Why don't the kids like me?
   (See Habit 3 about liking and getting along)
❖ Can I go if Dad says yes?
   (see Habit 7 about cooperation from others)
❖ You do it, why can't I?
   (See Habit 5 about minding your model)

Praise for Dr. McIntire's Books

"Outstanding." – Parent Council, Ltd.

"[McIntire] learned his lessons well and passes along his knowledge in a lively and readable book...filled with practical answers for all the common problems." – *Bookviews*.

First-Person History Series
Summit Crossroads Press also publishes memoirs, autobiographies, and travelogues that contribute to our understanding of history and humanity.

On My Own: Decoding the Conspiracy of Silence
by Erika Schulhof Rybeck. Sent by kinder transport to Scotland as a child in 1939, Erika was shielded from the facts of Hitler's Europe and the death of her own parents. Only as an adult did she finally learn the truth.
ISBN 9780983404996. $17.95

Return to the Shtetl
By Dorothy Sucher In 1992, Dorothy Sucher traveled alone to Russia and Belarus in search of information about her grandparents. She paints a vivid and moving picture of Belarus at the time.
ISBN 9780961451912. $17.95

The Twentieth Century Through My Eyes
By Isadore Seeman This is the story of a man at age 99 who lived through and played a part in the tumultuous events of the 20th century. As a leader in public health and social welfare, he helped shape those ervices in ways that affect us all.
ISBN 9780961451936. $18.95.

CPSIA information can be obtained
at www.ICGtesting.com
Printed in the USA
FFOW04n1858220616
25275FF